Praise for the Mead M‍...

"One of the freshest voices in fantasy romance! This book has it all: spice, humor, and a world I want to get lost in!"
—Katee Robert, *New York Times* bestselling author

"Sexy, witty, and fun as hell—*That Time I Got Drunk and Saved a Demon* is the instant mood boost we all need."
—Hannah Whitten, *New York Times* bestselling author

"Hilarious, hot, and full of heart, *That Time I Got Drunk and Saved a Demon* is exactly what you need in your life. Right now. Go pick it up because it is the cure to any reading funk and might even clear up acne. I'm serious. It's that good."
—Avery Flynn, *USA Today* and
Wall Street Journal bestselling author

"A hilarious, down-to-earth romance with magic, adventure, and intrigue. What's not to love?"
—Talia Hibbert, *New York Times* bestselling author

"Perfect entertainment for my stressed-out brain, and I was definitely rooting for those two wacky kids to have their HEA."
—*Smart Bitches, Trashy Books*

By Kimberly Lemming

MEAD MISHAPS

That Time I Got Drunk and Saved a Demon

That Time I Got Drunk and Yeeted a Love Potion at a Werewolf

That Time I Got Drunk and Saved a Human

MEAD REALM NOVELLAS

Mistlefoe

A Bump in Boohail

THAT TIME I GOT DRUNK AND SAVED A HUMAN

MEAD MISHAPS: BOOK THREE

KIMBERLY LEMMING

orbitbooks.net

Copyright © 2023 by Kimberly Lemming
Excerpt from *For the Wolf* copyright © 2021 by Hannah Whitten

Cover design by Alexia E. Pereira
Cover art by Mike Pape
Cover copyright © 2024 by Hachette Book Group, Inc.
Map by @Saumyasvision/Inkarnate
Author photograph by Kimberly Lemming

Orbit
Hachette Book Group
1290 Avenue of the Americas
New York, NY 10104
orbitbooks.net

First Orbit Paperback Edition: March 2024
First Orbit Ebook Edition: May 2023
Previously published in paperback in Great Britain by Jo Fletcher Books, an imprint of Quercus Editions Ltd, in September 2023
Originally published in ebook in Great Britain by Jo Fletcher Books, an imprint of Quercus Editions Ltd, in April 2023

Orbit is an imprint of Hachette Book Group.
The Orbit name and logo are registered trademarks of
Little, Brown Book Group Limited.

Library of Congress Control Number: 2023944722

ISBNs: 9780316570350 (trade paperback), 9780316570329 (ebook)

Printed in the United States of America

CW

1 3 5 7 9 10 8 6 4 2

To my husband, who always goes above and beyond to support me. And to my readers, who spread the word of my books with the speed and tenacity of wild jungle cats. Never forget that you are incredible and have the ability to change lives.

Content Warning

PLEASE BE AWARE: This book contains graphic violence, drugs, kidnapping, and sexually explicit content that could trigger certain audiences.

Chapter 1

Dante

"Gods, I am so fucking scared right now." Madam Shadow's voice shook as she spoke, yet she kept her hand outstretched. Behind her, Fallon leaned against the wall with his arms crossed. The shadow dragon watched our brief training session with bored nonchalance. It was a front of course. If his little human so much as yelped, I'd have a brawl on my hands.

He didn't possess the strength my seven centuries had afforded me, but he had an impressive amount of magic in his arsenal. By absorbing the false goddess Myva, Fallon had positioned himself as a formidable threat. Despite his young age.

"You're going to be fine," I reassured her. She would be. I'd been practicing all week. The first few attempts with Usha

1

were a little less than savory but it'd been a long time since I'd had to curb my strength. A dragon's power grew as they aged and the extra strength was something I never had to worry about in Volsog. Demons were so much more durable than humans.

I reached out to take her hand in mine.

"Wait!" Brie called out. She looked in between Madam Shadow and me and held her hands up. "Are we sure he's ready for this? Maybe we could start off with a porcelain doll or something. If he doesn't break that, then we can move on to hands again. It's only been a few days since his last attempt, and that did not end well."

Usha sighed from her spot in the captain's chair. "Agreed. He may not be ready." She rubbed at her shoulder absent-mindedly, as if it still pained her.

Irritation made my jaw clench. "Enough of your dramatics. I healed you, didn't I? Madam Shadow will be fine."

"You broke my shoulder," she hissed back at me.

"It was an accident." Truly it was. What was meant to be a friendly pat on the shoulder had sent the human flying across the ship's deck. Usha had been left with a fractured shoulder and had aimed a litany of colorful curses in my direction. Fortunately for her, the matter was easily fixed with a basic healing spell. Simple injuries were manageable, yet healing magic was by far not my forte. If the bones had splintered, then she would've been in for a long and painful recovery.

It wasn't until that minor incident that I realized I had never actually touched a human, despite having stayed on the *Banshee* for over a year. The ship's crew mostly comprised other demons. When I thought back on it, I realized I'd never actually been alone with the two humans on board. Or alone with any human, really. So how was I supposed to know how weak they truly are?

Felix threw his arm around his worried wife. "He's going to need to start with real people again at some point. It won't do Dante any good if he leaves to find a mate only to end up killing the poor thing as soon as he goes in for a kiss."

As much as I hated to admit it, he was right. The likelihood of my fated mate being one of the few demon women left in the world were slim to none. Fallon and Felix had found happiness in their human wives and I longed for that same companionship. Though I suppose Brie would soon be a werewolf. It was only a few days until the full moon and the bite mark on her arm was a constant reminder of what was to come. The circumstances of her bite were less than ideal, but the two seemed to have made their peace with it.

"I don't need to practice on another doll. Madam Shadow will be fine."

The co-captain's hand shook, but she stood firm. "I told you to call me 'Cin.' The whole Madam thing is weird."

"Right," I sighed. "You humans are an informal lot. Are you ready, Cin?"

She took a deep breath and nodded.

I stared at the outstretched hand, determined. It had taken a few shattered porcelain objects to get right, but I was confident in my ability to curb my strength now. I practiced on Felix the day before and he had deemed my grip safe enough for humans. Though the fact that he refused to let *his* wife stand in as my practice partner did not escape my notice. Not that it mattered. Cinnamon had proven herself to be a brave human and looked far more durable than Brie.

Slowly, I raised my hand to hers. She sealed her eyes shut and turned her head away. As gently as I could manage, I closed my hand around hers and shook once. When the fragile bones in her fingers didn't crumple under my grip, she peeked one eye open.

"Oh!" Cin gasped. "He did it!"

The room let out a collective sigh of relief. Which was more than a little insulting. I wasn't a monster. I just needed a little practice. Cinnamon patted our joined hands and smiled up at me. I returned her grin before releasing her. "Of course I did. I told you it would be fine."

Usha rolled her eyes. "A lot of confidence coming from a man who broke three of my fingers a few days ago."

My, that one could hold a grudge. "And once again, I'm sorry for the fingers as well."

The captain sighed and got up from her chair. "Doesn't matter. It's over now." She moved to my side and clapped a hand on my back. "Congrats on no longer being a walking threat. Does this mean you'll be flying off soon?"

Cinnamon pursed her lips. "You don't have to fly off right away, do you? We should at least have a send-off party."

"Rabbit," Fallon sighed. "Not every occasion requires a party."

She shot a glare at her husband and put a hand on her hip. "That is where you're wrong. There's no better way to start a journey than with a festival. He can stick around for one more night. Right, Dante?" she asked, turning back to me.

The sound of Brie's giggling caught my ear. I glanced over to see that Felix had leaned in close and was whispering some nonsense that had the woman slapping his chest. The werewolf grinned and kissed her temple.

Gods, they make me sick.

"No," I said, tearing my eyes away from the disgustingly happy couple. "I'd rather pack my things tonight and head out in the morning. Besides, I'm eager to see how much the world has changed since before Volsog's gates closed." It wasn't a complete lie. I was only a hundred and some odd years old when Myva rose up and banished all non-humans to a frozen hellscape. There is no telling how different the world looked after 600 years.

Her shoulders sank. "Right, I guess that makes sense. Damn, first Alexis flies off without so much as a farewell and now you."

"Not entirely sure we should mourn the loss of a murderous talking sword," Brie cut in.

Cinnamon shrugged. "I mean, she really only killed people we needed her to."

"So far," Brie replied.

"Don't worry, Cin, I'll be sure to drop by every now and then." I bid everyone farewell and headed into my quarters below deck. Packing wouldn't take long. I had little to my name aboard the *Banshee*. Any time we went out pirating, I took my share of loot and warped myself back to my castle in Volsog with the power of my Hearthstones. If I left one Hearthstone in the place I had last been, traveling back and forth was always an easy endeavor. So long as no idiot entered my quarters and took the stone from under my bed. Thankfully, no one on the ship was foolish enough to incur the wrath of a dragon.

I threw my sack onto the bed and knelt down to retrieve my stone. The smooth rock felt cool to the touch. Its travel rune was etched in glowing blue letters along the flat side of the rock's face. I turned to toss it into the sack then reared back at the sight of something darting across the sheets.

My back hit the wall and my horn scraped a gash into the woodgrain. A pure white kitten jumped out from behind my pillow. The tiny creature let off a loud yelp before rolling over onto the sheets. I cursed, irritated. That damn cat could be so unsettling. A slow burn set off behind my eyes and I rubbed my temples to ease the pain.

Every other day the little furball would find its way into my things, leaving me with white fur-covered clothes and a sharp headache. I didn't even know I was allergic to cats. Maybe I wasn't. Maybe it was just that little monster in particular.

Rebekah gave off another yowl before trying to claw my bag. I snatched it away from her and shooed the beady-eyed thing off my bed. Not that I didn't like cats, most of them never bothered me. There was just something about the way *this* cat stared directly into your soul that left me unsettled.

I opened the door to my cabin and shouted for Baraku to come get his pet. The orc barreled in from the deck above and thundered to a halt next to my door. He ducked his head low and snatched the kitten from the floor. "Sorry about that, my lord; not sure why she's taken such a shine to you." His hands trembled as he spoke. The motion irritated the beast in his grasp and she let off an angry snarl and then bit his hand. Baraku flinched but didn't let her go.

"You don't need to call me lord. This isn't even my territory." I sighed and rubbed my temples again. Most of the other demons on the ship were used to Fallon's and my presence. At least enough to drop the formalities. Yet, anytime I spoke to Baraku, he'd end up a shivering mess until he found a way to excuse himself. One would think that after a year it would be obvious that we didn't intend to kill and eat everyone on board. "It's fine, just make sure she stays out of my things for another night. I'm leaving in the morning and don't need the extra stress of a headache."

He nodded frantically and shuffled off with his pet. Rebekah's unblinking beady blue eyes poked over his shoulder and watched me as she was carried off.

Such a creepy little thing.

Chapter 2

Cherry

Drowning was getting real old. The familiar rush of panic lit pin needles under my skin. I clawed at the mud of the bank and felt hard grains of soil between my fingers, but I might as well have been grabbing at the sands of time. Searing pain shot through my knee as the creature twisted my leg and pulled me further into the water. I cried out for my sister, as I always did, but the words were torn away in a cloud of bubbles when murky water filled my lungs. Through the haze of thrashing water and pain, I could see Cinnamon dive in after me. She reached out and, for a fraction of a second, hope bloomed in my burning chest. Our fingers brushed, and I kicked harder against the beast in a feeble attempt to grab hold. But, as always, Cin was just out of reach. With another forceful pull, the dog-like creature shredded any hope of salvation.

Screaming echoed against the stone walls of my tower. I lurched out of my sheets with a start, then promptly fell on my face when the fabric tangled around my legs. Not a great start to the day. Sighing, I kicked myself free and stumbled over to the wall, picked up my stone and gave it another scratch. One more tally to mark the never-ending monotony of my captivity. Five years' worth of scratch marks stretched across the rounded walls before arching over the large window overlooking the sea.

Menacing-looking waves crashed against the rocky bank of my captor's island. No matter the season or time of day, the surrounding sea never let up its harsh assault against the shore. Or, at least, that's how it was ever since I attempted to escape by raft four years prior. When I first arrived here, I could have sworn the waves weren't that violent. Then again, I'd been stuck here for years. It was entirely possible that I was simply going mad.

Chilly morning breeze sent chills down my arms as I sat on the windowsill. "Good morning, asshole," I called down to the dragon below. As expected, the scaly blue dickhead didn't respond. Or move, for that matter. Day in and day out, the massive creature remained coiled around the base of the tower. Leaving just enough room at the front door for his little frog-like minions and me to slip through. For the most part, my captor didn't mind me wandering around the island, but if the tower was empty too long, he'd come running.

It was kinda funny in a way. When I was a little girl, my ma used to read me stories every night. Some were epic adventures with high stakes and exciting twists while others were of princesses trapped in towers guarded by fierce dragons. The pitiful princess would be stuck inside all day pining for her Prince Charming to come and save her. I always hated those princess stories. I couldn't imagine why the lazy thing didn't just get up and leave. Ironic, since I was now stuck in that same situation. Turns out, when a dragon holds you hostage, he doesn't just let you get up and leave.

Who knew?

The sound of pattering feet in the kitchen below alerted me that Amanda, the head frog, had already started on my breakfast. I had no idea if her name was actually Amanda, but it felt rude to keep calling the creature that cooked for me "frog 1." If she minded the name, she said nothing. Well, in common tongue anyway. She and the others did a lot of croaking I couldn't understand. They could be calling me every curse in their froggy language for all I knew. It's not like I did much else but insult their lord and pitch fits when my escape attempts fell through.

Freeing my hair from its wrap, I snatched up my comb from the dresser next to the window and began the morning ritual of styling. A few hair supplies, travel rations and a change of clothes was all I had in my satchel the day I was taken by that water monster. It was better than nothing, but—hot damn— the crimes I would commit for a freaking book.

"I'm thinking of bubble pigtails today. What do you think?" I called down to the dragon, knowing I'd never get an answer. Yet hurling insults and one-sided chats at him was the only conversation I ever got in this place. It had only taken about a week of silence until I had begun talking to myself like a madwoman. Then to the walls, then to the dragon, then I tried imitating the croaks of the frog people I'd seen skittering about. Judging by the angry hisses I had got in return, they did not appreciate my efforts.

The dragon below remained as silent as stone. With any luck, he was finally dead and I could leave. Unless the frog people were forcing food into his mouth, there was no way he'd eaten in the last few weeks. The damn dragon did little else but sit around and sleep. Which, I guess, was better than him trying to eat me. But it still made me wonder why he even cared if I escaped. Thwarting my attempts at leaving his island was the only time I'd ever seen any pep in his step. Well, that and the time he murdered a kraken that got too close.

If I were to try another escape, the crashing waves would still be a problem. It wasn't much, but at least the raft I was building was twice as sturdy as the haphazard ball of twigs I had tried the last time. If I played my cards right, and used up every bit of luck I had, it might just be able to make it out to sea where the sailing would be smoother.

Twisting the first bubble of my hair into a gold hair tie, I reached for another band and contemplated finding a stick to poke that dragon with later. If he didn't move, then I'd try finishing up my new raft.

On clear days like this one, I liked to imagine my home just beyond the horizon. With fall well underway, the trees lining the lanes of my family's farm would be a sea of yellows and reds, lighting up the canopy in a blazing display. My siblings and I would fight over who grew the largest pump-kin before we harvested the seeds into salty treats. Cumin always won. But we tried to beat him every year, anyway. As soon as I found a way back, I'd twist his arm until he told me what witch he paid off every year to make his crop grow so fast.

Glancing around my room full of scratched up stone, I finished my hair with grim determination. I'd try again today whether or not that damn beast was alive. I would not die stranded on this fucking island. There wasn't a cloud in the sky and the weather was perfect for sailing. I closed my eyes and took a deep breath, willing the Fates to grant me favor. "Please let today be the day. I don't care what it takes, just let me leave this place."

Yet when I opened my eyes again, the Fates had looked down on my plea and said "fuck your feelings." Angry-looking gray clouds spilled over the sky, dashing my plans onto the sharp rocks of the cove.

"Are you kidding me?" I screamed. The encroaching storm rolled closer to the island at a threatening pace. Streaks of lightning followed by booming thunder.

"Fuck my life." I swung myself off the window and pulled on my boots. A storm like that would rip my raft to shreds if I didn't get it covered in time. The weather had been completely cloud-free the past week. In my hubris I'd left the raft outside of my hidden cave to make it easier to work on, only covering it with a pile of banana leaves in case one of the dragon's minions passed by the area.

As I stood up, my life flashed before my eyes as my feet caught on the long fabric of my nightgown, almost sending me headfirst down the stairs. I grabbed the railing and took a deep breath. "Slow," I told myself. "Stairs are evil and out to get you."

Having second thoughts about going outside in a storm in my nightgown, I threw it off and traded it for a simple gray blouse and my favorite green skirt. It was my only skirt, as it was the one I was kidnapped in, but that was beside the point. I sped down the steps and bid Amanda good morning, before rushing out the door.

The dark blue of her cheeks puffed out before an angry croak in my direction. Pausing, I glanced back at the frog-woman to see her point her spatula at a spread of grilled fish and fruit.

"Amanda, I'm kind of in a hurry."

She slammed the spatula on the counter with a loud slap. Amanda was a menacing little thing that stood three feet tall with a temper just as short. The sharp, dark blue barbs jutting from her elbows promised a venomous sting I had no intention of experiencing. It was anyone's guess if she tasked herself with the job of feeding her master's captive or if she simply had drawn the short end of the stick. But gods help me if I ever decided I wasn't hungry. In my first year here, I had tried staging a hunger protest. I'd proudly declared my refusal to eat to the dragon, hoping he'd have a heart and take me home, rather than see a woman starve.

He didn't.

My grand protest lasted an hour. Then Amanda kicked open the door to the tower brandishing fish skewers like blades. The memory of her cold frog-hands shoving fish in my mouth will haunt me for the rest of my days.

"Alright, fine!" I hissed. With grace and civility, I crammed handfuls of food into my maw before rushing back out the door. "Thanks for breakfast," I called back, then whispered to myself, "Bossy little dart frog." A wooden spatula flew past my head, nearly severing one of my pigtails.

Note to self: frog-people have surprisingly good hearing.

Outside, the roar of thunder grew closer as the wind picked up around me. Slowly, I maneuvered around the wall of blue scales before jumping over the frilled tail of my captor. When the dragon didn't rear his head to rush me back into my keep, I tiptoed to the small path heading toward the beach, then took off running. Sand whirled up around me as the storm finally closed in on the island. In the distance, I could just make out my raft under the pile of leaves. The leaves shook violently against the rocks weighing them down.

White blinded my vision as lightning struck a nearby tree. The towering eucalyptus snapped, knocking into a handful of other trees before they came crashing down toward the mess of leaves hiding my raft. Panicked, I ran faster to find that the giant tree had barely missed the raft. "Oh, thank cheese and rice," I sighed.

As the wind howled, a banana leaf slammed into my face, knocking me on my ass. I sputtered and batted away the offending leaf just before another swirl of wind blew away the rest of my raft's cover. The sail I'd fashioned out of old blankets caught against the harsh gusts and blew open. In an instant, the wind lifted the raft and began sliding it out of the bushes toward the water.

"Oh, no you don't!" I screamed, diving onto the raft. My weight did nothing to slow the damn thing down. Ice-cold water splashed against my side as the raft launched itself into the waves. Cursing, I grabbed hold of the mast and tried to steer it back to shore. Instead, a full gust of wind snatched up the sail like a hawk would a mouse and the raft was airborne.

Roaring thunder drowned out my screams. I closed my

eyes and hung on for dear life as the wind whipped the raft back toward the shore. Seconds felt like decades as I waited for the wind to smash me against the sharp rocks of the coast or perhaps straight into the water to drown. Neither sounded like a pleasant death, but at least slamming headfirst into a rock would be fast.

The mast snapped under my grip and flung me off the raft. I went down hard into the sand and rolled to a stop. Dusting the sand out of my face, I peered down at my body and damn near burst into tears when I found every limb where it should have been.

"Burning hot ghost peppers, I'm alive," I cried, throwing my fists up in victory. I looked around for my raft, only to see it slam against a tree and shatter. Weeks of planning and sneaking around, gone in a flash. My hands dug into the sand.

"This is just fucking great," I seethed. Covered in freezing cold water and, if I was being honest, a little bit of piss, I made my way over to the cave, intent on waiting out the storm. Maybe have a good cry while I was at it.

The moment I ducked my head into the cave, the wind stopped. Angry gray skies receded into clear blue once more. My shattered raft and broken trees were all that remained of the once-raging storm. Jaw hanging open in disbelief, I held a hand out in the air. Nothing. No wind, no clouds, just nothing.

The gods hate me. There is no other explanation for this level of bullshittery.

Utterly defeated, I waded into the water to rinse the piss and broken dreams off myself before trudging back to my tower. Today was an absolute wash. Nothing left to do but shrug it off and plan for the next time. Maybe I'd enjoy a ganja cookie and have a tall glass of mead.

Yep. As I started on the path back, the day was already sounding better. The only good thing about my captivity was the wide variety of plant life. So, food and...well...more entertaining plants were never in short supply.

In the early days of my island exploration, I almost couldn't believe the copious number of caapi vines lining the edge of the cliffs on the west side of the island. Chacruna shrubs sat tall and proud in near perfect rows, while marijuana plants competed for sunlight among the tall grass. If I didn't know any better, I'd almost believe they'd been planted by the dragon himself. I'd never seen those kinds of plants grow together in harmony in the wild. Not that I was complaining. There wasn't much else to do on the island. Maybe that's why he hardly ever moved. The thought of my captor sneaking off to brew ayahuasca tea while I slept was laughable, but my grandma always said nothing was impossible.

A deep voice reverberated through the ground, making me freeze. **"Gideon, you could at least acknowledge that you hear me."**

Without thinking, I dove off the trail and hid behind a bush. My hands trembled as I struggled to pull a branch out of the way to peek out at the stranger. Then I clamped a hand over my mouth to keep from crying out.

Screeching pumas, it's another dragon. My mind whirled at seeing the massive creature maneuver its long serpent body, in front of my tower, to glower down at my dragon.

"Gideon," he said. *Could all dragons talk, or was the newcomer special in some way? If they could, why the hell didn't that blue bastard say anything to me for the past five years?*

The newcomer was smaller than my captor. One lone horn rose from the right side of his head. His silver scales glittered in the morning sun, casting rays of light on the surrounding grass. Smoke rose from his nostrils as he snorted, then grabbed hold of one of Gideon's long sea-foam green horns and shook violently. **"Hey!"** the silver dragon snapped. **"Don't ignore me, you beached whale. Get up."**

Gideon let out a long sigh, but made no move to stand.

So, he was still alive then, and his name was Gideon. Damn.

Annoyed, the silver dragon shook him again, then sat down. **"At least tell me you've eaten. You'll wither away if you keep on like this."**

His only response was another long sigh.

The silver dragon shook his head and looked off into the distance. **"You know, that damn lich is dead. The lot of us are no longer trapped behind Volsog's gate and the lands beyond are completely free rein. You'll miss out on all the**

excitement if you remain here. I understand your pain but—"

"You don't," Gideon interrupted.

So, he can talk. I was seething. Years of talking to the walls like a madwoman and that donkey's ass could have chimed in at any time.

His harasser paused, then lowered his head. **"You're right. I don't. But you were a friend to my father, and I owe it to him not to let you rot away. So, get up and go eat or I'm not leaving."** When the dragon on the ground didn't move, sparkles of lightning erupted from the silver dragon's body. They raced down his scales until they collected in a frantic dance at the tip of his tail. **"I'm not asking, Gideon."**

When Gideon didn't move, the silver dragon whipped its tail against the blue one's hide, provoking a snarl. Undeterred by my captor's refusal to budge, the silver dragon stared him down. **"Go eat,"** he said again, this time with a hint of a threat in his voice.

The blue dragon finally gave in, rising to his full height with a grunt. **"Fine. You win, Dante. I'll go eat. But I'm not leaving this place."**

Dante blew out a relieved breath, and the sparks died down. **"Thank you."**

The blue dragon started off in the opposite direction to my hiding spot. Dante watched him go, not moving until Gideon's blue scales receded into the ocean waves.

My heart was pounding in my chest as I mentally replayed what had happened. So, there were other dragons around. Some of whom were incredibly pushy. I waited, crouched down in my hiding spot to see what the newcomer would do next. A gust of wind blew behind me, sending loose strands of curls to brush against my face. Annoyed, I brushed them back and shifted to sit on my heels.

Dante's head snapped up, making me freeze.

Crap, did he hear me move?

His nostrils flared. The mane running down his back puffed up like an angry cat as he sniffed at the air. I didn't breathe. Couldn't even if I wanted to. After a few agonizing seconds, the silver dragon's body relaxed. His mane lost its poof as he let out a breath. **"I must be imagining things,"** he muttered, before gray smoke engulfed his entire body.

In the blink of an eye, a tall man dressed in a simple blue tunic and gray pants stood in the silver dragon's place. The only sign left of the monstrous creature was the long silver hair and the lone horn adoring the left side of his head. I bit back a gasp, never having seen a dragon transform before. The dragon-man-whatever turned and entered my tower, but not before giving the area one last sweeping glance.

I waited a few minutes, making sure he was gone before I dared move. When I could finally breathe again, I let out a shaky laugh. "Well, that was close."

I slowly stood up, brushing the dirt and leaves off my wet

clothes. "Alright, let's not panic," I said to myself. "There's another dragon-man-thing on the island and my raft is smashed to bits." My hands fiddled with the ends of my hair as my body brimmed with nervous energy. "Escape isn't an option, nor do we know if this new guy is friendly or a total dick. Judging by Gideon's weird abduction kink, that one is probably a dick too."

I glanced at my tower then paced back and forth to gather my thoughts. Walking up to a strange man and asking for a ride home wasn't the best plan, even if the man was human. Let alone a dragon big enough to swallow you whole. He could sooner kill me than just say no. But I was a desperate woman. Desperate women do desperate things.

Swirling leaves danced around my feet. I looked down to find a thin caapi vine entangling itself around my ankle. Smiling, I plucked it free and ran my thumb over the deep green leaves. The innocent-looking little plant could pack one hell of a punch when brewed into ayahuasca. A few sips in had me feeling euphoric even on my loneliest days. "Maybe the Fates don't hate me after all." A sober dragon might be a raging asshole, but perhaps a high one just might help me escape.

Chapter 3

Dante

The aroma was stronger inside the tower. My blood raced as an explosion of freesia-scented madness engulfed the room. I closed my eyes, gripped the table in front of me and tried to slow my breathing. Hints of vanilla intertwined with the sweet smell of spring. Sparks of my magic raced their way into my fangs until my jaw ached with the build-up. The need to claim the owner of the alluring scent tore at my insides until clouds churned in the sky. "Well…fuck."

It couldn't have been more than a few hours since I had left Fallon's territory. The desire to find a mate became too hard to fight after being surrounded by happy couples. Not to mention the bitterness I felt watching Fallon, a much younger dragon, find everything I had hoped for right in front of me. True mates were so rare it wasn't unheard of to go a thousand years without finding one. Yet the whelp had barely earned his fire and immediately stumbled upon his mate, Cinnamon.

I was happy for them both. Somewhere deep down, past all the unyielding envy. They had saved me and the rest of the world from the clutches of that evil lich, after all. But a man can only watch so many stolen kisses.

Who would've thought all I had to do was fly a few hours southwest to visit an old friend. Well, a friend of the family. I'd only met the once-proud sea-dragon-turned-insufferable-sad-sack a handful of times when I was younger. When Myva sealed all demons behind Volsog Gate, Gideon was nowhere to be found. My father and I could only assume he didn't make it and was slain in battle.

The collection of islands that made up his territory must've been just out of range of Myva's magic. Lucky son of a bitch. Not that it mattered; it seems the Fates had finally decided to put luck on my side.

I took a deep breath, savoring the scent in the air. Whoever she was, she couldn't have been gone long. There must've been a human settlement somewhere on these islands that I'd missed. It definitely wasn't the scent of a dragoness. Which was fine. With female demons so rare, I expected my mate would be human. Fragile as they were. A few years after taking in my magic, and even the frailest of humans would become a force to be reckoned with. I just needed to bite her as soon as possible to begin the process.

Would she allow me to claim her right away? I thrummed my fingers on the kitchen counter and cursed. It had been a few years since my last courtship ended. Akina, like most dragons, had a love of treasure and gifts so the courtship was easy enough. The rest of our time together was a whirlwind of stress and bad decisions but at least I had that part down. We weren't fated mates, so I never actually claimed her. Yet perhaps the rules were similar.

I should have asked Fallon how he went about courting Cinnamon. By the time I had met them, she had already taken his magic. The only other demon with a human mate that I knew of was Felix. He had mentioned that it wasn't the same as courting another demon.

"They don't care if you're a powerful dragon," he had warned. "They don't even imprint. So, you're going to have to actually speak to her and, let's be honest here, niceties are not your strong point."

Bah! What did he know? I could be nice. What other dragon could spend months cooped up on a ship with a bunch of insufferable idiots and not kill a single one? No one, that's who.

Still…perhaps it was too soon. The plan was to quickly check up on Gideon then head back to my castle in Volsog. There, I could find a proper courting gift from my hoard. At the moment, I had nothing of the sort. I couldn't approach her empty-handed. A dragoness would kill a man for such an offense.

"It's settled," I muttered to myself. Now that I knew where my mate was, there was no rule saying I had to claim her immediately. I could use my Hearthstone to send me back to Volsog and come back with a proper gift. Perhaps scry Fallon and Felix on the return trip for advice. As much as it would pain me to see the smug look on the werewolf's face.

"What is settled?" A voice called from the entryway. That damnable scent spilled into the room, so potent in its intensity that my knees nearly gave way.

Dammit. Dammit all. I took a deep breath to calm my nerves and released my death grip on the counter.

Relax. Niceties. Just be kind.

I noticed her mouth first. Her upper lip was larger than her bottom. Shaped perfectly in a crescent moon, creating an irresistible pout. Her round face was adorned with deep dimples as she smiled at me. Long lashes danced against her dark skin. Wet strands of curly brown hair clung to her face, while the rest was neatly tied back in a bubble pattern. One look in her big brown eyes and the courting gift was completely forgotten.

Fuck. She was stunning. There was no hope in this land or the next that I'd be able to leave her side for a moment. The magic racing through my blood crackled at the thought and a loud boom of thunder sounded off overhead.

Great. Now I'm storming. I dug my nails into my palm and

forced the erratic magic to still. It'd been centuries since I'd gained full control over my powers and I'd be damned if I let that slip now. The only thing to do was to claim her quickly. Give her my magic before she grew irritated with my constant pestering. Or noticed my lack of control.

My mate flinched and glanced up to the sky. Her voice strummed against my senses in the soft strings of a harp. "The weather today has been absolutely insane," she said with a smile. "I'm surprised you could fly in this."

"Yes, well, stormy weather has always been a favorite of mine."

She nodded politely and dusted sand from her skirt. Water dripped from the tips of her hair. Innocent little drops of rain slid down her neck, guiding my gaze down to the elegant ridge of her collarbone. What I wouldn't give to run my tongue against it.

"I know what you mean," she said. "I always sleep better when it's storming outside. Though the sudden uptick of wind nearly swept me out to sea while I was walking on the beach."

Dread pooled into my gut until thunder roared loud enough to shake the tower. "Are you hurt anywhere?" I asked, rushing over to her. *Dammit all.* I had barely met the woman, and I had already put her in danger.

She let out a small laugh and held up a hand to stop me. "No, no. I'm fine." She closed the door behind her and stepped around me to kick off her shoes, then turned to me again and held out her hand. "I'm Cherry, by the way, you must be a friend of Gideon's?"

"Friends might be a little too strong of a word. My name is Dante Remnac of the Mirrored Summit." I took her hand in mine, delighting in the thrill of pleasure that raced up my arm. Her lips parted in a soft gasp and immediately I knew she felt it too. A satisfied grin tugged at the corner of my mouth. Perhaps this wouldn't be so difficult after all.

She cleared her throat and pulled away. The absence of her touch left a gnawing ache in my hand and I fisted it at my side to avoid reaching out again.

"Oh. Well, it's nice to meet you. Gideon's out right now, but I'll put on some tea for us until he gets back." Without waiting for a response, Cherry rushed into the kitchen and pulled a silver tea kettle from the cabinets.

I made my way over to the table and took a seat. "Tea would be lovely, thank you." My mate gave a shaky nod in my direction, then busied herself with preparing tea. She uncorked a glass jar and put two scoops of the foulest smelling tea I'd ever had the misfortune of being near into the kettle. The stone hearth at the end of the kitchen still had small embers dancing under charred wood. She placed a few more logs on top and blew until it lit up again. Unfortunately, the smell only grew worse once the kettle was over the flames.

My eyes watered, and I rubbed my nose to keep from reacting to the scent. What kind of tea had Gideon been forcing on the poor woman? This wouldn't do. As soon as I stole her away, she'd need to be reintroduced to some proper food. As skinny as she was, I doubted she'd been eating well. Not that it mattered, Cherry would be in my care soon.

After a few minutes, a bubbling cup of questionable liquid was placed in front of me, along with a large bowl of assorted fruits. It was poor form to deny hospitality, and the last thing I wanted to do was offend her. I held my breath and lifted the cup.

Choke it down. You've done worse for less.

"I have to ask," I began. "When I flew overhead, there was no human settlement on this island. What are you doing here?" I took a sip of the tea and nearly gagged. It tasted like bark that was fermented in a mushroom for no less than a century before it was filtered through the dirty toes of depressed cyclops.

Cherry sat across from me on the table and set her own cup down. She leaned against her hand. A string of braided hair kissed the slope of her neck before it fell past her shoulder. Suddenly my entire existence revolved around following the action with my hand. I wanted to tilt her chin back, kiss my way down her neck and run a trail along her shoulder until she cried out.

"Well, I'm a bit stuck at the moment. I washed up here a while back and haven't found a way home yet."

So, her home isn't in Gideon's territory. Excellent. I won't have to challenge him for it. "Why hasn't he just taken you home?"

Her eyes widened as if my suggestion surprised her. She

recovered quickly and laughed. "He isn't too keen on moving about. To take me home or, well, anything else really."

He just let her rot here? Perhaps I'd end up challenging him after all. I hummed and took another sip of the terrible drink. The sooner I got her away from Gideon the better. It didn't seem like he wanted to take her as a mate, but I couldn't be too careful. "It must be your lucky day then. I happen to be quite fond of moving about. If you can grab your things we can leave whenever you're ready."

Cherry's body completely froze up. Her pouting lips opened in an O shape. "I'm sorry, what?"

"I mean I'll take you home. If that's what you want." *Keep those big brown eyes trained on me and I'll take you anywhere.*

She turned to glance out the window. "What about the storm?"

My shoulders tensed. "I'm sure it will clear up in a moment," I said, taking another sip.

Quickly, she reached across the table and covered the top of my cup with her hand. "Don't drink that," she said, her voice raising a pitch. I raised a brow at her as she closed her hand around the cup and pulled it from my grasp. "Oh, you know, now that I get a better whiff of the stuff, I think it's gone bad." A nervous laugh escaped her throat. "Let me get my things and I'll meet you back down here in a moment. I don't have much."

At my nod, Cherry smiled again and raced up the stairs of the tower. I couldn't believe my luck. Not only had I stumbled across my fated mate, she needed my help. On the flight to her village I could ask about what kind of mating gift she would be fond of. Get her some real fucking tea as well.

Excitement raced through my veins. I found myself feeling giddy to the point of euphoria. Sweat beaded my brow and my heart raced. I stood and paced about the kitchen. Unable to stay still. *Was it normal to be so nervous?*

"Might wanna calm down there, bud. You'll scare the poor girl off if she catches you jumping around like a jackrabbit in heat."

I stilled. "You're right. I need to get a hold of myself," I said. The roaring thunder outside simmered to a low thrum, as if in agreement. "Wait." I looked behind me for the source of the voice, but no one was there. "Who said that?"

"Me, buddy," said the bowl of fruits. A banana shifted and rocked its way upright, leaning against a mango for support. "Don't see anyone else in this dingy little kitchen, do ya?"

Slowly, I backed away from the table. "What is this?"

The world shifted, and I found myself on the floor, staring at the ceiling. The wooden beams cracked, then bent toward each other forming a circle. Water drifted up from the floor and pulled into the circle. Pools of yellow and blue swirled to and fro until they formed into Felix's face. "Oh, Dante. You're about to fuck this up with her so bad."

"I am not," I snapped back. The sound of Cherry's footsteps bled in from the floor above. The siren call of freesia had my fangs burning. She was so close. All I had to do was sink my teeth into her neck and she'd be mine forever. The lonely ache in my chest would vanish with my companion at my side and then I'd be able to claim whatever land she hailed from. I wanted that. I wanted that so fucking bad.

Felix let off an irritated growl and bared his fangs at me, bringing my attention back to him. I returned the gesture. Perhaps I was too nice to the *Banshee*'s crew, if a werewolf of all things thought they could get away with such insolence. "How did you even get here, what magic is this?"

"I'm not here, you idiot," he replied. The uncharacteristic sharpness in his voice had my head spinning. "Focus. Fly away right now, and don't come back. If you don't, your arms will leave you and your woman will hate you."

"Felix, what the fuck are you talking about?"

He snarled. His human-like features contorted with sickening pops until he took his wolf form. The beast snapped his jaw in annoyance. "You're talking to a banana, Dante. She drugged you. Get up and leave before you make an ass of yourself."

"Shit." I leapt up, then crashed to the ground when the world dipped again. "Why would ⌐he do that?"

"Could I offer you a mango for your thoughts?" the banana called from the table.

With a thud, the mango in question rolled off the table and out the front door. "You'll never catch me alive!" it screamed, before turning into a gaggle of bats and flying away.

"Dante, your arms!" Felix roared. Before I could even blink, my arms let off a terrible hiss. I jerked away from them and they popped off. Then slithered across the floor like snakes. One reared up to hiss at the bowl of fruits before they too, fled out the door.

"Oh gods, this is all wrong. I'm high, my arms are snakes, and they have abandoned me." In the distance, I could hear the low thrum of my own existential dread.

Chapter 4

Cherry

Alright, I fucked up. Maybe my years locked up in a tower have made me a little too untrusting. In hindsight, I could've at least heard the stranger out before I just immediately drugged him. The sight of my would-be savior sprawled out on the floor was enough to make any woman feel a little guilty.

His gray eyes looked unfocused as they stared up at the ceiling. When I stepped further into the room, he tilted his head and sniffed at the air. He let off a low groan before a scowl marred his face. The dragon-shifter snapped his attention back to the ceiling and grumbled threats into the wooden beams. I didn't know who Felix was, but he was in trouble. Dante's long silver hair was spread out like a fan beneath him. I noticed a few strands caught around a loose nail in the wood floor and plucked them free before he hurt himself. The silky strands were smooth in my hand. I couldn't help but take a moment to admire them.

"Hey, Dante," I called, kneeling next to him. "Are you feeling OK?"

Stupid question. You gave the man month-old ayahuasca tea, Cherry. Of course he isn't feeling OK.

Though, when I took in the large frame of the man on the floor, I never would have guessed him for a lightweight. He barely had half a cup. Not only that, it couldn't have been more than a few minutes since I left him. How in the world he was so far gone so fast was beyond me.

His voice was solemn as he spoke. "My arms have left me."

I coughed into my elbow to hide my laugh. "Oh no, hun. Your arms are still right where they always were." I took hold of his upper arm and gave it a squeeze.

Dante took in a deep breath, then let it out slowly. "I don't wanna live in a world where my arms can just leave me."

This poor baby. "Again, sweetheart, your arms are still on your body."

"All I wanted was the scent of spring."

It would be a lot harder to feel bad about my actions if he didn't keep giving me the giggles. "I...I don't know how to help you with that."

Dante tore his gaze from the ceiling to look up at me. His

hand came up to caress the end of my braid. The back of his knuckles dragged against my shoulder. Heat pooled in my skin from the small gesture, making me shiver. My eyes roamed down the expanse of his brawny arms. His large frame suddenly became a little too interesting, and I leaned away from him.

His hand fell away, and I tried not to read into the disappointed look on his face. "Don't you?" he asked, sounding almost accusatory. His head fell back and he let out a deep shuddering breath. Unfocused eyes scanned the room, his voice came out in a half-broken sob, "Why do I hear colors?"

My mouth quirked at the ridiculousness of his question. "I'm sorry, Dante. The truth is, I drugged your drink."

He scoffed. "Yes, I've gathered that from the talking banana."

This time there was no fighting the laugh that escaped my throat. "Please tell me what the banana is saying to you."

"It's saying I should have escaped you when I had the chance." Dante closed his eyes and relaxed as if to accept his fate. "Now I'm doomed."

Guilt weighed heavily on my shoulders. Poor guy just came to check on his friend. Now he's sprawled out on the floor talking to bananas. "I'm so sorry. I promise I don't mean to hurt you or anything. You'll be fine in a few hours."

The dragon-shifter barked out a laugh. "I know you will not hurt me. How could you? You're a human. It's you I'm concerned about." He lifted my arm and shook my wrist. "Look at these tiny things," he lamented. "A flick of my wrist and they'd snap."

Welp, no way he'll be any use to me now. "Can you stand?" I asked. "Tiny arms or not, I don't want you to have to sleep off the high on a hard floor. You can rest in my bed until you recover."

He gave me an incredulous look. "While I admire your ability to cut to the chase, I don't think I can perform under these conditions. I haven't even marked you yet."

I stared at him. "What? I'm talking about sleeping, you pervert."

His eyes became unfocused again. His hand feathered its way up my arm, before taking my hand and bringing it to his face. My cheeks burned as he ran his nose along my wrist. "Cherry, why did you drug me?"

There wasn't really a point in lying anymore. My *brilliant* plan had gone up in flames, and I was left with nothing but guilt and a very high dragon. I shifted to sit next to him and decided to come clean.

"The truth is, I've been stuck here a long time. About five years to be exact," I began. "If I have to spend another five, I may just hurl myself off the roof. So I drugged your tea to see if I could convince you to take me home. The other dragon won't let me leave or even speak to me, so I knew he wasn't an option. I thought maybe if you had a bit of ayahuasca in you, it would loosen you up and you would be more likely to say yes."

"Why didn't you just ask me?" Dante inhaled against my

palm. His breath came out in the warm tickle against my skin. Fireflies began swing-dancing in my tummy. I pulled my hand free and tucked it at my side. *What is wrong with me? First you drug him and then you ogle him? Get your shit together, girl.*

Absently, I picked at the edge of my skirt. "I wasn't sure if you'd kill me for even asking."

Dante shook his head. "I can't kill you; you smell like flowers," he said, sounding like he just revealed the great truth of existence, instead of just more high nonsense.

I nodded. "Not sure how that correlates, but thank you. Still, I didn't expect you to have a bad trip. It would be far too dangerous to fly in your condition. So, clearly I didn't think this through."

His brow furrowed. "You said Gideon won't let you leave. Why?"

"Wish I knew. It was his creepy little water dog that dragged me here in the first place. The only time I ever see that dragon move is to stop me from escaping."

In a flash, Dante shot upright. The sudden movement caused me to jerk and fall back. He looked around the room wild eyed. "Has he hurt you?"

"I mean, sort of?" I shrugged. Being thrown back into a tower several times wasn't exactly a pleasant affair.

He leapt to his feet and rushed to grab the satchel he had left by the door. "We need to get you out of here. I need to take you home."

My stomach fluttered. He was still willing to take me home, even after what I'd done? Dante staggered to the side, and I rushed to steady him. Turns out the incredibly tall man was also incredibly heavy. I grunted and braced myself as he put more of his weight on me. He threw his satchel on the table and quickly began rummaging through it.

"Dante, calm down," I began. "We're not, like, in imminent danger. You'll be fine." Lightning flashed outside the window. A chorus of thunder rolled through the air with the force of a pride of roaring lions. As much as I wanted to leave, only an idiot would try to brave this weather.

"Of course I'll be fine," he snapped. "You are the one with the fragile human body."

I shot him a glare. "Lay off my body, man."

Ignoring me, he pulled something out of his bag and clutched it tight. "That mad bastard has gone too far. I'll rip his throat out before he so much as looks at you wrong again," he snarled. "I'm taking you home. Now." He swayed again and caught himself on the table. "Damn it all." Dante rubbed his temple and glared at the banana in the bowl of fruit. "I don't need that from you right now." He cursed at the fruit, then snatched an arm around my waist and pulled me flush against his side.

"Wait!" I gasped, trying in vain to push him away. "At least let me get my things."

"I'll buy you new things. Let's go," he growled.

He raised his fist, revealing a gray stone about the width of this palm. Letters from a language I didn't recognize glowed on its surface. Dante muttered something under his breath, then the letters grew even brighter until I had to look away from the sharp blue light. Swirls of mist surrounded us on all sides, whipping around like a tornado, and I clung tighter to Dante.

As the small tornado raged harder, Dante's grip on me tightened. His large body completely enveloped mine. A hand slid to the small of my back pushing me further against him. His free hand tilted my head to the side. I gasped when I felt his warm breath on my neck. He shuddered. Then inhaled deeply. "Dante?"

"Gods, you smell so good," he breathed.

Logically speaking, I knew I should be more concerned with the strange tornado he just summoned around us. Or the litany of other things wrong with the situation. But when the heat of his body pressed against mine, I was all too aware that the strange dragon-shifter pinning me to him was also the first man I'd seen since I was taken. I didn't have much experience with men. Yet I imagined when a man whispers such things as "Gods, you smell so good" in a woman's ear, when said woman had not seen a man in many moons, I'd like to think she should be allowed to feel some...*things*. At least, I really fucking hoped so.

Dante lifted his head to look me in the eye. My heart

practically beat out of my chest. The silver of his eyes bled away to an ethereal-looking violet. A long scar ran down the right side of his face, giving his regal features a wild edge. Flickering lights appeared around the swirling tornado keeping us entrapped. My breath hitched when he took hold of my chin and forced me to look at him.

"I need you to say yes," he said.

My throat went dry. "Say...say yes to what?" His tongue darted across his lower lip. I wondered just how much softer it was than the rest of his chiseled features. The warmth of him radiated into me. My body felt icy anywhere he wasn't touching. He leaned in closer, as if he meant to kiss me. *Did I want him to?*

"Just say yes."

"Yes," I said instantly.

Wait, oh hot habaneros, I can't do that!

His body shuddered. I squeaked when his hands grabbed my ass and lifted me to wrap my legs around him. He pulled me closer, and I closed my eyes.

Then I felt his sharp fangs on my neck.

"Wait, Dante, what are you doing?" I asked. Sharp pain sank into my neck as he bit down. I cried out and banged my fist against his shoulder, trying to knock him away. His grip held me like a vice. No matter how much I struggled he didn't so much as flinch.

Something seeped into my body from every direction. It

beat against my insides with such an oppressive force that I lost my breath. Thunder rolled in from the world outside. Then that too shook through me. There was a flash, and it felt like every inch of my body was electrified. I screamed, the sound being choked out by the storm trying to rip me apart.

"Relax, Princess. I have you."

"Relax?" I snapped at him. "You fucking bit me!" I thrashed, frantic to escape whatever force was clawing at my insides. Thick gray clouds lapped at my waist, while little sparks of yellow danced in their wake. My breath caught, and I choked on what felt like syrupy fog. Whatever the force was looking for, it found it. I felt it in the jolt it sent through my body. I wasn't in control anymore. My limbs weren't mine to move. My lungs gulped in air, but it wasn't me that commanded them to. It pushed and pulled against me until the fight had been wrung out of my consciousness. Soon it settled somewhere deep in my body. Thrumming through my blood in an almost pleasant hum.

Dante let out a breath and placed a kiss on my temple. "There you are."

The swirling tornado dissipated, and the clouds faded away. Yet the room was covered in darkness. I heaved in air, then tested my limbs to make sure I was the one in control again. When my fingers clenched and unclenched at my command, I shoved at Dante as hard as I could. It did nothing, but he relented and set me down, then stumbled away. There was a soft thud, and I heard him groan. Cold air nipped at my skin, making me shiver.

Chest heaving, I whirled around trying to get my bearings, but I couldn't see a damn thing. "What did you do?" I snarled at him.

Dante snapped his fingers. Torches lit up all around the room, revealing that I was no longer in my kitchen. Judging from the size of the room, I wasn't even in the tower. This room was enormous. I saw blankets, and soft cushioning littered the floor in every direction. On the far end of the room, there was a small waterfall that fed into a peaceful-looking pond. Vibrant lilies glowed in a white light on the water's surface. I looked up to see that the ceiling was covered by a rolling storm cloud. No rain came down, but flicks of lightning and thunder rolled gently through the clouds.

I turned back to Dante, anger and confusion making me see red. "Where the fuck am I, and why is it so damn cold?"

He forced his eyes to open and blinked around as if he was the one that was confused. "I took you home," he replied. "Isn't that what you wanted?"

"My home!" I screeched. "I meant my home, you weirdo!"

His head lulled back against a pillow, his eyes drooped. "You should have been more specific," he said, before closing his eyes. In a matter of seconds, the dragon-shifter was snoring.

"Are you fucking kidding me?" My question fell on deaf

ears. The damn lightweight was completely passed out. I gritted my teeth in frustration, then took a deep breath to clear my thoughts. "Bright side, Cherry. There's always a bright side," I muttered. If I repeated the mantra enough, perhaps it would come true. When my breath evened out, I snuck a glance at Dante's sleeping form. From the looks of it, he wouldn't be moving anytime soon. Maybe that *was* the bright side. He didn't seem like a raging murderer, but he did bite me for some weird reason.

Gods, I hope it wasn't kink-related. My neck still tingled where he had bitten me. I gently touched the area to assess the damage. A tiny smear of blood showed up on my palm, but for the most part the bleeding had stopped. "It must have just been a scrape. Thank goodness," I sighed.

My heart flip-flopped violently in my chest, making me stagger. The memory of Dante's lips on my throat sent coils of heat rushing down to my lower stomach. The chill in the air became almost unbearable against my skin. Dante rolled to the side, and I became all too aware how warm he would be against me.

I pinched myself; the pain served as a distraction to get my shit together. "What is wrong with me?" Knees shaking, I backed further away from him. Dizziness nearly took me off my feet, and I leaned against the wall for support.

"Snapping gators, are dragons venomous?" I had heard about a mushroom that could mimic the feelings of sexual desire when eaten. It also made you shit your brains out for three days. So hopefully a dragon's bite wasn't exactly like that. Still, there was no telling what other effects the venom could have.

Fear made the hair on my arms stand on end. Blue Coral Snake venom paralyzes their prey. Once bitten, the unlucky mouse is just stuck there until the snake unhinges its jaw and swallows it whole. I shook my head to clear my mind.

"Cherry, you are reading way too much into this. A man got high and bit you. It doesn't mean it's going to end in cannibalism." I spoke with confidence, trying to trick myself into bravery. Besides, the man had snatched me up like I was a rag doll. If he wanted to kill and eat me, he didn't need to resort to venom.

And yet…a little distance couldn't hurt.

"Time to go," I whispered to myself.

As silently as I could, I took a torch from the wall and made my way out the room. When the door clicked behind me, the sound of rattling plates hit my ears. Panicked, I flattened myself against the door, ready to swing it open again in case I needed to flee. Tiny sparks of flame flickered all along the floor. As the hallway lit up, I could see hundreds of candles placed on small golden plates. They rose high into the air, better illuminating my surroundings. I gasped in both shock and wonder. "Jumping jaguars," I breathed.

Soft piano music fluttered somewhere in the distance.

Candlelight danced against elegant crystal chandeliers that lined the massive hallway. The area was decorated with high columns painted blue, the tops and bottoms of the column ending in gold-plated caps with intricate filigree. The walls and floor were a beautiful white marble that was polished to a high finish.

More golden filigree traced patterns around doorways and up the arches that led to the ceiling. My breath faded away when I took in the painting that stretched across the entire ceiling. It was of a beautiful blue sky with fluffy white clouds. Dragons wove in and out of the clouds in an almost playful pattern. Some had glittering silver scales, like I'd seen on Dante. Others were red and yellow and a rainbow of other colors. I followed them further down, entranced. They ducked and weaved together, some forming intricate knots I'd only seen in tattoos.

It was just a freaking hallway, yet every inch seemed to be handcrafted by masters who must've trained day in and day out for the simple purpose of making everything they touched breathtaking. They had succeeded.

In a way, the site of all the surrounding beauty made me feel more at ease. Dante was clearly richer than any king in the land. A man that wealthy probably ate nothing but caviar and the tears of the poor. He didn't need to resort to eating random women he found. I stretched my arms wide, then shook out my legs, checking for any stiffness. Aside from the urge to shove my hand down my skirt, my body felt fine. "I guess dragon venom is just an aphrodisiac. If people can get frisky after eating oysters then I suppose dragon spit isn't that crazy."

Relieved, I leaned against the banister to peer down the stairwell, then drew my hand back. Everything was so perfectly polished, I didn't want to touch it. I was sure a single candlestick in this room cost more than all the money I'd ever seen in my life. Just in case, I took the end of my shirt and rubbed it against where my hand had touched the banister.

"Focus, Cherry. You're supposed to be escaping," I chided myself, giving my cheeks a slap.

"No more sightseeing. Time to find a way out." I was pretty sure there weren't any giant castles on Gideon's Island. So that meant my plan to escape the island was a resounding success. With only the minor setback of being wherever the hell I was now.

Purpose renewed, I raced down the staircase, ignoring the beautifully painted portraits lining the way to what seemed to be a dining area. Nor did I stop to admire the massive statues of beasts that surveyed the dining room. Instead, I ran through the castle in search of the front door. Which I imagine would have been a lot easier, if they had put a fucking directory in this bitch.

Mesmerizing rooms blended together in an increasingly irritating blur the more I tried to search for the exit. After about an hour, I had managed to find two dining halls, what I assumed was a giant bedroom, a study, a kitchen, yet another dining hall in the east wing, about five unexplained giant rooms, two indoor hot springs, and a conservatory full of plants and giant beehives home to bees the size of my head. I ran out of that room with a quickness at the first angry buzz.

Chest heaving, I paused against a window to catch my breath. "How big is this fucking castle?" I screamed.

When another hour or so had passed, I was convinced I was going to die lost in a strange man's castle. There was no way any living creature needed this much space. I didn't even spy a single servant or any of the people from the portraits hung on the walls. Not even the windows gave me any sign of where I might be. Each one revealed nothing but darkness. I looked to what must've been the fifth grandfather clock I had run past. Seven o'clock at night. No wonder I couldn't see anything outside.

I took a deep breath and trudged into another room with yet more rooms off it. Maybe behind one of these doors was a bedroom where I could take a nap. There was no way I was going to escape the (possibly) dastardly clutches of my newest dragon acquaintance if I was ready to keel over.

With a shove, one of the doors opened, and more magic candles rose to illuminate the room. "Snapping gators, this library is huge!" I gasped in awe. Bookshelves lined every wall and reached up to the ceiling. More bookshelves were neatly lined up in rows along the room. A wooden ladder leaned against a particularly tall shelf with a stack of books lying on a table next to it.

My fingers itched to get my hands on all of them. Years of boredom had me aching to snatch up every book. My sister Cinnamon and I had what I always thought was a decent size collection of fantasy novels and folktales. Clearly, we were just two paupers who thought too highly of themselves. Not even the king's library in Goldcrest City came close to this.

"Why couldn't I have been kidnapped by this dragon in the first place? This guy has way better stuff." Each row was labelled with the subject of the books therein. Wasting no time, I walked down the aisle labelled Magic/Beasts. My hand skimmed past comforting leather bindings. The smell of old books nearly brought tears of joy to my eyes.

A row of four similar-looking books caught my attention. I peered closer to find that they were a part of a series called "The Big Book Of." If my scrawny arms had the strength, I would've greedily nabbed the entire series. Unfortunately for me, my upper body strength failed me like a disappointing lover after I had grabbed *The Big Book of Beasts* and *The Big Book of Magic*. The remaining books of fairytales and folk songs would have to wait.

I dragged my treasure to the sunken couch in the center of the room and placed the books down with a huff. Wiping the sweat off my brow, I wandered over to the liquor cabinet that sat beside the fireplace on the far side of the room. "Ugh,"

I groaned in distaste. "He's clearly a whiskey drinker." Which was fine. If you were just never burdened by things such as taste. Instead, I grabbed a bottle of wine, uncorked it, and returned to the couch with a full glass.

I groaned with satisfaction as my body sank into the plush furniture. It was the type of couch that was worn in such a way that you could flop onto it in any position immediately and have it soothe all your troubles away. I debated taking my comfort level up a notch and finding some wood to start up the fireplace. But that would mean having to get up, and I'd done quite a lot of that today.

The Big Book of Beasts was a thick leather-bound monster of a book. Its cover was decorated with the seven-headed serpent. Each head was adorned with vicious-looking fangs and a row of small horns cascading down its skull. Its body wrapped around the spine rising from the sea that decorated the back of the book. The name Victoria Remnac sat proudly above the title.

"Remnac," I whispered, skimming my finger over the silver letters. "Wasn't that Dante's last name?" So this book must've been written by another dragon. Excitement raced through me at the thought. A mythical creature making an entire book on other magical monsters? If my sister and ma were here they'd be squealing in excitement.

The index had the monsters broken down into understandably separated categories. The types of magic they could use, bovines, equines, level of danger, etc. I wasn't entirely sure what a bovine or equine was, but I noticed horse-like creatures down the equine section. Wasting no time, my eyes zeroed in on the page for my favorite mythical creature. Page 526—Unicorns. Quickly, I flipped to the page and noticed with no small amusement that page 526 was only about halfway through the book. Suddenly the failure of my arms seemed much less extreme.

Giddy, I swirled my wine glass and took a generous sip. The page for my childhood obsession started off with a beautifully drawn unicorn galloping in a field. Facts such as normal height and weight littered the middle section, while below held more in-depth details on their behavior and habitat. "Songbird Wood?" I scrunched my nose trying to recall if I had heard it before. "Where is Songbird Wood?"

Something clattered on the table. A round golden saucer shook as if being pulled by a frantic force. It ceased its movements, then split down the middle. The top half rose, then a bright flash shot up above it and I reared back. When the light simmered down a pinch, a sprawling map unraveled itself in front of my eyes. The words "Songbird Wood" appeared on the top half of the map. A ring of gold materialized in a small forested area in the bottom half of the kingdom of Kibar. The ring grew larger as did its highlighted area. Letters were written out next to it by an invisible hand. "Songbird Wood, 614 miles from your current location."

"Holy filé powder, it's a magic map!" I leaned in closer, taking in the impressive details of the map's terrain. Reaching out, I skimmed my fingers over the tops of the green forest area. Instead of feeling parchment, my fingers let off a strange tingle and I pulled my hand away. The map grew hazy, then faded away, only to reappear as a moving picture. Actual unicorns grazed in a field. One stomped his hoof and looked up. Its ears twitched as if sensing a predator. With another stomp, the entire herd took off into the forest. The movements were so elegant and regal, it made my heart soar. The moving picture stopped then restarted with the unicorns back in the field.

The invisible hand wrote more words below the image. "Unicorn. Primary habitat: Songbird Wood. Regal and majestic creature whose body can be used for numerous purposes. The mane of the unicorn has many medicinal properties. A single hair can turn a barren wasteland into a lush forest. Its horn, when boiled down into different potions, could extend the life of a dying man, or even make an immortal out of a healthy man.

"Caution: Taking the life of the unicorn may result in steady and intractable mental decline. Previous cases have become slowly mad over time until finally ending their own life. Those who survived the curse have stated that they wished they hadn't."

What kind of monster would kill a unicorn? That was absurd. Still though, a single hair could turn a ruined land into a lush field? Well, I think I just found out how I was going to beat Chili at our pumpkin-growing contest. I was already going to have to travel to gods knew where to get home. A little pit stop wasn't going to hurt.

Speaking of home. "Um…map, thingy. Show me Boohail," I said, clearing my throat.

The map zoomed back out to its full view. Instead of zeroing in on my hometown, the words "Unknown Location" appeared in the middle of the map. "Damn."

Well, I still knew where it was. My home was located just on the tail end of Kinnamo. So long as I got close enough to it I could find my way back. I reached out and tapped at the bottom tail of the heart-shaped continent. As expected, the map zoomed in to where I tapped. Wide grasslands appeared across the land. "That's not right," I said, tilting my head in confusion. Boohail was surrounded by swampland. There wasn't anything but the bayou and forest until you traveled closer to Wandermere. I knew I had been gone a good five years but there was no way the entire landscape had changed. "Map, how far away is that location?" The invisible hand wrote out the letters 2,794 miles. "Hissing puma, that's far."

"Map, where is my current location?" My fingers thrummed on the book as the map zoomed out again then highlighted another location. My eyes went wide when it circled a mountain ridge on the continent that took up most of the northern hemisphere of the map.

"Volsog," I breathed. My stomach did a wicked turn. "I'm in Volsog. How the *fuck* am I in Volsog?"

The frozen continent was only home to demons. No human in their right mind would ever travel there. Hell, I don't think any human has ever traveled there. Yet here I sat in a dragon's castle, sipping his wine and reading his books.

Anger and frustration welled up to tears in my eyes. There was no way I could get out of here on my own. I hadn't escaped at all. I just traded one dragon's tower for another.

As if to add insult to injury, the ache of desire I'd been trying to ignore ramped up into incessant need. My breath came out as an irritated hiss as I squeezed my legs together. "Great, I'm trapped and I'm poisoned with weird dragon slut venom."

The more I tried to ignore it, the more the image of Dante's hands on me came to mind. The way he lifted me against him, how warm his breath felt as he ran his lips along my neck. Sighing, I slammed the books onto the table and stood. "I need a bath."

Chapter 5

Dante

Fallon's laughter echoed through the room. I rubbed at my temples to stop myself from putting a fist through the mirror. "I'm glad you find my predicament so amusing."

"I do," he said through a chuckle. "I really do." His shoulders shook from the other side of the mirror. The ornate room he was sitting in was in sharp contrast to the simple gray tunic he was wearing. The space appeared to be much too large for the charming house he and his wife called home. Which implied that he'd finally finished setting up his new hoard below their farm.

It never crossed my mind to build my home underground, but shadow dragons were known to be rather secretive. When

I thought back on it, I had no idea where the old Castle of Shadows even was. We knew the general location of his territory, but none were allowed inside. For all I knew, that castle could have been underground as well. No one I knew had ever seen it. My sister had attempted to find it once in her early years, thinking she'd be allowed passage as a female. She returned shortly after with a singed mane and bruised pride.

Fallon's predecessor rarely ventured out from his territory to speak to any of us. It wasn't until I met the young dragon that I realized the previous Lord Shadow even had a child. Though if he already had a female to protect, it would explain the violent rejection of Kohara's advances.

"Did you find out why that sea dragon held her captive?" he asked.

I shook my head. "Who knows what's going on in that madman's head. He's completely unrecognizable from what my father described. At first, I thought he may have taken her to replace the mate he lost, but from what she said, he made no advances in the time she was trapped in that tower."

Fallon paused. "If his mate died, then how is he still alive?"

"It's possible she wasn't his fated mate. I'm not sure. Still, I'm not letting him anywhere near my wife."

He chuckled. "Sounds like she doesn't want to be anywhere near *you*."

My brow twitched. Admitting the need for his assistance was uncomfortable enough. However, Fallon was the only

other dragon I knew that had taken a human mate, and I'd
clearly messed things up with mine. I didn't even know how
much time had passed since I fell asleep, only to wake up
dry-mouthed and groggy. At the very least, the magic bond
between us had let me know she was still in my castle. "Are
you going to help me or not?" I questioned with clenched teeth
and bruised dignity.

"I'm not sure I can, Dante. Of all the things not to do,
getting high off your ass and biting her as soon as you met
her is arguably the greatest thing not to do. Even so, I guess
you didn't electrocute her by accident. So Usha lost that bet."

"You placed bets?" I asked incredulously.

"Of course we did."

With a deep sigh, I leaned back in my chair and ran a hand
down my face. "Please, just tell me what you gave Madam
Shadow as a mating gift." Our initial encounter had been a
complete mess. Yet if the little human could be swayed by the
perfect gift, then perhaps she'd forget the whole thing.

If there was one thing I had absolute confidence in, it was
my hoard. Centuries of treasure-hunting had left my clan one
of the richest families in history. Not that there was anyone
left but my sister and me to enjoy the spoils. Though Kohara
had little interest in the family fortune. As one of the few
remaining dragonesses around, all she had to do was snap
her fingers and any unmated male in the area would come
running with jewels in hand. Most of her time was spent away

from the castle, gallivanting around with her latest person of interest.

Which of course meant the majority of the spoils went to me, to do with as I saw fit. The ground level of my castle was meticulously arranged to entice even the most fickle dragoness. I could only keep my fingers crossed and hope that a human female would be equally pleased.

My jaw clenched as I glanced over my hoard. Gold coins blanketed the floor until the stone beneath was completely hidden. Chests filled to the brim with jewels and finery were tastefully strewn about the room to give the eye places to rest. Ivory statues carved from the legendary demon walrus Baldantu sat proudly on each side of a golden throne. If she didn't care for jewels, then perhaps a fur coat from the enchanted treasure room.

The corner of his mouth twitched into a grin. "Nothing," he said simply.

I froze. "What do you mean nothing?" I asked.

Fallon shrugged, "We were a little busy hunting down that lich's chalices. There wasn't time for tradition."

Baffled, I leaned in closer. "So how did you get her to fall in love with you?"

"I licked her cunt."

He had to be joking. "Is it truly so easy?" I asked.

Fallon crossed his arms and leaned back in his chair. "I

imagine it would help. Look, if you want my advice, pick out something nice and shiny and tell her exactly what's going on. I was a fool and refused to tell Rabbit from the beginning that she was my fated mate. Instead, I panted after her like a wyvern in heat for almost a full month before she gave in."

I shuddered at the thought.

"From what she's told me, that wait could have been cut down to a few days. She'll need time to get used to the idea, as humans don't choose partners the same way we do. But if your woman is anything like Rabbit, then she'll come around after mulling it over. It's not as if she'll have much choice now that you've given her your magic. The honeymoon phase is impossible to ignore for long."

"Don't remind me," I said. The pull to return to Cherry's side had gnawed at me ever since I had woken up from my stupor. I went to the nearest chest and plucked a string of pearls from its contents. I turned back to Fallon and held it up for inspection. "What about this?"

He tilted his head, considering. "Pearls are fine, I suppose."

"You suppose?" I countered.

His mouth formed a thin line as he inspected the necklace further. "Try something with a more lustrous shine. Pearls are nice, but they don't shine and catch the eye as much as diamonds."

I nodded in understanding. "You're right. This is far too dull." I tossed the necklace aside and turned back to the chest, only to nearly leap out of my skin when a blur of white jumped on top of it. "Gah!"

Rebekah let off a yowl before leaping off the chest to rub her head against my ankle. In an instant, my headache returned.

"You snuck off with Baraku's cat?" Fallon asked.

I backed away from the creature and dusted the fur off my pants. "I didn't sneak away with anything. The damn beast must have hidden itself away in my bag."

The cat stretched herself out on a pile of coins and turned her back to us.

"Well, the little intruder may work in your favor," Fallon said, eyeing the beast. "Women like small animals."

Annoyed, I turned away and dug further into the chest. "Fine, but if it pisses in here, I'm turning it into a handbag."

Focusing on the task in hand, I disregarded anything made of pearls or opal. Neither seemed to suit Cherry. Thinking back, I couldn't recall Madam Shadow or Brie wearing much jewelry. Usha, on the other hand, had been quite taken with a pair of golden earrings we'd looted off a Toska naval ship back in spring.

"Dante, is that what I think it is?" Fallon called from behind me. When I glanced around, I saw him pointing at a trident protruding from a cluster of sapphires.

Shit. I should have hidden that before I scried him. Fallon and I may have been on friendly terms, but he was still another dragon.

His dark eyes grew wide. "That's Mokas the Blight's trident, isn't it?"

"It may be," I answered, my eyes narrowing in his direction.

Fallon remained transfixed by the trident. "What would you exchange it for?"

"Nothing," I growled.

Unfazed, Fallon's eagerness caused his magic to fail, and a fog of shadowy mist spilled all around him. "I'll give you the weight of your dragon form in rubies."

"Bah," I scoffed. "I wouldn't give it up even if you gave me enough rubies to drown a whale. Besides, the trident is useless to you without—"

"The shield and crown?" he cut in. Fallon leaned closer into the mirror. "What if I told you I had them?"

My jaw fell open. "You have King Mokas' shield?"

"Yes."

"And his crown?"

He nodded. The rest of the room was obscured by a rising black mist. "You possess his trident. If we put the three pieces together..." He trailed off.

"We could open his tomb," I finished. King Mokas the Blight was a legendary woodland dragon with a lifespan of nearly 3,000 years. He had used magic to create an oasis with streets made of pure gold and abundant fruit hanging from every vine in the middle of a barren desert, and from there he had created the nation of Mokyr. He had a reputation for bestowing enormous wealth on any wizard who could increase the force of his magic, out of his insatiable need for more power. It was rumored that, in his final years, his magic was so potent that even his shadow would bring ruin to any kingdom that stood in his way. According to legend, when he passed away, his trove and all the magical objects contained inside were locked up in a tomb somewhere in the desert.

I had no intention of releasing the tomb's key. Not when there was so much treasure at stake. Fallon and I stood in silence for a moment, assessing one another. "You know, King Mokas was a notoriously paranoid man. The traps he put in place will be far too daunting for a young dragon."

His eyes narrowed. "Yes, and the curses he undoubtedly placed on his treasure would be impossible for anyone to remove, unless they'd absorbed the magic of a powerful lich."

Dammit. He was right. Even if I was successful in stealing the other two keys from him, venturing out on my own would be a recipe for disaster. If we worked together, though, we might just have a shot at winning. Not to mention, there were so few dragons left it was highly unlikely that we would ever have to contend with one another for territory. We could split the treasure evenly and go our separate ways. Or even form a united kingdom fierce enough to rival King Mokas himself.

I straightened my shoulders and held his gaze. "Fallon Ozul, will you join me on a quest to retrieve King Mokas' treasure?"

Fallon grinned. "I thought you'd never ask."

Just then, Madam Shadow opened the door to the room. She waved away the black smoke around her and coughed. "Honey, could you tone it down on the smoke? It's wafting into the next room and we're in the middle of book club."

"We?" Fallon asked, turning to his wife. "Who is we? Did you let other people into my hoard?"

She set a hand on her hip and waved more smoke away. "Well yeah, you spent weeks digging a hole in the yard like a dog with a bone. People got curious. Low and behold, Brie and I find an entire library under the farm. What else was there to do but start a book club?" Her eyes widened when she took notice of the mirror. "Oh, is that Dante? Hi Dante!" She waved, then rushed forward and lifted the mirror and turned it around to inspect it. "How are you in a mirror?"

"Hello Cin," I called, waving back.

"Give that back," Fallon growled, reaching for her.

She ducked out of his reach. "No way, you didn't even tell me you two would be chatting today. Besides, I'm sure the gang would love to say hello too." With that, she darted off to another room, Fallon hot on her trail. She nudged open a door and held the mirror above her head. "Everybody, say hi to Dante!"

A chorus of greetings sounded off from a group of women sitting on a sunken oval sofa in the center of the room. I recognized Brie, Holly and Usha, but drew a blank on the other two.

Fallon's library was decorated in a similar fashion to mine, though the shadow dragon seemed to greatly prefer darker tones. A little too Gothic for my taste, but to each his own.

"Hey Dante!" Felix called from the bar.

"What the hell is he doing in here?" Fallon snapped, pointing to the werewolf.

"Felix joined the book club, obviously. He also makes the best cocktails," Cin replied.

As if to prove her point, Felix leapt over the bar, shaking a silver canister. Usha held up her drink to him and Felix topped it off with a grin. "So," he began, turning to look into the mirror. "Did you piss off your woman already?"

"No," I snapped.

"Oh, but you found her?" Usha asked excitedly.

Felix laughed and shook his head. "And so the time has come for you to ask your good buddy Felix to help you out." He sighed and waved a hand at me. "Not to worry, Dante, we'll fix that attitude problem of yours in no time."

Before I could respond, Fallon snatched the mirror from his wife. "He called me, not you lot. Now if you excuse us, we are right in the middle of a conversation." Fallon turned and made his way out of the room, then paused at the door to glare daggers at Felix. "And if you scuff my silver, I will gut you like a fish."

He returned to his study and locked the door behind him. "What were we talking about? Oh right, selecting a gift for your wife and then joining forces to find King Mokas' treasure."

Concern crept down my spine when I thought further on the traps undoubtedly lining his tomb. "What will we do with the women when we go find his treasure?" I asked, not liking the idea of leaving them unguarded.

Fallon raised a brow. "We bring them."

"Is…that safe? They're both human."

Fallon lifted his chin in pride. "Of course, if your woman takes to your magic as easily as Rabbit did, then in a few years they'll both be as powerful as any wizard. With the help of their magic we should be able to take the tomb in no time. You've already bitten her, so if things go well then we can set things in motion in about four to five years."

An extra pair of mages would certainly help. "Would they want to go? I didn't think Madam Shadow enjoyed adventuring."

"She'll be fine," Fallon said, waving off my concern. "Rabbit will invite her most annoying friends and start a book club in his library." He placed the mirror down on its stand and dropped himself into his chair. "Now the real question is where do we build our new kingdom? Have you found out where your wife lives yet?"

I shook my head. "I haven't had a chance to ask her about that."

He nodded and clasped his hands under his chin. "I'm

obviously partial to my territory. If you could convince her to move into the surrounding area, we can simply build up what we have here."

"Fine," I said. "On the condition that the first order of business is building a proper aqueduct system. I want running water and real toilets. If I have to shit in an outhouse like an animal for another second, I will go mad."

"I've already hired the contractors. I can't live like this anymore," Fallon said. He slammed a fist on the table and leaned back in his chair. "We're getting ahead of ourselves. Let's pick out a gift for your wife." He paused and looked me over. "Oh, and Dante?"

"Yes?"

"Comb your damn hair."

Chapter 6

Cherry

Captivity was a little less of a bitch when your captor had indoor hot springs. It was still awful, obviously. But there was just something about a steaming hot bath that managed to temper your anger just a tad. Even the black stone floor beneath my feet was warmed by the water beneath. After a few moments rummaging through the dressers lining the wall, I found towels and some nice-smelling soap.

Like the rest of the castle, the hot spring was designed with elegantly carved stonework. There were no murals, most likely because of the steam, but the room made up for it in the lush flowering vines that crept up the walls. Pale pink petals fluttered down from their flowers to scatter on the water below.

"Absolutely gorgeous," I muttered. "If Dante decided to kill or eat me, at least I'd die in a pretty place." As morbid as the thought was, I just couldn't bring myself to care. Escaping an island had seemed so doable in my head. I had spent each year fully believing that one day, if I could just get past the waves, I would be free.

But this was *Volsog*.

Even I wasn't brave or stupid enough to believe I could get out of here on my own. The only hope was that Dante had a bigger heart than Gideon and would take me home. But, after so many failed attempts, my hope was in short supply. So, if this was really where I was going to die, then I should at least take advantage of what I could.

I tossed my clothes on a nearby bench and took my hair out of its pigtails to wrap in a bun to keep it dry. Once the hair safety procedures were complete, I sank into the warm water and let out a satisfied sigh.

Of course, every moment of my life had to be met with contention, so the satisfaction didn't last long. The ache in my body went from a gnawing annoyance to a ferocious need. "Stupid dragon slut venom," I growled.

I reached behind me for the towel and folded it into a pillow. Once comfortable, I peeked around the room to ensure I was alone, then spread my legs.

My eyes fluttered closed as the image of Dante pinning me against him showed crystal clear in my mind. Slowly, I slid my hand down my body until my fingers teased at my pussy. With how pent-up I already felt, it didn't take more than a few strokes until I was gasping for breath. My free hand slid to my chest to tease my left nipple while I worked my clit. The steam from the bath turned to dragon-shifter's breath on my neck.

I bit my lip as the pressure built, my legs spread a little further as I dipped a finger inside me. The water lapping against my shoulders imitated his lips as he ran them across my skin. I craved the sensation of his long hair tickling my arms. Who was I kidding? I was so desperate I'd settle for the feeling of his teeth sinking into me again. As fucked up as it was. Heat raced through my core at the idea, and I worked myself faster, moaning his name.

There was a creak at the door, and my soul left my body when I saw the man in question standing in the doorway. Dante had changed from his simple clothes into more formal wear I could only assume was tailor-made to make him look upsettingly good-looking. His silver hair was draped over one shoulder to rest on a black coat with matching silver dragons coiling at the ends of the sleeves, while smoke lines rose above them. His dark blue tunic was unbuttoned, leaving a generous amount of sculpted chest in full view. White pants hugged muscled thighs before they disappeared into black leather boots.

And then there was me. Naked as the day I was born, eyes wide, touching myself in his bath while wantonly moaning his name.

Just fucking kill me.

Situations like these really made a girl question things about life. Like why didn't this grown-ass man know how to knock, why was he holding a tiara, and why was he walking over here?

Oh Gods, he's walking over here.

I tried to speak, hoping to form something witty to the tune of, "*Hey man, can you get the fuck out? I was in the middle of something.*" Instead, all that came out was a jumbled mess of intangible panic noises.

The panic-jumbles silenced into open-mouthed dismay when the dragon-shifter shrugged off his coat and stepped into the pool, with not a care for his clothes. Dante's expression was unreadable, and I wasn't sure if I should beckon him closer or get up and run.

Both?

He advanced on me, and I watched every step with increasingly oppressive hunger. It was a rather odd mix of dismay and desire. I wasn't entirely sure if I hated it. Dante stopped in front of me, then placed the tiara on my head without a word and sank to his knees. He glanced up at me. The hint of a devious smile touched the corners of his lips.

Then he lowered himself further, his head sinking under the water while streams of gleaming hair fanned out around him. My ass was suddenly lifted and I let out a yelp when he drew his broad tongue along my pussy. His figures dug into my writhing hips, pinning me in place. Sparks ignited across my skin, as if every nerve came alive every time he lapped hungrily against my clit.

"Wait," I panted, as my legs clenched around his head. My new friend added a finger into the soiree and I moaned, forgetting my own name for a few hot seconds.

I shook my head, forcing reason and sense back into my body, then grabbed his horn and pulled him off me. "I said wait."

When he ceased his movements, I scrambled my way out of the water to sit on the ledge. Dante followed, placing his hands on each side of my waist and pressing himself between my legs.

His face was mere inches from mine as he peered down at me. "What's wrong?"

"What's wrong?" I squeaked, trying to remember how speech was formed. "How about you say a couple words before trying to *enter me*?"

Gray irises receded to ethereal violet. The surrounding air simmered as if it were a breath away from combusting. His hand skimmed its way up my side before he gave a gentle push to my shoulder. "Lie back."

Sweet screaming meemies, that was way hotter than it should have been.

I shoved his hand away and scooted back. "You know damn well that's not what I meant. You can't just walk in here, put a tiara on my head and expect me to sleep with you." I tore the tiara off and went to throw it, only to stop when the glittering rubies caught my eye. The gold tiara was breathtakingly beautiful. Massive rubies encased in a ring of diamonds were set in the center. Another row of diamonds lined the bottom while other precious gems lined the five points.

Yup. Way too expensive to throw. Instead, I placed it gently at my side and crossed my arms over my chest.

Dante rested his arms on the edge of the pool, never taking his eyes off me. "What else would you want, then?"

"Well, I don't want to be trapped in Volsog. I want you to take me home. *My home*," I snapped at him.

"Granted. What else?"

Wait, really? I stared at him for a moment in disbelief, then snatched the tiara back up. In for a penny in for a pound. "I want to keep this too."

A grin tugged at the corner of his mouth. "It's yours."

"...And two books from your library."

He reached out to trail his hand along my ankle. "Think bigger. Take the entire library."

How much did this man value pussy? No wonder women have sugar daddies.

Dante let off a low chuckle. "You seem disappointed."

My fingers thrummed nervously against the rim of the tiara. "I guess I was just expecting more of a fight than this." Nor did I expect the day would end with me giving my virginity to a dragon in exchange for transport and riches. But the more I looked at him, the less of a hardship the idea seemed to be. "You're really going to give me all this stuff if I just sleep with you once?"

He raised a brow. "Once? No. Our situation is a little more permanent than that."

Dammit, I knew there was a catch. "What do you mean?" I asked.

He grabbed my ankle to drag me to him. A small noise escaped my lips as he settled me on the ledge. The stroke of his hand on the bite mark he had given me earlier sent fireflies straight to my tummy. "I mean, you've taken my magic."

I narrowed my eyes on him, then placed the back of my hand on his forehead. "Are you still high?"

Grinning, he took my hand and kissed my palm. "I'm a lot of things, but drugged is no longer one of them. If you'd like me to explain further, then we'll need to revisit this once you've dressed." His violet gaze raked over me with unabashed hunger. "Or I could taste your cunt again. I'm eager to draw more of those noises out of you."

Stay focused, girl.

My voice came out as a broken stammer. "Clothes."

"Just a little," he begged. "Please?"

Sweet peaches, someone put my soul back in my body.

"No thank you," I said. Resenting every syllable.

"Pity," he sighed. "When you leave this room, go three

doors down and enter the bedroom on your left. The wardrobe in that room should have something that will fit you. When you're done, join me in the dining hall." He gave my palm one last kiss, then released me and moved away. Water dripped down from his soaked clothes as he lifted himself from the pool. Dante slung his discarded coat over his shoulder and made his way out the door.

"Wait!" I called after him.

He paused and glanced back at me.

"Um...could you tell me where the dining hall is? This place is a maze."

Chapter 7

Cherry

One successful closet raid later, Dante and I were sitting in the dining hall. The extravagant yellow dress I had pilfered, from whoever's room that had been, hung loosely off my shoulders. It fell far past my feet and I had to bundle it at my side to walk properly, but it was better than slapping on dirty clothes.

Plates of meat and cheese were brought out by little creatures. I did a double take; they looked like a family of warrior weasels that had turned to a life of crime, and who relished in the fruits of their labor. They were about the same size as the frog people on Gideon's island. Were all dragons assigned tiny butler animals or was it a rite of passage kind of thing?

I shuddered, thinking back on the spiked doglike creatures

Gideon also had at his disposal. Unlike the butler frogs, the water dogs didn't often come inland, much to my relief. Yet at night, I could hear their haunting cries along the shore.

"So let me get this straight, you bit me because my scent called to you. Which created a soulmate bond that ties us together as husband and wife and now we've entered a…" I waved my hand in the air trying to remember how Dante put it.

"A honeymoon phase," he finished, biting into a slice of pork.

"Yes, thank you. Which is the reason for this…intense attraction for each other."

He nodded.

I rested my elbows on the table, clasped my hands in front of my face and smiled at him, waiting for him to finish the joke. Yet he merely sipped his drink and continued eating.

My shoulders shimmied in a little dance before I wagged a finger at him. "No," I giggled. "You hear what I mean?" I took a sip from my mug and took a deep breath. "Because forget it…" Another sip for my suddenly parched throat. "On no account, you hear me?"

The giggling ended as my denial turned to a rage that settled into the stillness of my fists on his table. "You're going to start off with a no, sprinkle some paprika on that no, mash the no together with yeast, water and butter, roll it into a ball of no, and then bake it in the oven for an hour so it comes out with a nice flaky no. I'm not gonna lie, you had me at sexual favors, I'm a little desperate at this point. But I draw the line at holy matrimony to the same type of demon that I just escaped from. It's not gonna happen, sorry you wasted your time, I'm gonna go take my chances with freezing to death outside. Where is your front door?"

"Gods, you talk fast," Dante sighed, resting his chin on his hand. "You didn't feel the need to breathe during any part of that declaration?" He swirled a finger between us as if to mock my rushed panting.

In truth, I was breathing rather fast, but the situation called for it. The walls in the room I thought massive only moments ago, shrank further in on me with every tick of the clock. "I mean it, Dragon," I snapped, then pushed away from the table and stood. "Where is your front door?"

"I understand this can be a lot to take in." Dante paused, the grip on his goblet increased as he took in my trembling form. "Are you alright, love? You look rather faint."

I shook my head. "Don't call me that."

He stood and moved to my side, but I stepped away from him. "Cherry, sit down."

"Don't tell me what to do, either," I barked at him. The room swayed, and I gripped the table to steady myself. "I need to get out of here."

The dragon-shifter took a step back, apprehension forming a crease on his brow. "Alright. I'll take you outside, but first I'd like it if you took a sip of water." Slowly, he took a glass from a tray in the center of the table, filled it and slid it over to me.

Water spilled as I picked up the glass with shaking hands and drank. After a few sips, Dante nodded in approval. "Good, this way then."

Heart pounding, I followed him out of the dining hall. He remained silent, only glancing back at me occasionally to ensure I was still following. Relief flooded through me when he stopped in front of a door, then turned to fury when I didn't see the outside world on the other side. "That's just a closet!" I snapped.

"How very observant," he said, sarcasm dripping from his voice. Dante rummaged through articles of clothing before he emerged from the closet with a light blue fur coat. "Put this on," he said, holding it out for me.

Frustrated, I snatched the coat and pulled it on. "Are we at least close to the exit?"

He jerked a thumb to his left and turned away to continue digging in the closet. I followed the direction to spot two huge double doors with lion-head handles at the far end of the room. With his back still turned, I bolted toward freedom.

The soles of my boots squeaked against the marble floor as I skittered to a stop and flung open the front doors. A blast of cold hit me like a slap and I reared back momentarily before forcing myself forward into the night. White completely blanketed the ground in front of me, while more white dots swirled through the air, smacking against my skin in freezing little bursts. I swatted away the offending flakes in a panic before I fell back on my ass with a scream.

"What the hell is this?" I cried out, crab-walking back into the castle before kicking the door shut. Frantic, I beat the white stuff off me and shook as much of it as I could out of my hair.

"It's just snow," a voice called from behind me. I turned to see Dante leaning against the closet. He had a hand covering his face while his shoulders shook from laughter. "I swear to you, wife, it will not kill you." His face broke out in a grin as more laughter floated through the entryway.

Embarrassment made my face heat, and I stopped my frantic patting. "Right," I sputtered. "I knew that, I just...I never saw it in person before."

He cleared his throat then nodded. "Of course. Completely normal reaction." The last of his words came out in a laugh as he lost his composure once more.

"Listen you, it's been a very rough day. Just point to the direction of the nearest port and I'll be out of your hair," I hissed.

"Princess, you'll be dead before you even make it down the mountain if you try to leave on your own. Come back to dinner and I'll fly you wherever you want to go in the morning."

I narrowed my eyes at him. "Do you plan on staying wherever I am once we get there?"

"Obviously."

"Then I'll take my chances on the mountain." Thunder boomed. Its deafening roar nearly made me fall to my knees.

Screeching pumas. How is it storming so bad here too?

The dragon-shifter let out a breath before leaning away from the closet to make his way over to me. Instead of waiting for him, I hoisted myself up and shoved my way out the door. The wet cold slapped against me once more but this time I was ready for it. I pulled my hands into the coat sleeves to protect them against the bitter frost before trudging forward. My boots sank into the calf-deep snow. I looked around trying to see if there was any sign of a path. Yet each way I turned there was only endless white and darkness.

"Cherry, stop being foolish and come back inside," Dante called from the doorway.

"Foolish?" I snarled, turning to face him. "I'm trapped in a castle with a psycho dragon who thinks we're married. You could be a deranged cannibal for all I know. Besides, I just escaped the clutches of one dragon. You really think I want to be snuggled up next to another?" Angry tears welled up in my eyes, then froze on my face. Quickly, I scrubbed them away and turned to leave. "What is it with you guys and kidnapping? Get a hobby, damn it."

Lightning flashed and the wind picked up to blow the hood from my head. I reached back to pull it over my ears, shielding them from the harsh cold.

"I understand that you're upset," he bit out. "But there are better ways of expressing discontent than marching off to certain death. Now get back inside before you get hurt."

I gritted my teeth, irritation making me clench my fists so hard my nails dug into the skin. "What did I tell you about telling me what to do?" I yelled before continuing down the path in snowy darkness. The aurora above didn't give off much light, and I had to squint to make out a stone archway that appeared as I trudged further away from him. As I got nearer, I could just make out snow-covered steps leading down through it. Without looking back, I placed a hand on the railing and made my way down.

His deep voice rose to shout over the wind. "Oh, wise and stubborn princess, won't you grace my halls with your presence once more?"

The sarcasm in his voice had me seeing red. Which was probably why I didn't see the consequences of my (admittedly foolish) actions before it was too late. There was a squelch under my foot where there should have been the crunch of snow. I looked down to see the offending boot covered in red. Backing away from the mess, my gaze followed the blood trail to a dark moving lump a few paces away from me. The shadowy mass paused, then dropped something on the ground that fell toward me. It was the severed head of a deer. Its long antlers were the only thing still intact, while its face was half eaten, the eyes plucked clean out.

I shivered and backed away. My heart pounded against my chest as if trying to escape through the lining. The mass moved forward, revealing two large fuzzy antennae that swiveled in my direction as if tasting me in the air. A set of orange eyes bulged out of a furred head. With a hiss, the giant moth spread its wings wide, the painted eyes on its wings shooting me a deadly glare. Blood dripped from its mandibles as it reared itself up higher and let out a piercing screech.

"Oh, shit!" I yelled.

The demon moth flapped its wings, the force nearly knocking me back before it screeched again. A flash of blue lit up the world around me as a lightning bolt shot forth and severed one wing clean off. The monster's screeching morphed into terrified clicks as it fell back. Another bolt of lightning shot forward, striking the monster in its torso before it screamed and curled up into itself, then fell very still.

Sparkles faded when the lightning fizzled away, leaving me in a world of near-darkness once again. I stood frozen. Footsteps approached from behind before Dante placed a hand on my shoulder. "Have you finished your little tantrum?"

Some deep stupid part of me opened my mouth before I could stop it. "No."

"You can't be serious," he replied. His silver hair draped over my shoulder as he pulled me back against his chest. I turned to look up at him, letting myself admire his handsome features for a moment. If he were a normal man, the sinful way his lips curved into a brooding scowl would've had me on my knees. The thin scar that stretched from his brow to the corner of his mouth gave him the appearance of a hardened warrior mixed with a devilish rake. In every sense of the word, the man was unfairly sexy. But the sharp curved horn jutting out of the left side of his head buried any notion of normality.

Maybe it was the shock or maybe it was the fact that my life had once again been laid at the feet of dragons, but I wanted nothing more than to continue on my path. If nothing else, just to spite him. The dead monster in front of me should've filled me with a fear of what else was lurking around the castle. Yet I felt calmer than I had in years. "Honestly, I think I am," I said, before shrugging off his hand and making my way around the moth's corpse.

Dante let out a frustrated noise and caught up to me. His long legs had no trouble carrying him through the heavy snow, whereas I was half crawling. Which only added to my irritation. "Are you insane?" he asked.

"That's a strong possibility," I admitted. It would explain why I was crawling off into certain death. Though I doubted I was the only woman in the world who chose death over marriage. Men were often more trouble than they were worth.

My boots made a sucking noise as Dante plucked me off the ground and threw me over his shoulder. He ignored my indignant squawks of protest and turned to head back into the castle. "What do you think you're doing?" I snarled, slamming a fist against his back.

He remained silent, then slapped my ass when I struggled further. "Stop your flailing or I'll drop you."

Heat flamed my face. "Did you just spank me?"

"Was that too hard?" he asked, shutting the doors behind him. "You'll need to let me know if I'm being too rough. Humans are terribly fragile." In an instant, the sharp bite of the cold vanished.

My fingers throbbed and I ran my breath over them to force more warmth into the tips. "Whatever," I mumbled over his shoulder. "Just put me down, we're back inside now." Instead of letting me slide off him, Dante locked an arm around my legs keeping me in place. His shoulder dug into my gut as he made his way up the stairs and into the library where I had been relaxing before.

The pitter-patter of tiny paws raced toward us until a tiny white kitten appeared and wrapped itself around Dante's feet. He cursed under his breath and nudged the cat away from him. Undeterred, the cat followed close behind, yowling as Dante approached the liquor cabinet.

"What are you doing?" I asked.

"I've come to the realization that your shenanigans are going to cause me a lot of stress. The drink is for my fortitude." He reached back to hand me the bottle of whiskey. "Hold this."

Obeying, I grabbed hold of the bottle and debated whether

I should try hitting him over the head with it. "You were a lot nicer back in the tower."

"My patience tends to wane after someone drugs me to use me as a beast of burden," he said, sardonically.

"Alright, I deserve that one."

He waved a hand at something in the corner. One of the fluffy butler weasels peeked out from a door that was disguised as a painting. Its little head tilted up at its master, waiting for instructions. "Start a fire, please."

Without a word, the weasel bolted past us to fetch wood from a cabinet next to the fireplace before setting to work. In a few quick moments, the kindling caught and the tiny demon fanned the flames into existence. Then as quickly as it appeared, the creature vanished back into the painting from which it had come. Dante carried me over to the sitting area then placed the drinks on the table next to the bottle of wine I had pulled out earlier. "I see you made yourself at home," he remarked.

"Well, I couldn't find your front door in this labyrinth of a castle. So I took a break."

He hummed. "Princess, if I put you down are you going to run?"

A tempting thought. "No, and stop calling me princess."

He hesitated, as if unsure whether to trust my answer, then deposited me on the couch. He took a seat next to me and handed me a glass of whiskey. I placed it back on the table in favor of popping the wine open and filling up my old glass. "I can't drink that stuff."

He shrugged and downed his glass before picking up the one I had discarded. "So, what did you choose to read?" he asked.

I slid further away from him and drew my knees up to my chest. "Are we going to ignore what just happened?"

He leaned back in his seat, getting comfortable. "We can. If it were up to me we'd skip to the part where we're madly in love with each other. Go on dates, watch a thunderstorm with a steaming cup of tea, overthrow a reasonably sized kingdom and bend it to our liking, then get a dog," he mused, swirling his glass.

I took a sip of my wine, letting the smooth taste ease down my frozen throat. "You want to run the second to last one by me again?"

"That was a joke." Dante shrugged and cocked his head. "Unless you want to. Know that we have options. I'm just over the moon that you're here."

"Even though I almost died trying to get away from you?"

"What's a relationship without a few trials and tribulations?"

"Isn't this your kingdom?" I asked, motioning to the surrounding castle.

He took in the room with indifference, as if displeased with the surrounding opulence. "Yes, but I've been trapped in

Volsog long enough. That's why I had planned to rebuild my castle after I claimed whichever land my mate hailed from. Where is that, exactly?"

I ignored his question with one of my own. "Don't you have to rule over the local populace or something?"

He shook his head. "Absolutely not. I'd sooner abandon this castle and all its treasures than be burdened by the mundane trials of their everyday lives."

"Then why do they let you rule over them?"

"They don't *let* me rule over them. I allowed them to live here." With a sweep of his hand, the map disk sprang to life. The map grew when he tapped a region in the northwest corner of Volsog, revealing a mountain range with a river running through its bottom half. "This region is absolutely devoid of other titan beasts," he began. "Those who reside here need not fear giants trampling their crops or rocs destroying their communities. Do you know why?"

"No."

A confident grin spread across his face. "Because I'd kill them for trespassing."

"Intense," I offered. In a way, being in a dragon's territory was similar to what my village did with our goddess temple. Myva's protective barrier shielded us from all manner of demons that came knocking. It made sense that the more intelligent creatures would gravitate to a safer area like us.

"Where did you say you lived again?" he pressed.

I didn't. Nor did I want to. Not with a complete stranger informing me he planned to move in and build a freaking castle. Before being kidnapped by Gideon's minion, I was just a few months short of being assigned my own section of my family's farm. Each of my siblings and I knew growing up that at the age of eighteen, our parents would section on a part of the family farm as a gift.

Or in my brother Cumin's case, help him buy a particular piece of land a little further out. He'd always been the picky sort. So none of us were surprised when he pulled out a "Land for Sale" flier at his eighteenth birthday celebration. At twenty-three, I was a good five years overdue. Still, I couldn't imagine whatever small plot I was to be given would be enough to fit whatever Dante had in mind.

Speaking of age. "How old are you?" I asked. If I had to guess, the dragon-shifter looked to be in his late twenties or early thirties. His face was free of any imperfections such as laugh lines or sunspots. Yet the commanding aura around him projected something far older. Maybe thirty-five. Some folks were just born with the gift of younger-looking features.

"I'm seven hundred and four."

I choked on my drink. Red wine spilled all over the front of my borrowed dress. "Seven hundred and four!" I choked out between coughs. "How is that even possible?"

Dante's weight lifted from the couch. At a speed no human could match, he rushed over to the bar area and returned with a cloth. I snatched it greedily and wiped what I could of the mess off me. "Age does not have the same effect on dragons as it does on other species," he began as he returned to his seat. "We age at a considerably slower rate, and our human forms reach adulthood at the age of forty. Our dragon forms never truly stop growing. It slows to roughly half an inch every few years after we reach one hundred years of age."

My voice came out in a hoarse squeak. "How long do dragons live?"

"Until we're killed," he said, as if it were the most natural thing in the world. "Both my parents lived well into their 8,000s before they met their end."

A friggin immortal is sitting next to me. Endless questions flew into my head. Dante, if he really was as ancient as he claimed to be, would have lived through the era when demons were not locked away by the Goddess Myva. My ma would regale me with tales of adventure and creatures of all shapes and sizes, but I always dismissed them as just that: tales. But here I was, sitting next to physical evidence of that era. I gazed around the library in wonder, as though seeing it for the first time. This place held at least 8,000 years of history. My hands itched, eager to get my mitts on every page.

Not only that, the walls outside of this castle led to land that was home to the very same creatures I'd always dreamt about. If I weren't positive they'd gut me as soon as they saw me, I'd love to meet them.

Excluding any other dragons. I've had enough of them.

"How old are you?" he asked, snapping me out of my thoughts.

"Hmm? Oh, I'm twenty-three."

He blinked. "I apologize for not being more precise. I'm unaware of how humans age. Are you an adult?" His tone became more suspicious as he scanned my face. "Please tell me you're not a child."

Indignant, my fist clenched at my side so I could hold myself back from swatting him. "No. I'm an adult," I bit out.

His shoulders dropped in relief. "Oh, thank the gods," he sighed.

"Do I look like a kid?" I huffed.

"Do I look over seven hundred?" he asked, sipping his drink.

"Fair point," I conceded. If they really aged so slow, then a dragon in their twenties probably looked like a gangly preteen. I guess I couldn't fault him for being confused.

He reached for the bottle of whiskey and refilled his glass. Its delicious caramel smell mingled with Dante's. Without meaning to, I leaned forward, drawn in by the earthy scent of fields after a good rain.

"Are you ever going to tell me where you live, or should I simply pick out a sunny spot on the Southern continent and build your dream home there?" he asked, his tone teasing.

I cleared my throat and leaned back, grateful for the

interruption before I did something stupid. Like crawling in his lap to get more of that scent.

Damn this dragon slut venom!

"I don't want to tell you," I said.

"Why not?"

"You're an immortal stranger fully capable of killing me or destroying my home. If you chose to do so, there would be nothing I could do to stop you."

His brow furrowed. Then he tilted his glass up as if inspecting the remaining liquid. After a moment of deep deliberation, Dante nodded. "I can't fault that logic. Would you believe me if I told you I'd never do that?"

"No," I said flatly. "Besides, I doubt you'll be able to fit a giant castle on my little farm, so maybe we should just call it quits here."

"Well you never know," he said casually. "Why don't we go take a look? With winter well on its way, I imagine you're far past the growing season. Now would be the perfect time to build."

"Nice try, we don't even have real winters. The growing season stretches far past this."

A satisfied smirk pulled at his lips. "No winters, huh? I take it you're from the far South then. Somewhere in Kinnamo I imagine."

I froze, then schooled my features. "Nope."

Smelling blood in the water, Dante leaned in closer. "Why

not just tell me where? If you've truly been gone so long, I'm sure you're missing your family terribly. I was just visiting a small village in Kinnamo before I found you. Lovely area."

His words sent a chill down my spine. If a dragon was wandering around near my home, who knows what that meant for my family. I cleared my throat and tried to keep calm. "Oh, what village?" I asked.

He opened his mouth to speak, then closed it and tilted his head. "Dammit, I can't remember the name."

"Seriously?"

"Human settlements often look the same," he said with a shrug. "I think it started with a D. Though I suppose it doesn't matter."

YES IT DOES!

I wanted to scream. A fire breathing mythical monster was casually sightseeing around my home and he couldn't even bother to remember the name! How was I supposed to press him for answers like this? It wasn't as if I could just ask him about Boohail directly. He'd know right away that's where I was from.

If the village he was in started with a D, then it may have been Doncaster. That was a good three-day journey on horseback. Probably a short jaunt to someone who could fly.

Snapping gators, this is so frustrating.

"Would you like me to take you there?" he asked.

The offer was tempting to say the least. If he took me to

Doncaster then I could slip away from him and be home in a matter of days. But then he'd know I lived nearby.

Not wanting to seem eager, I casually sipped my drink and kept my tone uninterested. "No thanks. That far south might be a bit too hot for me. Why don't you just drop me off anywhere outside of Volsog and I'll find my own way home?" I asked.

Dante tilted his head. "Let me get this straight. You want me to drop you off at an unspecified location on the Southern continent and believe you can make your way back home without being murdered?"

"Yes, exactly!" I said with a smile.

He rumbled with a deep chuckle. "Alright."

"Really?"

"No."

"Why not?" I snapped, drinking the last drop out of my glass. Dante picked up the wine and opened it before I could even reach for it. I offered him my glass, and he slid his free hand over mine to balance it as he poured. Wherever my fingers touched his skin, there was a surge of searing heat, and the screaming need I'd been attempting to tame flooded back with devastating force.

Fucker. He did that on purpose.

Violet seeped into his eyes before they quickly receded back to gray. "Well for starters, you are my wife."

"Hey, you bit me! I didn't agree to anything."

"If memory serves, neither did I. You drugged a dragon; thus, you must now deal with the consequences of your actions. Whether or not you agree, we are now irreversibly linked."

"Unless one of us dies," I grumbled around my glass.

"One? No," he said, shaking his head. "What part of irreversibly linked did you not get? If I die, the magic inside of you will grow too strong and kill you."

My mouth fell open in shock. "This is so unfair."

He hummed. "I imagine this is one reason drugging people is frowned upon."

"You could have at least brought me somewhere that wasn't Volsog."

He scoffed. "All I heard was home and the low drawl of my own existential dread. Woman, there were faces in the walls and their words were extremely cutting. Be happy I didn't warp us into the jaws of a beast."

I buried my face in my hand. This is all too much. "So what do we do, big guy?" I asked. "You want a wife and I have no intention of marrying a stranger."

There was a twinkle of mischief in his eyes. "Isn't it obvious? You give in."

The confidence in his words brought a grin to my face. This man had no idea of the gauntlet he just threw. "Oh, honey," I drawled. "Bless your heart."

His eyes closed on an inhale. "Call me that again, I liked it."

It was at that moment that I completely scrubbed the word

honey from my vocabulary. The softening of his voice, the way his long hair moved and glistened as it fell down his chest at the slightest tilt of his head. All of it should have been out-lawed for the sake of women's undergarments everywhere.

The cat jumped onto the couch, snapping me out of my stupor. Swallowing around a lump in my throat, I gave a terse reply. "Nope. I'm good."

Dante grimaced and rubbed at his temple before pushing the cat off his lap. "You should be nicer to your kitty," I scolded.

He grabbed it by the scruff when it tried to fight its way onto his lap again, then gently set it down on the ground. "She's not mine, just a stowaway I'll need to return soon."

"Alright," I nodded toward the map. "Tell you what, why don't we give this 'bond' thing a trial run?" I asked, reaching for *The Big Book of Beasts*. When I removed it from on top of *The Big Book of Magic*, the book rattled, then blew open. Its pages flipped wildly until it stopped dead on a banishing spell. The spell labeled itself as suitable for mid- to high-level threats and had a list of various herbs and incantations needed to perform it.

I glanced back at the dragon sitting beside me. "I think your book is trying to tell me something."

He sipped his drink. "It's an old castle. I wouldn't be sur-prised if there was a ghost or two milling about."

"What?" I looked around, half expecting a ghost to pop out at any moment. When no specters leapt out to grab at my feet, I let out a breath. Dante looked away from me, his shoulders shaking.

I shot him a dirty look, then found the scrap of paper in *The Book Of Beasts* I had been using as a bookmark and I quickly flipped it open to the unicorn page. "Anyway, would you be open for a brief trip to see unicorns? I always loved them as a kid and had no idea they actually existed until I picked up your book."

His lips twitched. "You're having a drink with a dragon and you want to go see a horse with a horn?"

Embarrassment simmered in the tips of my ears. "I just like them, alright? Besides, we can use the trip as an excuse to get to know each other. I won't tell you where I live, so if I ever feel the need to escape, I will just disappear into the forest and you will never see me again."

A hint of amusement lit his features. "I understand you think you have a choice in this matter, so I'll humor it," he remarked, setting his glass down. "Fine, in the morning we'll pack a few things then set off to see your precious unicorns."

He stood and held a hand out to me; I took it and let him help me off my seat. "You're going to agree to it, just like that?" I asked.

Dante gestured for me to follow him as he exited the library. "I have a vested interest in gaining your favor, Princess."

"Not a princess," I corrected.

Ignoring me, he continued. "Besides, I enjoy traveling. It's been too long since I was free to do so."

Oh, I didn't even think of that. Few demons were found beyond Volsog. The goddess' magic should tear them apart as soon as they try to leave. "How were you able to resist Myva's magic enough to travel to Kinnamo?"

He halted, and I nearly bumped into his back. He turned to me with a frown etched on his face. "Is this a poor time to tell you that Myva is dead?"

The glass slipped from my hand to shatter in a million pieces on the floor. "What?"

A weasel darted out from a painting with a broom in hand to clean up the broken glass. I stepped away from it, swaying before Dante placed a hand on my back to settle me. "Perhaps you should sit back down. I imagine you have a few questions."

"A few?" I asked, wide-eyed. "You just told me the goddess was dead, I've got more than a few questions." Stepping out of his embrace, I whirled around to jab a finger in his chest. "Start talking."

"Alright, well let's start from the beginning." He made his way back to the couch, and I followed. "The goddess you knew as Myva was actually a lich masquerading as a goddess in order to control you. Around six hundred years ago she sacrificed many of my kind in her dark magic." He looked away, his eyes grew dark before he took a deep breath.

"We rose up to destroy her, but failed. After that, she

sealed us away in this frozen wasteland, then placed a curse of madness on Volsog Gate. If any of us tried to leave, we'd go insane and kill anything in sight. As if that wasn't enough, she'd open those gates every fifteen years, letting the madness spill in until we tore at each other like animals."

Dread sank in my gut. "The Hero's Call," I whispered.

He nodded solemnly. "I imagine it was a useful ruse to keep humans in line. No reason to turn your back on a goddess who saved you from bloodthirsty monsters."

"You said you were seven hundred and four, does that mean you fought against her?"

"I did. Three of my brothers were some of her first victims. The remaining two fell in the war that followed."

Tears pricked my eyes and he placed a comforting hand on my knee. "Don't cry for me, Princess. It was a long time ago. I consider myself lucky that I still have my sister, Kohara, though she was born well past that time of pain. Besides, I had the honor of helping bring that evil bitch to her knees."

I let out a breath. "This all sounds insane."

"Yes, I imagine it does. Madam Shadow was rather surprised to hear the truth herself, before she helped us."

"Who's that?"

The darkness in his eyes receded as he leaned back. "Madam Shadow is the brave human that helped free us from the curse. Albeit by accident. In the last Hero's Call, as you called it, she was attacked by a shadow dragon named Fallon Ozul. She struck him with a stick of cinnamon and his curse was lifted. It was then we found out that that's how we break the curse."

"Why do you call her Madam Shadow?"

"She married the shadow dragon. That makes her Madam Shadow. Just as you are now Madam Storm."

"Madam, huh? Sounds fancy. So then what happened?"

He took a sip of his whiskey. "I'm a bit hazy on the details of the first two chalices, but from what I understand, she and Fallon went on a quest to destroy each of the chalices Myva used as her heart in order to break her curse once and for all. In an attempt to stop them, Myva attacked me here and embedded one of the chalices in my mane. With the source of her magic so close to me, the cinnamon did nothing to bring me back from that hell."

He paused, a smile gracing his lips before he continued. "Unfortunately for that damned lich, nothing stops Madam Shadow when she puts her mind to it. She flew on her pegasus and dropped onto my back, then broke the chalice with a hammer, freeing me. After that, I joined forces with them and the other demons they freed. Together, we destroyed Myva's remaining chalices and killed her."

"Wow. This is…this is a lot to take in," I admitted. My fingers tugged at a seam in the dress as I tried to calm my heart. "How does cinnamon even break a curse?"

Dante shrugged. "You'd have to ask a magic scholar for that. Though most remedies to ailments can be found in nature. For example, the bark of a willow tree can make a wonderful pain reliever. It shouldn't be too surprising that certain herbs and spices have a hand in counter-magic."

Most of my childhood was spent running through fields of cinnamon. Who would've thought that was the very thing that could have broken such a dangerous curse. It was almost unbelievable. I supposed it could be. There was nothing stopping him lying to me. Yet the pain etched in his face when he spoke of his brothers seemed all too real to simply pass off. "I don't know what to think," I said finally.

"Then perhaps we should stop here. As you said, it's been a long day. Why don't we retire for now?"

I nodded, taking his hand when he offered to help me up. My mind whirled with all of the new information, and I wanted nothing more than to sink into a soft bed and sleep.

Chapter 8

Cherry

Ocean water glittered in the morning light. The waves were calm, giving the water an almost glass-like appearance. A bubble floated to the surface, causing a ripple effect. More bubbles floated to the surface. I peered closer, trying to find the source of the disturbance. Faster than I could blink, a wall of teeth shot out of the water and swallowed me whole.

I awoke with a start. Chest heaving, I sat up on the bed and clenched at my rapid heartbeat. The room was covered in darkness and the same terrible foreboding I felt in the dream remained strong.

Something low hissed in the dark. **"Too sour."**

Movement caught my eye at the edge of the bed and I

looked over to see something shift. A lone shadowy figure crouched at the end of my bed. It let out a horrible hiss as it rose. Higher and higher until its head scraped against the ceiling.

Screaming, I threw a pillow at the creature then snapped my fingers together to try to light the torches the way I'd seen Dante do when I had arrived at his castle. When the room didn't immediately illuminate, I clapped, banged on the headboard and snapped again for good measure. When the flames lit up along the walls, the hissing stopped and the dark figure seemed to warp into nothingness. At the edge of the bed, the small white kitten tilted its head at me.

"A...cat?" I looked around the room, yet no monsters were hiding in the corners. Skin prickling, I glanced up, expecting a monster to swoop down from the ceiling. Instead of antlers and teeth, all the ceiling held was a painting made to resemble a calming night sky. Flecks of light from the crystal chandelier cast star-like glitters across the purple and blue hues.

The kitten stretched and jumped off the bed. I shifted upright, knocking away the absurd number of decorative pillows that took up a third of the bed. My heart pounded so hard in my chest it made my head spin. "It was just a nightmare," I muttered, swinging my legs off the bed. The soft fabric of my borrowed robe spilled well past my feet to pile on the floor.

The robe, along with the yellow dress I'd worn yesterday, apparently belonged to Dante's sister. By the looks of it, the female dragon shared her brother's impressive height. Judging by the soft pastel colors that decorated the bedroom, I'd say this room was hers too. Hopefully she wouldn't return home anytime soon and wonder why there was a strange human pilfering her clothes. Not that I had much of a choice. The weasel creatures had taken off with my clothes as soon as I got out of the bath.

Kneeling down, I checked under the bed to see where the kitten had gone. "Here, kitty," I called, tapping my fingers on the floor. Not bothering to even glance my way, the bundle of fur scratched at its ear before darting off through the crack in the doorway. "Well fine. I didn't want to pet you, anyway."

"Now what?" I asked the empty room. There was no way I was going to sleep after that. Even before the weird nightmare, my mind had been too jumbled to rest.

Myva, the goddess I had worshiped since birth, was dead. Killed by a demon uprising led by a shadow dragon, his mate, and apparently a few barrels of cinnamon. An uprising Dante was apparently a part of. Not only that, she wasn't even a goddess. Either way, demons were now free to roam the world unchecked. I bit my lip, trying not to imagine the worst. "Is my family OK?" I wondered. "Gods, is Boohail even still standing?" Without Myva's protective barrier, Boohail had little in the way of defenses.

I took a deep breath and sat on the bed, trying to gather my thoughts. "OK, let's not panic. Dante said it's been about a year since Myva got taken out. Boohail's at the tail end of Kinnamo, which is about as far away from Volsog as you could get. If demons are spilling into the Southern continent, then there's a chance that they haven't reached that far yet."

Even if they had, was there really anything I could do about it? Aside from scrapping with a few assholes back home, I wasn't exactly a trained warrior.

Soft music drifted into the bedroom. The low, deep thrum of a cello pulled me from my thoughts, and I opened the bedroom door to better hear it. Gentle piano music danced around the dramatic resonance of the cello.

I quickly shut the door and rummaged through the closet to find fresh clothes. One red dress in particular was shorter than the rest. If I had to wager a guess; I'd say it was meant to be knee length on its owner. On me, it fell down to my ankles. But beggars can't be choosers. I slipped it on, then did my best to wrangle my hair into submission. The tiara Dante had given me sat proudly upon the dresser. After a moment's deliberation, I put it on.

What can I say? I'm vain and it matches the dress.

Satisfied with my preening, I made my way out of the room and followed the sound of music up a flight of stairs. When I reached the source of the music, the melody changed into something more somber. The piano music faded away, leaving the cello to play a wistful ballad that seemed almost forlorn. I cracked the door open to peek inside.

The space was half-circular in form, and it was decked out with musical instruments. At the far end of the room was a wall of windows through which one could see strange dancing lights in the night sky and a dazzling array of stars. Waves of green, purple and pink rippled through the sky like water.

Dante was playing the cello with his back to me. The sky's gentle illumination bathed him in a bluish radiance. I sat there, mesmerized, while he kept playing. His hair was perfectly bunched up, so I could see the defined muscles in his broad back, and the way they moved with each note that poured out of the cello.

Flaming flamingos, why did he have to be so damn mouth-watering?

I shut my eyes and propped myself up against the doorframe. Letting myself get lost in the music for a bit. If he noticed my presence, he didn't let it show. Instead, he kept at his melancholy tune until my chest hurt from the anguish in it.

The words "I'm fucking lonely" were basically woven into the melody. The row of portraits lining the hallway entered my mind. Not one of those people seemed to be anywhere in the castle. Nor anyone else for that matter. From what he had mentioned yesterday, Myva's reign spelled disaster and death for most demons. I knew his sister was off somewhere on her own, but it didn't take a genius to figure out the rest of the people in the portraits were dead. So how long had he been in this castle alone?

Tears welled up in my eyes. That kind of loneliness was something I understood all too well. The only thing that got me through the years of mind-numbing loneliness was the thought of someday making it back to everyone. I had even planned out my homecoming meal down to the sides. Shrimp and sausage gumbo, an unholy amount of devilled eggs, and pudding with bourbon sauce for dessert. Then we'd all spend the day by the river. Swimming and catching up until the fireflies came out to signal the end of the day. I closed the door and sank down to sit against the wall. Fuck, I missed home. I missed my family and friends and eating meat that wasn't fish.

Maybe I could give in to his proposal. He said that dragons act as a bodyguard for everyone in their territory. There was no reason he couldn't guard Boohail. That would solve our problem of the missing protection barrier.

Then again, for all I knew, he might decide to set fire to the whole place. I had planned to just slip away once we reached the Southern continent. Get to the nearest town, rob a stable, and ride the horse back home. Though, when I considered the new state of the world, a guard dragon seemed like the ideal solution. Provided he wasn't a psycho cannibal.

Fuck. I'm going to have to actually consider this marriage. It was too risky to bring him home to meet Ma and Pa just yet. I needed time to sort out whether Dante could actually be trusted. Best-case scenario, he was just lying to get me to go along with him. After all, a guard dragon in the face of a demon-infested world was awfully convenient.

I fiddled with the end of my braid. I used to dream about going on fantastic quests when I was a kid. Joining forces with the heroic band of explorers to vanquish a demon overlord or retrieve a priceless relic. The world had been full of adventure and possibility in the ancient stories my ma used to tell me about the time before Myva. With the gates wide open and the demons at large, the potential for exciting new experiences looked to be limitless.

Instead, fate saw fit to give me a fucking marriage of convenience.

Fate is such a bitch.

Alright, that's enough of a pity party. It's like Grandma Nutmeg always said: being a whiny little twat never solved anything. Well, that and how to hide the taste of arsenic in case your husband ever manhandles you.

Resigning myself to my fate, I stood and entered the music room. Dante's head tilted in my direction and the music paused. "Um, hi," I said with a wave.

He set the cello down and turned to me. "Cherry, sorry, did I wake you?"

Holy crows, so much chest. I bit the inside of my lip, trying to tear my mind away from the descent into madness that was Dante without a shirt. Light brown skin stretched over sculpted muscles. The only blemish belonging to a few scars on his stomach. Which, somehow, made it worse. Gods, I wanted to run my tongue along each—

FOCUS WOMAN. GODS.

"Oh, no," I said, waving him off. "I just couldn't sleep. Then I heard the music and came to check it out. You play beautifully." Looking around the room, I spotted the piano I'd heard before. But no one was around it. "I thought I heard piano music alongside your cello. Who was playing?"

He glanced at the piano feet away from him. "No one."

"Pardon?" I asked.

He waved his hand at the piano, and a soft tune started playing. "It's enchanted. If you play something on it once, it will remember the keys and repeat the song back at your command."

Right, my *husband* owns an enchanted castle. I should've guessed as much from the floating clap-on candles. "So, do you know if it will be morning soon? I don't think I will be able to go back to sleep."

Dante nodded toward the window. "It is morning, can't you tell?"

I tilted my head, confused. "Are...are the dancing lights the sun here?"

He laughed and shook his head. "No, that's called the aurora. You see them more often now that it's the dark season here in Volsog."

"So when does the sun come out?"

"In about three months."

I stared up at the dancing lights. Beautiful as they were, they didn't cast much light on the land below. Anything below the tips of the mountains was still rather dim and hard to make out. "Are you serious?"

He nodded. "The dark season is one of the many reasons I'm inclined to leave this place. Shall we start packing? I'd hate to keep you away from your dazzling horses with horns." The sarcasm in his voice was so thick you could slice it with a knife.

I chose to ignore it, instead letting him lead me out of the music room. Turns out when Dante said packing, what he actually meant was having his weasel brigade stuff a few necessities like the map, rations and extra clothes into a travel pack. I stuffed *The Big Book of Beasts* and *Magic* into the pack as well.

My old clothes were returned to me, freshly pressed. The rips and tears of the years had been mended. Even the worn-out soles of my boots had been patched up as best they could. They still ran a little tight around the heel, but I was used to it. I gave my thanks to the weasels and followed Dante further into the lower floors of the castle. "What are those things, anyway?"

Dante glanced back at the retreating weasels. "Kobolds." He continued when the confusion was plain on my face. "They're shape-shifting sprites. To put it simply, there's nothing they love more than gold and riches. Dragons tend to have a lot of gold and riches. So they often work for us in exchange for access to our hoards."

"You have a hoard?" I asked. That made me feel a bit better. At least the little guys were getting paid.

He stopped at a room at the end of the stairs and swung open the wide double doors. My jaw fell open. All the books I've read about brave adventurers risking life and limb to steal from a dragon's hoard suddenly made sense. Piles of gold stretched as far as the eye could see. Treasure chests lined with jewels, pearls, and other shiny things were scattered about the room. I tucked my hands in front of me to avoid instinctively reaching out and snatching something he might not want me to touch.

"Does that answer your question?" he replied with a smirk. I turned back to see that he was watching my face intently, judging my reaction. Apparently, he liked what he saw. If the satisfied grin on his face was any sign.

Embarrassed, I crossed my arms and looked away from him. "I mean, it's nice."

It's fucking amazing. I wanna bathe in gold.

Dante chuckled, then pulled out two small drawstring pouches and handed one to me. He made his way further into the room and picked up a handful of gold coins and put them in the pouch. "Humans still barter with gold, right? I'll take a few silver, just in case, but I don't know what the exchange rate is these days. It'll take us a few days to reach Songwood if I fly. So we'll need to stop for a rest in a few towns along the way."

"Um...yeah," I said dumbly. Even if the economy had gone down the drain during the time I'd been gone, I was pretty sure the small handful he just picked up was enough to buy whatever small town we stopped in. That being said, if his goal was to simply stop at an inn for a few nights, it was unlikely that they were going to have enough money on hand to change for even a single gold coin.

I looked at the pouch in my hands. Wondering if he expected me to fill that too. I mean I would, no need to ask me twice, but talk about overkill. If I decided to escape him after all, I'd leave a very rich woman. I reached out to grab a few coins, then glanced back at Dante to make sure the dragon wasn't about to set me on fire for touching his hoard. When he nodded that I should continue, I gingerly took a few gold and silver pieces and placed them in the bag. "So do you have any copper? That's usually what we used back at home."

His lips curled in distaste. "No, I've never been fond of the color."

I paused from my pilfering and raised an eyebrow at him. "You...don't like the color of copper?"

"No, it's terribly bland."

My eyes narrowed. There was no way things could be so expensive that he had to use silver or gold for everything. "How do you buy food and stuff? There's no way Volsog is that expensive."

He shrugged. "I don't. The kobolds have always handled

that. Well, I've been traveling with a pirate crew for the past year, and they had a team of kitchen orcs that did most of the shopping." Dante bent down to grab a handful of diamonds and stuffed them into the bag. When he couldn't fill it anymore, he tied it up and held it out to me. "Do you think this is enough?"

It was enough to bitch slap the king of Kinnamo.

"You know, lemme grab a few more. Just in case," I said, quickly stuffing a few rubies and more coins into my little pouch. If he wanted to blow his money on a road trip, who was I to say no? He said he'd buy me new things after all. "Are you sure it's OK for me to take this much?"

He rolled his eyes and gestured to the room. "Take whatever you want, you're my wife. My hoard is yours."

Be still, my greedy little heart.

I looked around the room full of treasure, wide-eyed. An excited squeal escaped my throat as I stuffed an emerald in my skirt pocket, then raced over to a treasure chest sticking out of one of the piles of gold. A pair of glittering ruby earrings caught my eye. The style matched the tiara Dante had given me, and I immediately snatched them up, then made my way over to a mirror to inspect them.

With the tiara sitting proud on my head, and the matching earrings glittering right along, I felt just like a princess. Fitting, since I had been trapped in a dragon-guarded tower for so long. Though I couldn't say I'd ever read a story where the knight in shining armor was another dragon.

Speaking of…

I tilted the mirror a little to the side until Dante came into view. As expected, the dragon-shifter was still watching me. Well, more like burning a hole in my back. The look in his gray eyes so hungry and full of longing it made my stomach clench.

Right. He wasn't sharing an endless amount of treasure out of the goodness of his heart. Slowly, I set the earrings down, noticing how his gaze turned pensive as soon as the jewelry left my hand. I decided to test his reaction and picked up a necklace, then pretended to inspect it. After turning it around in my hand, I set it back down and watched him through the mirror. His mouth formed a thin line, and he pushed himself off the chest he was sitting on and wandered off.

The Big Book of Beasts didn't have a chapter on dragons. If it did, I'd bet money that there'd be an entire section dedicated to the importance of treasure. This didn't feel like a normal man trying to impress a woman with money. I got the very distinct feeling that Dante didn't just want me to take something from his hoard. He *needed* me to.

The weight of the emerald in my pocket suddenly felt very heavy. I fished the jewel out of my pocket and placed it next to the necklace. Boohail would need a protector from the demons that were now roaming free. For that purpose, I was willing to give Dante a chance. But there was something so…final about the way he watched me pick through his treasure. Sure, he says we're married, that doesn't mean I'm fully ready to jump all in yet.

I shivered, thinking about what normal couples would do in their first few days of marriage. Last night, Dante had guided me to my room and then promptly left, much to my relief. The last thing I needed was for him to push for sex. Even though the rush of dragon magic in my veins kept telling me what a fantastic idea that was. But the separate bed situation might change if he thought I'd fully accepted him. I reached for the tiara on my head, and set that down too.

"What are you doing?"

His deep voice came from right behind me. I whirled around to find him mere inches away. The earthy scent of rain and crisp apples curled through my body, making my senses flutter.

"What?" I brushed a braid behind my ear. "Oh, I'm just looking around still." I gave a friendly smile and gestured to the door. "Are you ready to go?"

"In a minute," he murmured in that smooth, rich voice of his. He reached out and took my hand, before sliding a gold bracelet onto my wrist. Instead of letting go, his thumb found the vein at the base of my wrist and stroked it gently. An action that had no right to be so arousing. Yet my lower belly fluttered, as if my lady bits had just woken up to say hello.

"I thought this would match your tiara well," he said, nodding at where I'd placed it next to my other discarded pieces. "Unless you find that it's no longer to your liking?"

"I like it just fine," I said. Hating how rushed my voice came out. "It's just…I figured we should travel light, ya know? If we're going to be gallivanting around a forest, I don't want to risk losing it."

"Hmm." His gaze was piercing, and even though the grip on my wrist was gentle, it felt like a trap pinning me to him. And I was so drunk off the heat of his body that I walked into the snare like a suicidal doe. "Yes, that would be a pity."

His hand came to rest on my hip. My breath hitched as he leaned in close, only to reach past me and pick up the tiara. "However, I enjoy seeing you wear it," he said, placing it on my head once more. Goosebumps raced along my arms as the hand on my hip tightened. His rough fingers sank into my skin. Just tight enough to hold me in place. "You'll keep an eye on it for me, won't you?"

"Yes," I blurted out.

Fuck.

How does he do that?

Dante's grin came straight for the cartilage in my knees and I had to focus to stay upright. "Good." Satisfied, he released me and made his way out of the treasure room. "I'll grab our things and meet you at the entrance. Try not to get lost this time."

Absently, I touched the tiara. Then flinched when I heard the bracelet clink against it. There was no engraving etched in its band, but the message Dante sent was clear: you're mine.

When the sound of his footsteps faded, I sank to my knees. All he had to do was touch my wrist and I snapped to give into his demands like an excited dog. Even now, my skin tingled wherever he touched.

"Get it together, Cherry," I growled, slapping my cheeks. If this was going to work out in my favor, then I couldn't let myself get turned into a simpering ninny anytime he looked my way. Sure, maybe he was freakishly good-looking. Did I wanna get carried around in those strong arms like a pampered princess? Gods yes. *Also, ya know, the fact that he's stupid rich ain't bad either. But snapping gators, I will not be pushed around!*

I breathed in deep, forcing the fireflies in my tummy to cease their infernal dance. The first order of business would be to get out of Volsog. Luckily, Dante was on the same page with that one. Next, I'd have to see if he was really being honest about Myva. *I'll know he is telling the truth if we run across any demons outside the gate. If he's lying, then I'll do whatever I need to in order to get away from him. If he's not lying then… well, I guess I'll have to figure out whether I can trust him to protect Boohail.*

In the meantime, I guess I'm actually going on a road trip with a dragon.

To see a unicorn.

I snorted, then burst into giggles the more I thought about the situation. "If I live through this and make it home, Cumin and Cin are going to split a rib at this story."

Chapter 9

Cherry

My face hurt. Why would anyone live in a place so fucking cold that their face hurt? I brushed the snowflakes off my half-frozen eyelashes. Every last part of my body aside from my eyes was covered in several layers of thick clothing. So much so that I had to waddle my way into the courtyard after Dante. At least it was a little brighter outside. The dancing aurora still couldn't hold a candle to actual sunlight, but it was better than nothing.

Even though I was freezing my ass off, the dragon-shifter only had on simple travel clothing and a black cloak. The bastard even had the audacity to look comfortable. How, was beyond me.

Two kobolds strapped our travel pack to a long rope and tightened down the small cage holding the white kitten I had seen before.

"You never told me your cat's name," I said, waddling over to the cage.

Dante glanced at the creature with a scowl, then continued to check over the supplies. "It's not my cat, but her name is Rebekah. She belongs to an orc on the pirate ship I was traveling with. The damned thing must have stashed away in my bag when I flew off to find you. Once we're done with our trip, I'll fly her back to where she belongs."

"Aww, did you sneak away from your home?" I cooed, bending down to get a better look at the little ball of fluff. I removed my mitten to rub a finger against her soft fur through the bars of the cage. Then promptly stopped when Rebekah's little body rattled with a menacing growl. "Well, not the friendliest cat, are you?"

Rebekah hissed and swiped at me.

I pulled my finger away just before she could sink her claws in. "Now I'm just determined to win your affection," I said, smiling at the little murder ball.

"Alright, this should tide us over until we get to the first town," Dante announced. "Stay by the pack while I shift. I don't want to throw you back."

Excited, I watched on as Dante moved a suitable distance away from me. I'd never seen a dragon transform before.

Would it be a cloud of smoke like when he shifted into his human form?

He turned his back to me and shifted his weight from side to side, then remained still. I watched on, waiting for a bolt of lightning to come down, or whatever magic explosion that came from a dragon shifting. Dante glanced back at me again, a reddish tint spread across his face.

No way. Is he blushing?

His signature scowl returned, and he waved a hand at me. "Turn around."

"Why?"

The reddish tint spread to the tips of his pointed ears. "It feels strange to have you staring at me while I shift." He made a twirling motion with his finger, indicating I should face away.

"Are you kidding me?" I asked. "You've been eying me up like a wolf near a flock since we met!"

"Exactly. You're very aware of the destination I have in mind for this relationship. But you are staring at me with wide-eyed unidentified intent and it's making me nervous. Turn around."

"Gah!" I threw my hands up in frustration then turned around. "You're being ridiculous."

Thunder rolled in from behind me. Gray smoke spilled across the snow and—damn everything—I wanted to sneak a peek so bad. After a few seconds, the smoke dissipated.

I waited a few more seconds out of politeness then looked over my shoulder. Dante's dragon form took up most of the frozen courtyard. He stretched like a cat, then shook his head. "Can I look now, Your Highness?" I asked, filling the question with as much sarcasm as I could.

He snorted and reached past me to grab our pack. Using the long rope, he tied it around his neck then laid himself down in front of me. **"Can you climb up on your own?"**

His voice rang so deep it rumbled the ground beneath my feet. I shook off the jitters and approached him. "Probably," I said.

Even lying down, his neck was taller than I was. It took a few tries, but eventually I was able to climb up his scales to sit against the luggage. To my relief, his mane was soft and cushioned my bum from the hard scales. Once situated, I grabbed hold of his mane like a rein. "OK, I'm all set!" I chirped, giving his neck a little kick like I did with my horse back home. The dragon was a lot bigger than my stallion Crash, but I figured the concept was the same.

Dante's tone was flat as he spoke. **"Did you just kick me like a horse?"**

Shit. I guess it wasn't the same. "...Maybe?"

The dragon sighed. A stream of flames shot from his nostrils and melted the snow in front of him. **"You're lucky you're cute."**

I patted his mane in apology. "Sorry about thaaAAAAAAA!"

My scream was drowned by the wind as the dragon shot up faster than a snake's strike. His mane slipped from my mitten-covered hands and my back slammed against the luggage. Rebekah yowled, I screamed, my stomach rolled. All in all, it was a very noisy affair.

When he finally evened out high above the trees, a wave of nausea rocked through me. I grabbed at his mane again, desperate for something to hold on to. Beneath me, the dragon's body shook. "You're laughing," I said, slapping at his scales. "You jerk, you did that on purpose!"

Dante laughed harder. His breath turned into frozen wisps of smoke in the chilly morning air. **"Never kick me again."**

I gritted my teeth and gave him another little kick. Why? Fuck if I knew. Maybe it was my hatred at being told what to do, maybe I simply had a death wish. But that one little defiant kick filled me with satisfaction.

Until I saw his toothy grin. Then it just felt like my heart shot out of my ass.

Dante flung himself higher, then barrel-rolled over a mountaintop. I dug my heels into his neck and held on for dear life, screaming as he dove back down to scrape against the tips of tall pine trees. My hood flung back, and I quickly grabbed my tiara and stuffed it in my coat.

When he evened out again, my hair was a wild mess, my heart was pounding, and I may or may not have lost my breakfast. I wasn't sure. The sound of his laughter rang through the air and echoed through the mountains below. In his dragon form, laughter sounded more like someone beating on a massive drum. Yet it was surprisingly pleasant…and contagious. Even though my heart was beating a mile a minute, I found myself laughing along.

I gave another kick, screaming in delight when he dove straight down to a river, only to pull up at the last second. His tail hit the water like a whip and sent waves through the air. I couldn't remember the last time I felt so excited by anything. Each dive below made my blood race, and I felt more alive than I had in years.

Water skimmed along his neck and belly as he followed along the river's path. I pulled off a mitten and stuck my hand out. Laughing as the freezing water slapped my palm before shielding it back into the mitten. He rose higher, and I noticed something white in the water up ahead. Shifting to my knees, I gripped his mane tight and leaned over to get a better look.

There, just below the river's surface was a massive skeleton. Its long spine poked out in certain places above the water. Its head had broken off at the neck and lay next to the crushed remains of what looked like a hand. Rows of vicious-looking teeth littered its jaw, with a few missing around the front. As we flew closer, I counted several more heads littering the water. Confused, I followed the spine up the creature's body to find that it ended in not one neck, but seven!

My eyes widened. "Is that a hydra? Like a real hydra?"

"It was a damn nuisance is what it was," Dante snorted. **"I leave my territory for a little sabbatical and every idiot with a pair of fangs thinks they can move in."**

The urge to reach out and touch the legendary creature had my hands tingling. Its skeleton alone looked far bigger than Dante. "Did you kill it all on your own?"

As if sensing my desire, Dante flew lower and stopped close enough to where I could reach out and touch the long spines that poked free from the river. **"No, Kohara had returned home and found it first. Hydra are difficult prey, so she summoned me back to help kill it."**

I removed a mitten to run my fingers along vertebrae the size of watermelon. The tingle in my fingers turned into teary-eyed elation, and I had to quickly pull myself together to avoid freezing my eyes shut. "Tell me everything!" I demanded. "How did you kill it, why did it come here?"

A hydra! I just touched a hydra!

"Is this place a part of its mating grounds? How old was it?" A rush of questions flooded out of me, probably faster than anyone could understand, but I couldn't help it.

Dante craned his neck to look back to me. **"Did you develop a secondary organ to allow you to talk and breathe at the same time?"**

"If I say yes, will you tell me?"

His large body rumbled beneath me. **"I didn't sit down and have tea with it, love. I just killed it for trespassing. If**

you want to know more about it, open *The Book Of Beasts* **and hold it up to the skeleton."**

My excitement soured at the endearment. "There you go with that 'love' bit again," I grumbled, digging through the pack to find the book. With a tug, I was able to free it from the rest of our tightly packed luggage. "You have no idea who I am. It's going to take more than a day to fall in love with someone."

"A day? Princess, I fell as soon as I saw your reaction to snow."

"I hate you."

"We'll work on that."

I rolled my eyes. "What if after two days you find you don't like me? What if the way I snore keeps you up at night?"

"I like the sound of your heartbeat. If your snoring is truly that ferocious then I'll focus on that."

My heart sputtered as if it were a mere puppet at the mercy of strings wound tightly around his claws. *Can he hear that?*

"Yes, I can hear it. In this form at least."

"Can you read minds too?" I squawked.

His lips pulled back in a grin, revealing fangs the size of swords. **"No, your face is just incredibly honest. I hope you had no desire to become a gambler. That profession is far beyond your reach."**

"Well, it's a good thing I married rich." When I opened the book, the pages flipped themselves to the chapter regarding hydras. Then, the pages glowed before a new blank page appeared at the end of the chapter. An image of a fierce-looking hydra materialized in the top corner of the page, while details like height, weight, and probable age appeared below it. "It can record a monster on its own?" I asked, marvelling at the new entry.

"Who has the time to make every entry themselves?" he asked.

I merely stared at the page in disbelief. "Most people, Dante."

"Sounds exhausting," he mused.

A shrill cry drew my attention away from the book. I glanced up to see what looked like the love child of a peacock and hawk skimming over the water. The bird flew up high, letting its dazzling red and blue feathers catch in the light. Then, it dove into the water with practiced precision before it came up with a fish in its talons.

"Oh wow. I can't believe that bird still dives underwater despite how cold it is. It's a wonder how it doesn't freeze." I was bundled up head to toe and was still freezing.

"Keep watching."

The bird flapped its wings hard and erupted in flames. The surrounding air sizzled as the water evaporated.

"Snappy caimans, it's a phoenix!" I cried out, scrambling to open the book to its chapters on flaming birds. "Go after it, I wanna record it!"

The dragon looked at the retreating bird. **"You...want me to catch a phoenix?"**

"Yes!" I cried out, slapping at his scales. "Go, go! It's getting away!"

"Hold on tight," he sighed, then shot off into the sky.

The wind blew so hard against my face that my skin pulled back, baring my teeth and eyes to the bitter cold. I gripped his mane tight with one hand and secured the book against my chest with the other. When we came up behind the phoenix, the bird squawked in terror, nearly dropping its fish. It tucked its flaming wings tight against its body and dove into the trees below.

"Oh no you don't," Dante growled, then took a deep breath and roared. The sound was so fierce that an entire flock of birds flew out of the trees in a panic.

I searched the fleeing birds for a sign of the phoenix's colorful plumage. One bird flew more erratically than the rest and I zeroed in on it to find the phoenix still struggling to fly away with its fish. "There!" I shouted, pointing to the bird.

Dante shot off after it. The phoenix veered hard to the right before we could close in, using its superior maneuverability to elude the dragon.

"Cherry, hold the book out in front of you and stay as still as you can."

The book was far too heavy to hold out with one hand. Let alone while darting after a bird. "But I need two hands for that. I don't want to fall."

"Don't you trust me?"

I glanced down to the icy river below. "Not at all."

"Then close your eyes," he said.

"Oh shit," I cried out, my heart leaping into my throat as he sped up. Swallowing my fear, I scrambled to lift the book up and faced it toward the bird. When the phoenix tried to speed away, Dante flung us upside down to loop around the bird, cutting its path. The phoenix cried out and erupted in flames once again before shooting straight up away from us.

When he evened out, I was left panting hard. Blood rushed through my veins in a frenzied dance until I giggled like a madwoman. I turned the book around to see the page still glowing. After a few seconds, the glow died down to reveal an image of the phoenix. Its fiery wings were spread wide while the half-fried fish still dangled in its talons. "You did it!" I cheered.

"Are we good to continue, or do you see any other creatures to terrorize?"

"I'll let you know," I said, happily flipping through the pages.

The dragon snorted then veered us back on the path where we fell into a comfortable silence. Volsog was vast and strangely beautiful in a way, and I was content to sit back and enjoy the view. It was so different from anything I'd seen in Kinnamo that it almost looked like another world entirely. Instead of endless trees and water, Volsog was wide open. Sparse clusters of trees bundled together against the wind. Rolling hills of white blanketed the landscape, while a wall of mountains lined the horizon. If it wasn't so unbearably cold, I would have liked to touch down and explore awhile.

"Hey Dante, this is gonna sound crazy but, do you think we could ever come back to Volsog? You know, after we get settled if we work this out and stay together."

"I refuse to dignify your 'if' with a response. You are my wife, and we are *clearly* **falling in love**."

Touchy thing.

"Such confidence," I teased. "Alright, fine. Dear husband," I cooed, adding as much sugar to my voice as I could. "Will you take me back to Volsog someday?"

His body trembled, and I had a feeling that it wasn't from a laugh this time. Heat radiated off the silver strands beneath me until the air sizzled. The aurora lighting our path cast its rays against the shine of Dante's silver scales. Snow-brushed mountains lit up in the reflected light. Hills of greens, trees of pink, and everything that danced in between. When he spoke, the dragon's voice commanded the surrounding sky. As if the noise of the world knew to fall away at his vow. **"Cherry, I'll take you anywhere."**

Anywhere.

"I like the sound of that."

Chapter 10

Cherry

After what seemed like hours, Dante landed near a large manor nestled in a valley. The valley was fenced off with walls made of tightly packed snow. Smaller houses and buildings were clustered together in an oval at the valley's center. I looked around for any inhabitants, but the little town seemed completely devoid of life.

Eyeing him warily, I slid off his back when he knelt down to let me off. "Is this the part where you kill me?" I asked.

He laughed. **"This is the part where we rest for the day so my wife doesn't freeze to death."**

"I'm not—"

"I can hear your teeth chattering." Dante carefully

removed our luggage before shifting back into his human form. He slung the pack over his shoulder then made his way inside the manor. The creepy, very clearly abandoned manor. "Grab the cat, would you?" he asked.

Despite the fact that I was freezing my ass off, the thought of stepping into what was clearly a haunted building didn't seem like the best idea. "Should we really be going in there?"

"It's fine, the manor belongs to an old friend of mine," he said, waving me in. "Though from the looks of it, he's already migrated to the Southern continent."

"...Right." Warily, I stepped inside. The sound of the door closing echoed against the stone walls. Goosebumps rose on my arms. "And when you say *old* friend?"

"Kaspar and I have known each other for about—" he paused and tilted his head in thought "—350 years I think? Time blurs together after a while." My companion paid no mind to the manor's general spookiness and sauntered in as if he owned the place. Rebekah, once freed from her confines, glared daggers at the both of us before darting off down a hall.

"Damn, the longest friend I had was twelve years." There was a rumble in the air, and I glanced out the window to see clouds churning in the dark sky. "Man, we have been having the worst luck with weather. I hope there isn't another storm."

He glanced up at the sky and cleared his throat. "Did you break up due to a fight?" He shrugged off his cloak, then took a few pieces of firewood from the stack against the wall and lit them in the hearth.

I rushed over to warm my fingers. Damn near moaning in relief when the warmth spread across my chilled limbs. "No, Fern just moved away when her pa found work in another town. Is Kaspar another dragon like you?"

"He's a fae," he said on a yawn. "Where did her pa find work?"

"Stop sleuthing for answers. I'm not telling you where I live."

"Worth a shot," he said. "What can you tell me then? Any hobbies, or exes I'll need to shoo off?"

I thought about that for a moment. Most of my hobbies consisted of running around the bayou with my friend Brie and my older sister Cin. But I couldn't just say that without giving out too much information. He'd already guessed which country I was from based on the growing season alone.

Low thunder rumbled outside, and the manor shook. Dust kicked up from the rafters, making me sneeze.

"What's his name?"

"Who?" I asked, turning back to him.

Dante's posture grew stiff as he unpacked our things, yet he kept his voice calm. "Your ex," he called over his shoulder. "What was his name?"

Ah, so he's the jealous type.

Giggling, I sat closer to the fire and basked in its warmth. "Take a breath, Dante. I'm not pining over any lost love."

A thud brought my attention back to the dragon-shifter,

who had slumped to the floor. I rushed to his side and knelt beside him.

"Are you alright?" I asked.

He ran a hand down his face and nodded. "Just a bit drained. Our bonding transferred a large amount of my magic into you. It'll take a few days before I've fully recovered."

I took his hand in mine and pulled him to his feet. His large body sagged, and I wrapped my arms around him to hold him steady. "Alright. Let's get you to bed, big guy."

He smirked.

"Oh, keep it in your pants."

Dante threw an arm over my shoulder and guided us toward the bedrooms. "I didn't say anything."

"You didn't have to."

"I see, my wife is a mind reader. Maybe I should be on my best behavior." He stopped us at the end of the hall and opened a door. Its rusted hinges creaked in protest. Inside was a modestly decorated bedroom with chestnut furnishing and a large bed in the center.

"You better be," I huffed, walking him over to the bed. "Don't think I'm a pushover just because I'm human. Push me too far and I'll have ya begging for mercy."

The arm around my shoulders fell as his hand slid to the small of my back. My heart sped up. Mind reeling as the seductive tenor of his voice played against my ear like the strings of his cello. "Is that a promise?"

I leaned away from him, putting my hands up against his chest. Good lord, what a mistake! The hard muscles of his torso felt like heated steel beneath my fingertips. I shook my head and glared up at him. "Ease up with the sexual tension, will ya? I thought you were going to be on your best behavior."

A devilish grin pulled at his lips. "The key word was *maybe*. No promises were made." Dante sat on the edge of the bed and pulled me to him. The hand on my back led an electrifying trail down my spine, before his fingers dipped beneath the waist of my skirt, just above my ass. "What happens if I misbehave?"

In the corner of my mind, the sensible part of me was fighting for her fucking life. I knew I should push him away. Untangle myself from his upsettingly temping arms and go dunk my butt in a pile of snow until my pussy remembered who was in charge.

When I didn't pull away, Dante hooked a hand behind my thigh and tugged until I straddled his lap. "Come here," he whispered, before grabbing the back of my neck and pulling me in for a kiss. His mouth teased my lips apart, while warm hands slid the coat from my body to trace the outline of my curves. Once again, his palm travelled slowly down my back, finally dipping beneath my skirt to cup the pliant weight of my ass.

Trembling hands gripped his shoulders as I tried desperately to regain my senses. "Wait, maybe we should slow down?"

His lips curved against my neck. "The taste of your cunt on my tongue is burned into my memory like a brand, and you ask me to slow down? My princess is a cruel little thing." Heat flooded my lower belly as he gave a playful nip at my collarbone.

I whimpered as the warmth of his breath teased the top of my breasts. My nipples hardened, and I would have given anything to have his mouth travel just a little lower.

"Just for tonight," he rasped. The playfulness bled from his voice, leaving something hungry and hot in its wake.

"What?"

"Let me take care of you tonight. In the morning we can go back to slow and careful. Grant me this and I swear to you that I'll drink from your cunt until your legs shake. I want your voice hoarse from screaming my name. Use me. Punish me if you must. Give me a taste of what it feels like to sink into my princess and I'll worship you until you beg me to stop."

I cried out as a finger slid against my slit, coating itself in my juices. I muffled a gasp into his shoulder as my skin burned at his touch. "Why do you have to feel so fucking good?"

That damnable finger dipped inside, and I ground against it as if possessed. "Say yes, Cherry." The heat in his voice nearly caused me to come undone.

Just before the submission could leave my lips, something moved outside the window. I peeked around him to see a shadowy horned figure staring at us. I leapt up with a scream, my back hitting the wall behind me as I scrambled away.

Dante shot up immediately and whirled around. Fire engulfed his arms as he poised to strike. "What's wrong?"

I pointed a shaking hand toward the window. "There's something watching us!"

He caught sight of the large head before his shoulders relaxed on a sigh. "It's a moose."

"What the fuck is a moose?" I asked, flatting myself against the wall.

"A terrible interruption, apparently."

"Dante, I'm serious, what the hell is that thing? Some kind of demon deer?" Without waiting for a response, I raced to the pack to grab *The Book Of Beasts* and held it near the creature. And by near, I mean safely behind my dragon-shifter bodyguard.

He clicked his tongue as he glanced back at the creature. "Demon, no. Though I suppose you could say it's related to a deer."

When the book didn't start its signature glow, I took a tentative step closer. "Why isn't the book recording it?"

Dante chuckled and sat back on the bed. "*The Book Of Beasts* was created to catalog the different magic beasts that roam the land. That is no magic beast, that is a moose."

"But it's huge!" I yelled. "It looks like some evil wizard mashed together a few deer then melted its face."

"The moose has feelings, Cherry," he said dryly.

"Well...why is it just peeking into the window like some kind of stalker?"

"I imagine it's curious as to why the strange woman on the other side started screaming at him."

"You are very catty," I snapped.

"And you are petrified of snow and a moose."

"I am not petrified, I just didn't know what they were!"

"And yet, you chase after a phoenix and marvel at the bones of a hydra. I'm starting to have serious concerns over your ability to process danger."

I narrowed my eyes at him.

The heat of my glare only caused him to grin back at me. "Has anyone ever told you how adorable you are when angry?"

Without a word, I set the book down on the bedside table. Then snatched a pillow from the bed and whacked him with it. Dante merely laughed and let me strike him a second time.

When I stormed away, he called after me. "Where are you going?"

"In a room you are not in. Goodnight."

The grin in his voice nearly had me turn around for a third strike. "Goodnight, Princess."

Chapter 11

Cherry

The next morning, we cleared the last of the jagged mountains on Volsog's border and soared over the Dreaded Expanse. Even from high in the sky, I could see the crashing waves the sea was known for. Almost as if it was the goddess' last attempt to keep the demons locked away in Volsog.

By the time the shores of Kibar came into view, Dante slowed and swayed in the air. "Feeling alright, big guy?" I asked.

His speech was slurred. **"Tired. I'll be fine long enough to reach Kirkwall."** So he said. But as soon as the words left his mouth, we dipped down toward the raging sea at an alarming pace.

Frantic, I kicked at his side until he straightened back out. "Not to be a backseat rider, but I think we should just camp on the nearest bit of land. I don't think you're going to make it to the city."

"It's right on the coast," he yawned. **"We should be there soon."**

I scanned the shore in front of us. Instead of a city or a bustling port, it was nothing but towering woods. I fished the map out of the bag. "Show me Kirkwall." In an instant, the map sprang to life and circled the coastal city. "According to the map, Kirkwall is about fifty miles east of us. Can you make it that far, or should we just land on the shore?"

In response, Dante plummeted out of the air. I screamed and kicked him awake again. "Alright, I'm putting my foot down. Just land on the beach and we'll find Kirkwall tomorrow."

To my relief, the dragon listened, and sank onto the sandy shore. Then collapsed into an exhausted heap. I leaped off his back and fell to my knees on dear sweet precious land. **"My apologies, Cherry. It seems our transfer of magic took more out of me than expected."**

"A man who apologizes *and* admits when he's wrong? You really are after my heart," I said, then stretched out my sore muscles. My back gave a satisfying pop, and I sighed in relief.

He chuckled, then gently removed our luggage from his back. His clawed hands were careful not to jostle the cat's cage too much. He set Rebekah and our things a good distance away from the shore then shuffled off to a line of the biggest trees I'd ever seen. He swung his long body around, then whipped his tail against a tree. The towering tree snapped like a twig under the blow and came crashing down with a booming thud.

"Did...did the giant tree do something to you, Dante?" I asked.

He responded with a snort then began clawing at the fallen tree. When the trunk of wood was bare and had suffered enough carnage, he dragged the resulting branches and splinters a little closer to our travel sack, divided them into two piles, setting one on fire. **"Redwood burns slowly, so this should last you until morning,"** he said, nodding to the bonfire.

Enough was an understatement. The amount of wood he had casually piled up would have been enough to last me the whole damn winter. A branch from one of those honkers would have been enough.

"Will you be alright with travel rations, or should I hunt for you?"

By the way his eyes were drooping, I doubted he could take another step. "I'll be fine," I said, trying my best to sound reassuring. "If Rebekah and I get sick of dried meat and nuts, I'll just catch us a few fish. Please sleep before you keel over."

He sat, but kept his eyes trained on me, considering my words. Then, he fiddled with the pile of firewood and scanned the woods behind us. When he shifted to stand again, I held out a hand to stop him. "Dante, we do not need more firewood."

"Yes, but I smell a deer nearby. Perhaps you should save your rations." He stood and made his way over to the treeline. **"Wait here. I'll fetch it for you."**

"No!" I barked out. "You look like you're ready to pass out. Just go to sleep. We have enough food, fire, and water. We're fine. Sleep!" Not to mention we were only a short flight away from Kirkwall. Even if we somehow tore through our rations, the over-prepping dragon had loaded our pockets with enough gold to buy a table at every restaurant in the city. I guess no one could ever accuse him of being underprepared.

He looked over our supplies once more, then lay down. **"If you're certain. Wake me if you need anything."** At my nod, his violet eyes gave into their exhaustion and finally closed. His body relaxed into the sand before the low rumble of his snoring joined the sound of the waves crashing along the beach.

"Huh. I thought he'd shift back into his human form." Not that I was looking forward to it. I wandered over to the pack and helped myself to a little snack, then pulled out a few pieces of dried meat and brought them to Rebekah's cage. The cat sniffed at the meat indifferently then turned her nose up at it.

"Now is not the time to be picky," I scolded. "We aren't exactly anywhere near a pet shop so try to eat at least a little bit of it." To no one's surprise, the cat didn't listen. I sighed in defeat and didn't offer her any more. "Alright, well you probably have to use the litter box. Good news for you, we're kind of camping on one." I reached a hand up to the latch on her cage then paused. "You're not going to like, scratch the hell out of me if I open this cage, are you?"

Rebekah tilted her head but gave no indication of the level of violence she was considering. Cats hardly ever do.

"Well, here's to trust, I guess," I said, opening the latch. The cat shot out in a white blur and darted toward the forest. I watched her disappear into the thick trees with grim annoyance. "Immediate betrayal."

I ran a hand down my face and pushed myself to my feet. As much as I'd love to flop down and sleep the day away like Dante, I couldn't get behind the thought of letting the fluffy little shit get eaten by a fox or something. That would definitely make me feel guilty.

I shoved the rest of the dried meat back into my pack and followed Rebekah. She was already out of sight, but I knew where she had gone.

Maybe I should have put a leash on the damn thing?

The forest was an odd place. It felt like I was walking through the woods at home, except everything was ten times bigger and twice as eerie. The trees were enormous, even the underbrush that clung to their branches was enormous. There was enough space in between each tree to fit an entire carriage, while slivers of sunlight broke through the dense canopy overhead.

"Just how big do these things actually grow?" I muttered to myself.

As I walked deeper into the forest, the ground got progressively softer until it was almost mud. The air was thick with the smell of damp earth and the faintest hint of rotting vegetation. I passed several sets of animal tracks, but none of them looked anything like a feline print.

"Hey!" a voice called out. "Lady with the blue coat, come over here!"

I whipped around, trying to find the source of the voice. "Up here! To your left!" the voice shouted again.

I brushed some ferns out of my eyes and peered through the woods to spot a blade embedded in a massive rock. The rusted metal of the sword shone in the sunlight that passed through the canopy. No one else seemed to be in the area, though. "Hello?"

"I'm right in front of you," the voice said, taking on an edge of impatience.

"Where?" I asked.

"I'm the sword in the stone," it said. "Please, for the love of all that is good, pull me out of this thing. And if you have some vinegar I could soak in, that would be lovely. I'm so rusted it's disgusting."

"I'm talking to a sword," I said in disbelief. "How am I talking to a sword?"

The sword gave a little wiggle. "All your questions will be

answered if you just please, please pull me out of this stupid rock!"

Well, it's not like my life could get any weirder. I carefully clambered my way up the face of the rock, nearly losing my footing when the moss gave way under my fingers. As I neared the top, I grabbed the sword by its hilt and pulled. It...barely budged. Which was a little embarrassing.

"Come on, put your back into it!" the sword yelled.

I rubbed my hands on my skirt, steadied my footing, and gripped the sword once more. With some very ladylike grunts, I pulled the sword with all my might. The sword sprang free of the stone, and I immediately lost my balance. All the air escaped my lungs as I landed hard on my back. Groaning, I rolled over and dusted myself off. Then I looked up to see the sword scream in joy and float happily around the stone. "You can float?" I asked.

"Float, talk, sing a jaunty tune, I'm full of surprises," it giggled. "Name's Alexis, by the way. Thank you so much for getting me out of that situation."

"OK..." My mind spun with questions as I took in the floating sword giggling happily above me. "Are you like some princess who got trapped in a sword or something?" I read a story once about a princess in a far-off land who got cursed and turned into a hamster after rejecting a suitor. Perhaps this was something like that. Or the food Dante gave me was full of shrooms. That was also a possibility.

The sword floated closer down to my eye level. "No, but I haven't had anyone to talk to for a few days so sit back and listen to my woes."

"Yeah, alright," I said, crossing my legs. *When else was I going to have the opportunity to listen to the tale of the talking sword?*

An orange glow illuminated behind the bits of brown rust covering her blade. Alexis huffed angrily and paced back and forth.

Is it pacing if she's just floating?

"So there I was," she began. "Just your average cursed sword who only recently gained the ability to move on her own, ready to take on the big wide world. Maybe make some new friends, go on fun adventures, touch a merman's butt. And what do I find in that big wide world?" she asks.

"Hopefully merman booty?"

"No! Well yes, but the correct answer for this story is *treachery*, that's what!" she shouted.

I gasped.

"Gasp is right!" she bellowed. "So after some time of living my best life doing what I want to do, I think to myself, 'Alexis, why don't we take this to the next level? What if we got a human body so we could actually feel?'"

"So I decide to team up with a merry band of adventurers to retrieve a genie's lamp to grant us some goddamn wishes. After some squabbling and maybe a little bit of stabbing, we came to an agreement. They get the first two wishes to ask for gold and fame, and the last wish was to be used to give me a body. Look at me, blue coat lady," she hissed.

"My name is Cherry," I piped up.

Alexis floated closer. The flat end of her blade pressed against my leg as she leaned in. "Look at me, Cherry. Do you see a human body?"

"I do not."

She growled and twirled herself higher in the air. "You do not!" Alexis swung herself around, as if beheading an invisible betrayer. She swung again, and I crawled backward to be further away from her striking range. "That's because those swindling bastards took the lamp after they were *completely fine* with having me do all the dirty work. Then waited until I used up all of my strength and slammed me into this stupid, STUPID ROCK!" The last of her words came out accompanied by a stabbing motion.

I covered my mouth in shock. "Oh, that's terrible!"

"Yes, thank you!" she said. Her orange glow faded into a dull hue as she floated closer to the ground. "Gods, it feels so good to talk to someone about this. All I had for company for the past few days was the trees and this uppity squirrel named Patricia. But between you and me, Patricia is kind of a judgmental ass and I just can't with her anymore."

A high-pitched chattering echoed from the distance.

The orange hue flared into an angry red. "I will dance on your grave, Patricia," Alexis simmered as she turned herself toward the trees. I waited with shallow breath until the red faded into the dull gray of the sword's natural state. Alexis turned back to me, her voice taking on a chipper note. "So anyway, enough about me, what's going on with you?"

It probably wasn't the best idea to spill my guts to a random talking sword I just found in the forest. But I was also dying for someone to talk to. "Well, I'm traveling with this dragon— the one I accidentally married, not the one who kidnapped me." I proceeded to regale Alexis with the weird happenings of my past few days. "I just don't know what to do about him," I said finally.

"You don't know what to do with the hot rich man with the magical castle, who vowed to take you anywhere you wanted to go?" Alexis hummed and leaned against the rock. "Honey, I'm gonna be honest with you. I don't understand the problem."

"It sounds dumb if you say it like that," I grumbled.

"How else am I supposed to say it? You don't want your hometown destroyed. In a convenient turn of events, your rich dragon husband has a thing for guarding hometowns. It's a match made in the stars."

"I know, but..." I sighed, too frustrated to form the right words. "Five years of my life were snatched away from me by a dragon. I don't want to be bound to another one without even a day of freedom between the two. It's just so damn frustrating to have all my choices taken away. At first, I assumed he just wanted to sleep with me, and that was alright by me. To put it bluntly, he's hot. But married?" I lamented, throwing up my arms in the air. "I don't even know him. What if he's weird? Maybe he eats people or is one of those nutcases that eats pasta with no sauce. Just buttery recklessness."

"I am a sword; I lack the cognitive abilities necessary to comprehend the act of eating. But I see what you're getting at."

"You do?" I asked. If a talking sword, of all people, understood my plight, then maybe I wasn't crazy.

"Yes, I despise being ordered around."

I drew my knees up to my chest and buried my face in them. "Why can't I just get railed, see a unicorn, and go home? I don't want all this extra shit."

"Extra shit is for the birds," she mused. "What's the verdict so far, do you hate him?"

I thought about that for a moment. Dante was pushy, and a little aggravating. Yet if I took out the whole marriage aspect, today was…kinda fun. I couldn't remember the last time I had fun. He took the time to answer any questions I threw at him, made pit stops anytime I wanted to look around, and made damn sure all my needs were met. Even if he was a little overzealous about it. "No, I don't think I hate him. I'm just frustrated."

"Well, that's something, I guess." Alexis turned toward a spot up in the trees, then rotated herself to point her blade. "Hey, is that your man up there?" I followed her gaze to see the head of a dark-haired woman, peering at us. Blood-red lips curled back in a wicked smile as our eyes caught.

"No," I said, swallowing. "No, she is not." I stiffened when a twig snapped behind me. My head whipped around to find another woman with red hair leering at us from high in the trees. The redhead stepped closer, revealing long bare breasts that swung like pendulums as she moved. The skin of her torso bled into the feathery body of a bird. Upsettingly sharp-looking talons adorned her feet and dug into the tree bark with each step. A winged shadow passed over us and a third bird woman landed next to the first one.

"Harpies," I whispered. Enough of them had made appearances in my fantasy novels to be recognizable. Unfortunately, they were never exactly nice or friendly in any of the books I had read. I could only hope they were much friendlier in person. Judging by the way the redhead was licking her lips, I wouldn't have bet on it. Slowly, I got to my feet and put my back against the stone.

The dark-haired harpy swivelled her head to the side like an owl. "Lost?" she asked.

Her gleeful tone made the hair on the back of my neck stand on end. "No, I'm not lost. Just looking for my cat."

The newest harpy cackled. Her long black hair fell in front of her, shielding her chest. "We are looking for food."

Yeah, I bet you are.

"Well, I have some travel rations at my camp if you're

hungry," I offered. If I could lure them back to Dante, maybe I stood a chance.

Black talons impatiently clicked against tree bark. She leaned closer and shimmied her shoulders. "But I see food right here. And we've flown such a long way. Haven't we, ladies?"

The other harpies murmured in agreement. "I just don't think I could fly any further for a bite," said the redhead.

With a screech, the first harpy launched herself off her perch. I dove to the ground, narrowly avoiding her talons. They scraped against the rock as she pivoted herself and flung toward me. Screaming, I rolled out of the way, then grabbed fistfuls of mud and threw them into the harpy's eyes.

When the harpy stumbled back, Alexis slashed her side. Blood sprayed from the wound and painted the surrounding ferns in red.

I staggered to my feet only to be slammed into the stone by the red harpy. Ignoring the ringing in my ears, I punched at the harpy's face. She reared back then stabbed at my gut. I grabbed her foot in my hand, stopping the blow. Pain raced up my wrists as her back claw dug into my skin. The foul stink of her breath made me recoil. "Just die quickly, we're starving!" she hissed.

My arms strained with the effort to keep her at bay. "Alexis, a little help?" I yelled. Instead of answering, the clang of metal rang through the air. I chanced a look to see that Alexis had her hands (blade?) full with the other two harpies.

Panic seeped into my bones when the harpy pushed harder. The tip of her sharp talon jabbed against my stomach. She smiled cruelly. "I'm going to enjoy plucking those pretty brown eyes right out of your head." The harpy jumped back with a flap of her wings, grabbed my wrist and used momentum to throw me to the ground. My back scraped against a fallen log, tearing my skin.

Time slowed as I watched the harpy rear up for the killing blow. The steady pounding of my heart drowned out the noise of the world.

"GET THE FUCK AWAY FROM ME!" I screamed, raising my hands up. Lightning shot out of my palms and struck the harpy dead in the chest. Burning feathers and hair sizzled, sending putrid waves of stink through the air.

The two harpies attacking Alexis paused to look back, but by the time they did it was too late for their friend. The red-headed harpy was fried to a crisp on the ground. Silence fell over the clearing. The defeated harpy twitched, then gurgled and fell still.

"She's dead," the black-haired harpy whispered.

Alexis slashed at the black-haired harpy, slicing a gash in her cheek before darting over to me. The black-haired harpy cried out and slapped a hand to her face. Blood dripped from her raven wings and onto the mud. "Damn right she's dead!" Alexis shouted. "Unless you want to end up like her, I suggest you take your pendulous titties and get the hell out of here!"

"You," the dark-haired harpy hissed. Her feathers puffed up and her talons dug into the ground beneath her feet. "You'll pay for this!" she roared, before the two of them charged forward.

Alexis floated behind me and tapped my shoulder. "You may wanna do that little zap zap again," she said.

I jumped to my feet and held my hands up. The harpies flapped to a halt, fear lacing their expressions. Blue sparks pricked at the tips of my palms but no lightning came forward. "Umm," I murmured. I flexed my hands, trying to get lightning to come out, but nothing happened.

Alexis laughed and nudged at my side. "OK, stop messing around. Light 'em up!"

"I can't," I whispered.

She floated closer to my ear and lowered her voice. "What do you mean you can't? You just did it."

"I don't know, it's just not working." I tried rubbing my hands together and flicked them out in another frantic attempt.

"Cherry, they're starting to realize there's a problem," she hissed.

The two harpies exchanged looks then advanced forward. Drool spilled from the black-haired harpy's maw as she licked her lips. She sprang forward just as the blue sparks ignited in my palm. Frantic, I shoved my hands forward, pleading with whatever magic I had tapped into to listen. The harpy flung herself back, screaming. White light blinded my vision before fiery pain erupted in my hands.

"FUCKING DICK BISCUITS!" I yelled. Smoke simmered from my burned hands. The skin was angry and red as if I'd been holding a scalding-hot pot.

"Oh shit, that looks like it hurts," Alexis said.

"YA THINK?" I cried out, clutching my hands to my chest.

"Is that the best you can do?" The dark-haired harpy sneered. "Well, looks like your luck has just run out."

Chapter 12

Cherry

In a flash, the sunlight peeking through the canopy vanished. Thunder boomed so loud my ears rang. Wind picked up, snatching the raven-coloured harpy's body like a leaf in a storm, and slammed her against a tree. Before the other harpy could blink, Dante was on her. She screeched as he pulled back her wings until they made a sickening pop. I looked on in shock as he ripped the wings from her body and threw them to the side. Blood splattered the ends of his black cloak.

His gaze turned to the last harpy, who was struggling to get up. One of her wings was broken. The white of her frail bones peeked out among black feathers as she desperately tried to flap away.

She didn't get far. Sparks danced along his arms as he advanced on her. I shielded my eyes, only opening them again when I heard her scream cut short.

"Dante!" Alexis cried cheerfully. "Cherry, you didn't tell me Dante was your dragon." She flew up to the dragon-shifter and twirled happily. "Man, am I glad to see you. You wouldn't believe the week I—" Her words cut short when Dante turned to her. He said nothing, but she sank lower to the ground then backed away from him. "You know what, I can wait." Alexis retreated to the other side of the rock and laid herself down, far away from the man's path. "I'm just gonna wait right here. Yup, don't worry about me."

That can't be good.

Lightning flashed and the dragon-shifter was suddenly in front of me. His face was calm, but the surrounding storm whipped with fury, as if mirroring his wrath. Startled, I backed up against a tree, then hissed in pain. He tugged me toward him, then inspected the damage. Blood from the cuts on my back left their mark on the tree. His grip on my shoulder tightened painfully. I winced and he let go just as quickly. The wind picked up around us, howling so fiercely that the giant redwoods began to sway and creak under the storm's pressure.

"Are...are *you* doing this?" I asked, gesturing to the wild weather around us. The idea was ludicrous, yet the skies had been clear until Dante showed up.

He nodded once, then instructed me to turn around. When

I did, gentle hands slid the ruined coat from my shoulders. I bit my lip, trying to put on a brave front. Yet I couldn't stop the whimper from escaping when the coat brushed against my cuts. I felt Dante tense behind me. Lightning struck a branch, snapping it in half before it plummeted to the ground.

"Are you—?"

"Do not ask if I am alright when you were moments away from being taken from me." The deep gravel in his tone sent a shiver down my spine. Even with the pain in my hands, and the rush of my near-death experience, his nearness did terrible things to my psyche.

"Alright, I won't." I pressed my lips together, vehemently trying to ignore the gnawing ache between my legs.

Snapping gators. Read the room, dragon slut magic!

He gingerly took hold of my wrists and inspected my hands. "These burns, did you use my magic?" he asked.

"Yeah, it just sort of happened while I was being attacked. My second try ended up backfiring."

His voice turned wary. "Hmm, you shouldn't be able to do that yet."

"Is that bad?"

"It's unsafe," he said, releasing my hand. "Storm magic is erratic and requires careful concentration. Normally, it takes years to tap into magic gained from a mating bond. If you can, try to avoid using it further. You may not be so lucky the next time it backfires." Smoke spilled past my feet as Dante placed his hands on my upper back. He took a deep breath then the hands on my back grew cold. As they did, the searing pain in my cuts faded away. Replaced by a rushing tingling feeling, somewhat similar to what I felt after he had bitten me. When the feeling spread to my ruined hands, I lifted them up for a look. Right before my eyes, the angry painful burns faded into mostly clear skin. When the tingling sensation stopped, my hands were still a little red but not nearly as painful as they had been.

I felt Dante slump, and his head came to rest on the tree in front of me. He put a hand on my shoulder to steady himself as he breathed deep. "This is all I can do for you right now. Most of my magic is still depleted."

I placed a hand on the one on my shoulder. "Thank you for saving me," I whispered.

Alexis cleared her throat.

"Us," I corrected, rolling my eyes.

His fingers clasped mine, before leaning further against my back. As if trying to occupy as much of my space as he could. With my coat gone, the warmth of his body was much appreciated and I leaned back against him. The scent of petrichor and man bled into my senses like a drug.

"Why did you run off, Cherry?" His tone remained calm, yet the rolling thunder gave away his mood.

"I wasn't trying to escape," I huffed. "Your cat ran off, so I was just trying to find it."

Booming thunder faded into a low rumble. The wind died

down, stopping its relentless assault against the canopy. Dante regarded me with a withered expression. "You risked your life for a cat?"

"Well, I didn't know there were harpies in the area. I've never even seen one before." Though they proved he was telling the truth. If harpies were this far outside of Volsog, then the world I knew was gone. Not only that, if it wasn't for that freak accident with the lightning I'd be dead. When it was just my life on the line, I didn't really care what happened. But if there were demons here, then it was only a matter of time before they reached Boohail. If they weren't there already.

The thought of my family and friends trying to fight off a flock of those terrifying creatures sent a chill down my spine. I thought about the kraken that had attacked Gideon's island, and the gargantuan hydra skeleton in the river. There's no way my village would survive that kind of attack. Not without Myva's magic barrier.

Or a guard dragon.

A grin pulled at the long scar running down his face. "You're doing it again," he said in that low voice that sent fireflies to my stomach.

I tilted my head. "What am I doing?"

"You're staring at me with fierce, unidentifiable intent. What's on your mind, Princess?"

Whether I can trust you to not eat my family. Well, that and shredding our clothes and climbing you like a tree.

I smiled up at him. "Just thinking about how great it is not to be harpy food."

"Hmm."

"What are you thinking about?" I asked.

Strong arms slid around my waist. Dante rested his head against my shoulder and squeezed me to him. "I'm trying to decide if I should bother finding the harpies' colony or just burn the entire forest down until not even cinders remain. At least then I'll be sure I've gotten them all."

His hold tightened with each word until he was squeezing the breath from my lungs. My feet left the ground as he held me tighter. I tugged at his wrist, but it didn't budge.

"She can't breathe, Dante," Alexis called out.

He gasped and released me. I dropped to my knees and gulped in precious air. Dante backed away further and put his hands behind his back.

"We need to work on your hugs," I coughed.

"Cherry, I'm so sorry. I didn't realize I wasn't curbing my strength."

I waved him off, silencing his nervous apology. I was starting to think I needed to add my own chapter on dragons to *The Book Of Beasts*. Fact number one: dragons are very strong. "Yeah, I know. Look, just call off your vendetta against the harpies and I'll call it even."

He tilted his head, clearly bewildered at my request. "They could have killed you."

"Yeah, so could any predator. Or a really enthusiastic fla-mingo. Humans aren't that hard to kill. Are you going to wipe out all flamingos on the off-chance one tries something?"

He looked away and shifted on his feet as if considering.

"Dante," I warned.

"Fine," he scowled, crossing his arms. The storm surround-ing us had simmered down to a dark overcast. Judging by his distemper over my unwillingness to let him commit bird genocide, I think that's as good as we were going to get.

Fact number two: dragons are fucking dramatic.

"Let's get you back to camp," he said, motioning for me to follow him. "I have some Kiboon honey we can put on your hands. It should soothe the burn."

"What about Rebekah?" I asked. He kept a wide berth between us as we made our way back to the beach.

Dante lifted a branch out of my path and guided me through. But I couldn't help but notice the way he flattened himself against the tree to avoid touching me. "We'll leave some food out for her. She'll come back if she doesn't want to be left behind."

"Who's Rebekah?" Alexis asked, coming to float at my side.

"She's a little white ball of fluff about this big," I said, wid-ening my hands to show the length of the little kitten.

"Oh, you mean that freakish horror creature?" she asked. "I saw it run off just before you showed up."

Her eyes may have been a little beady but calling the kitten a freakish horror creature seemed like a bit much. "I mean, it's a cat."

"Hehe, sure it is," Alexis said.

For a man on the brink of exhaustion, Dante sure was determined not to stay still. I shifted on my feet awkwardly, unsure of what to do. The dragon-shifter busied himself with setting out food for Rebekah and setting up camp. Any attempt at helping was met with him herding me back onto the blanket he'd set by the fire.

"I'm getting dizzy just watching him," Alexis whispered to me.

So was I. The inhuman speed he used to move around the beach was hard to follow. Instead, I settled myself down by the folding table he'd set up and picked at the food. All of which he had arranged in a tasteful display, complete with a small vase with fresh flowers. Where the flowers came from was an absolute mystery.

"How do you two know each other?" I asked.

The sword sank herself a few inches into the sand and let out a contented sigh. "We helped fuck up a sexist cult together. He's good people."

Of all the ways I thought she was going to answer that statement, fucking up a sexist cult was not one of them. "So, he saved people then?"

"Yup. The cult was full of a bunch of gross men nobody wanted to bang, so they stole a bunch of women to sacrifice to a giant lobster. It was wild. On a good note, we managed to get all the victims out safely and I was able to steal their magic and gain the ability to move."

I narrowed my eyes at the sword in the sand, yet her lack of a face made it kind of hard to tell if she was serious. "Are... are you messing with me?"

She laughed. "I swear on my creator, it's all true."

I sat down beside her and mulled over her story. It sounded like the weird ramblings of someone on too much ganja. Yet when I considered the fact that I was chatting with a cursed sword, while a dragon set up camp, it didn't seem so far-fetched. If the sword was telling the truth, then maybe Dante wasn't such a bad guy. "I think I'm gonna give him a shot," I whispered to Alexis.

"Wasn't that the original plan?"

I shook my head. "No, plan A was to buy a horse and abscond into the night."

The man in question paused from his work. "Did you need something?" he asked.

"She wants to know how you eat pasta!" the sword shouted.

"Alexis!"

"What? Oh, was that told in confidence?" She turned back to Dante and took on a chipper tone. "Disregard that! We have no pasta-related questions at this time."

A white ball of fluff came waddling out from the trees. Rebekah's belly was rounded so far, I feared she might very well burst. The kitten dragged herself to the edge of the blanket and let out a burp at a volume you normally associate with a large drunkard, not a small kitten. Bits of feathers came out of her mouth and floated onto the sand.

"Looks like she caught her own dinner." I reached over to pick her up but found that I couldn't. The kitten flicked her tail in annoyance as I struggled to heave her onto my lap. "Shrieking pumas, did you eat rocks?" I asked. There was no way such a small thing could be so heavy. When she had enough of my fussing, Rebekah's claws unsheathed while an angry rumble shook the kitten's body. I took the hint and backed off.

Once the firewood had been rearranged into a neat stack, and the rest of our belongings had been tidied up, Dante finally joined Alexis and me. He took out a jar of purple liquid and set it on the table.

"What is this?" I asked.

"It's the Kiboon honey," he said, taking a seat on the edge of the blanket. "Rub a bit on your hands and it should soothe any remaining pain. Kiboon bees are venomous, but their honey temporarily increases your magic. Since you now have half of mine, it should heal you faster if given the push. It's also much sweeter than regular honey, though you'll be in for a nasty stomach ache if you overindulge."

I opened the jar and sniffed at the purple honey inside. It smelled fine, but I had never seen honey any other color than well…honey. "Is it safe for humans?"

"I don't know why it wouldn't be," he yawned.

"Guess that's good enough," I muttered. The dull ache in my hands finally vanished when I spread the honey over my palms. Curious, I licked some off my wrist. Impossibly sweet goodness invaded my tongue in a hostile takeover, and to my utter shame, I moaned. Loudly.

Dante cleared his throat. "You're supposed to keep it on your hands, Princess," he said, pointing to the palms I'd nearly licked clean.

Quickly, I slathered more honey on my hands then shoveled a spoonful in my mouth. Through the bliss, I was able to eke out a meager response. "I told you to stop calling me Princess."

"You're right, I'm starting to think honey badger is more apt." He turned his back to me and laid down, the tips of his ears turning a dark shade of red. If the divine taste of the honey didn't have me so caught up, I might have felt embarrassed at the noises I was making. But fuck, I'd sell my soul for another jar.

I greedily shoveled another spoonful in my mouth. "Dante, we have to go back."

"Back to where?"

"Your castle. I need more honey." Mentally, I was kicking myself for running out of the bee room so quickly. If I had known bee demons made something so precious, I would've bowed down and erected a shrine in their honor hoping to be given some of their bounty.

"You're going to make yourself sick," he scolded.

"It's worth it," I sighed. "Please, dear husband, just keep me in an endless supply of this stuff and I'll be yours forever."

"Keep testing me and all those wicked assumptions of yours will come true." His voice lowered to something hungry and hot. The deep baritone of his words sank into my body to caress my core.

I tilted my head back, groaning, and licked the remaining demon honey from my lips, savoring its impossible sweetness. "Say that again."

He let off a frustrated growl as his back tensed. With his cloak cast off, I could see the hard muscles straining against the fabric of his shirt. The thin layer of white loosened around the collar, allowing glimpses of tawny skin, as if it was tempting me to grant it freedom.

It should be free.

I realized then that fabric was the true evil of this rotten word. And it had to go.

I crawled on top of him and ran my fingers over the bare skin of his collar. The sensation alone sent sparks of desire down my body. "Maybe you should clarify which assumptions."

His arms came around me, sure and hard as I knew they would be. He took my chin, tilted my head and kissed me until the world spun. I didn't waste any time slipping my hands over the broad expanse of his back. An approving growl rose from his throat, and his tongue pillaged my throat like the dragon he was. If I were a kingdom under siege, there would have been no survivors. I caved immediately, responding with each stroke of his tongue in kind, while melting in his arms.

Breaking the kiss, he fisted my curly hair at the nape, and his gaze bored into mine before he froze. "Your eyes are violet," he said. Realization seemed to dawn. "Right," he groaned, releasing me to bury his face into his hand. "The honeymoon magic must have been increased as well."

Why was he talking about honey when his tongue belonged down my throat?

Dante rested his face in the crook of my neck as his power-ful arms pulled me tighter to him. My hands slid lower down his back until I could slip my fingers underneath that damn shirt, gasping at the reward of warm skin. I shivered as he ran his lips against the bite mark. "Alexis," he called.

"Yes?"

"I need you to knock me out."

"Why would I stop this?"

"Damn voyeur," he growled. Icy wind frazzled my senses when he fell back, throwing an arm over his eyes. Something twitched, and I looked down to see proof of his arousal. Pant-ing, I slid my hand down his body, running my fingers over the ridges of his abs. When I traveled lower, his hands shot out to grab my wrist. He lifted his arm to regard me with a calm expression, mismatched from the feral want in his eyes. Gently he brought my hand to his face and pulled my fingers away to kiss my palm. "Cherry, go back to the blanket. Right now." The command in his voice brokered no room for argument.

But fuck, I love to argue. "I'd rather stay here with you."

He rubbed my ass gently, before smacking it. "This must be penance for some past crime I've committed." With a grunt, he lifted himself up and sat on the opposite end of the fire.

Why am I sweating? My mind felt hazy and euphoric. The stress of the day melted away as my entire body relaxed. If this resulted from mixing purple honey and dragon magic, then we'd need to figure out a way to bottle this stuff and share it with the world. "Aren't we supposed to be bonding on this trip? Kissing by a campfire seems like the perfect idea to me."

Dante's head fell into his hand. When he spoke, his voice sounded hoarse. "Honey badger, take a step further and I'll remember this when I have you underneath me and completely sober."

"I still think your clothes should answer for their crimes, but fine," I relented, and returned next to Alexis on the blanket.

"What crimes have my clothes committed, Cherry?"

"Existing. Obviously."

He laughed, but made no move to undress. "Just stay on your side of the damn fire."

Sweat beaded my brow, and I fanned myself. A bout of dizziness struck me and the world spun. My back hit the blanket with a soft thud. I blinked and tried to focus on the fluffy clouds in the sky, but they too were swirling.

Alexis floated closer, the glint of her metal causing me to squint. "Um…Cherry?" She said something else, but her voice was too far away. As my vision grew blurrier, I saw a blob of gray and black rush over to me, before my mind drifted to sleep.

An ocean of blue stretched out beneath me. Just like in my dream before, the waves were calm. Yet the serenity did nothing to soothe the growing animalistic fear nipping at the edge of my consciousness.

There was something in the water.

Chapter 13

Dante

"I'm doing everything wrong," I said, running a hand through my hair.

The mirror's image flickered as Fallon flipped through the pages of his book, his brow furrowed in concentration. "There's nothing in here that says Kiboon honey can be harmful. Though I suppose there is no record of humans trying it." He flipped the book closed and crossed his arms. "Where did you even get that stuff? I thought they were one of the species that went extinct after Myva banished us. Insects aren't exactly made for the cold."

"My mother was obsessed with medical research. When it looked like we were going to lose the war against the lich, she gathered a colony of bees and hid them away in her horde." Along with every other useful plant she could get her hands on. Her apothecary had been damn near a jungle by the time Volsog's gate had finally sealed.

Exhaustion weighed heavy on my shoulders. I rubbed at my tired eyes and tried to stay focused. Seeing my mate passed out on the beach chased away any thought of sleeping. Instead, I hauled her all the way to Kirkwall in search of a healer. Yet, even after forcing the healer I found to check her thrice, he couldn't discover anything wrong and suggested she merely sleep it off. Still, the fact that she hadn't woken hours later was worrying.

"What about before the mess with the honey?" Fallon asked. "You must've made at least some progress with her."

My fingers thrummed against my seat. "Well, we were."

"But?"

I thought back to when I had her in my arms. The rage I felt was so consuming that I didn't even notice her discomfort. Humans are incredibly fragile, I should have known better. Fuck, I'm a terrible mate. "But I may have crushed her a little. I don't think I heard any bones pop so she should be fine."

Fallon's mouth formed a thin line. "You don't think you heard any bones pop." His head fell into his hands. "Dante, I think we may need outside help."

"I said I *didn't* hear any bones pop!"

The shadow dragon merely shook his head at me. "I'm getting Felix."

"No," I groaned.

He rose from his chair with a sigh. "There's only so much I can do to help you in the face of you. Hold on, let me check my notes." Fallon paused and held up his fingers to count my mounting indiscretions. "Biting her without consent, kidnapping—"

"That was to save her from another kidnapping," I cut in.

"Semantics," he said, waving me off. "Almost breaking her ribs and now drugging her. Is there anything else I should add to the list?"

"Well, I saved her life after harpies attacked her. Surely that must count for something."

Fallon rested his chin on his fist and paused. "Follow-up question, did you destroy those harpies in front of her?"

"Of course. I tore the wings from their bodies so she knew they'd never hurt her again."

Fallon tsked. "I'm going to add potential traumatization to the list of infractions."

Frustration had my nails digging into the wood of my armrest. "You burned down a city in front of your mate," I pointed out.

He shrugged and gave a wry smile. "We're not talking about me here. My wife likes me just fine. Face it, there's a good chance your wife is terrified of you. Luckily, Felix has experience with that." With that Fallon rose from his chair. Presumably to go get the werewolf in question.

"She is not scared of me," I grumbled. If he heard me, Fallon didn't acknowledge it as he left the study. As much as I hated to admit it, he was right. I needed more help. Felix may have been irksome, but he possessed an amiable smile and sunny disposition that humans found reassuring. Even when he was possessed by a love potion, his own human wife was wrapped around his finger in a matter of days.

With Fallon gone, I took the opportunity to check on Cherry. In the center of the kitchen, my Hearthstone flashed. Kobolds emerged through the portal carrying more furniture from my storage. There hadn't been time to find decent accommodations in my rush, but the small house I had managed to acquire would do. One kobold snapped her jaws to get my attention, then looked around the room as if to ask where I wanted the dresser in her hands. I instructed them to place it in the corner of Cherry's bedroom.

My wife was sprawled out on the bed. At some point she had kicked away her covers. A small line of drool ran from her mouth to form a puddle on the pillow. Alexis had laid herself down at the end of the bed and fell silent soon after I placed Cherry there. I wasn't entirely sure if the cursed object could sleep, but she seemed to be in some sort of stasis. Not that I minded, I was in no mood for company.

By the looks of it, Cherry had no plans to get up anytime soon. Carefully, I undid the laces on her boots and slid them off. Her face scrunched up when I removed the second boot. I looked down to see that the heel of her foot was bleeding. Not only that, the leather boots clearly had been mended time and time again, yet they were still barely holding on.

Anger and shame simmered in the pit of my gut. "I didn't even notice she was in pain." She was supposed to be in my care yet she felt she couldn't even ask me for shoes. Another failure Fallon could undoubtedly add to his list. "Dammit."

I grabbed her ruined boots and stormed out of the house. The streets were alive with humans bustling about. There were a few demons thrown into the mix but not many, from what I could see. It was surprising when I considered how close Kirkwall is to Volsog. With so many demons migrating out of the frozen wasteland, I assumed the city would be packed full of them.

The entire street was lined with tiny homes all scrunched together with shops dotted in between. A street vendor bellowed about a sale on apples while an angry woman with a baby strapped to her back haggled over the price of fabric. Yet no shoe store appeared when I scanned the area. With a city this large, it was damn near impossible to find what you were looking for.

I looked around and spotted a red orc loitering about. He didn't have the same sense of urgency as the shop vendors, but he looked able-bodied enough to be of use. "You, Orc, stop!" I called. The orc turned and his red face paled at the sight of my horn. A dead giveaway for what I was.

"A dragon," he stammered, backing away.

I grabbed him by the front of his cloak and pulled him close to my face. "I need you to do something for me."

He held his hands up. "Please don't eat me."

"I need you to go to the shoe shop, and get every pair of boots that are a similar size to these." I pushed Cherry's boot into his chest as I released him.

He grabbed it back from me. His mouth fell open in bewilderment. "I'm sorry, you need me to buy shoes?"

I nodded. "When you have them, put them in front of my door here. Fail me in this endeavor and your family line will end with you."

The orc had enough sense to look terrified and rushed off. "At least that's one problem solved." I returned inside and started heating a pot of coffee. My body felt ragged and I was desperate for sleep, but my mind was far too jumbled to even consider rest. I heard Fallon call my name from the magic mirror and returned to my seat.

Fallon and Felix were sitting beside each other in the dragon's study. The werewolf's normally chipper smile was downcast, and he regarded me with a stern look one would give a naughty child. Felix ran a hand down his face then leaned back in his chair with an exasperated sigh. "She is terrified of you."

"What do I do?" I asked, scowling.

Felix leaned forward and rested his chin on his hands. "Bring her here and leave."

"What?" I growled. "Why would I leave my wife? The whole point of asking you for help was to get in her good graces."

He took a deep breath. "Dante, my beautiful disaster of a friend, if you had called me earlier I might have been able to help you. As it stands, this dynamic is too twisted to continue. She's scared, and she's backed into a corner. Give her to Usha for a while and back off. Your wife will most likely find comfort in another human woman, and there's no woman alive more fearless than the captain. Then, if she wants, Usha can take her home."

"She doesn't seem afraid of me," I argued.

Felix shook his head solemnly. "She is going to say and do whatever it takes to not be crushed or eaten. At this point, it's basically a hostage situation."

"Dammit," I sighed. As much as I was loath to admit it, Felix was making sense. Cherry wouldn't even tell me where she lived. Nor did I know her last name. Those weren't the actions of a woman unafraid of the man she was with.

Every instinct in me screamed to lock her away and never let her go. The last of my magic churned the clouds above the city. Ready to strike lightning down on anything that could take her away from me. Which was exactly what she was terrified of. I closed my eyes, steadied my breathing, and forced the clouds to stop churning.

"Fine," I said, meeting Felix's gaze. "I'll bring her to you and leave. But if anything happens to her while I'm gone—"

"You have my word, she'll be safe here," Fallon cut in.

Felix let out a breath and smiled. "It's not forever," he amended. "She's your fated mate after all. When the time comes, I have no doubt she'll seek you out."

Fallon scoffed. "He's already bitten her. That much is a given."

I nodded, bid them farewell and cut the connection. When the mirror's image faded, I sagged into my seat. "It's not forever," I told myself. As a dragon, I had nothing but endless time. Centuries had come and gone without Cherry at my side. Yet now the years all faded into nothingness. When I thought about spending a day away from her, time seemed like an awful thing.

A hurried knock at the door pulled me out of my ruminations. The red orc I had tasked before stood on the steps with a stack of boxes in his hands. He set them down on the steps and lowered his head. "Here are the shoes you wanted, my Lord," he stammered.

"You've done me a great service." I reached into my pocket, pulled out a handful of gold coins and set them in his large hand. It had been a while since I had done any shopping myself, but the astonishment in his eyes told me the payment was sufficient.

"Holy shit!" he shouted, then hurriedly stuffed the coins in his pocket. "Is there anything else you need?"

"No, that will be all," I said. With that, I gathered the

boxes and returned inside. Far too exhausted to unbox them, I deposited them by Cherry's door and lay down on the couch.

Without a sound, a kobold set a mug of coffee on the center table and scurried off. I heard the portal open once more before it fizzled with each kobold that passed through, then fell silent. I breathed a sigh of relief and finally allowed my eyes to close. When all else failed, at least I could rely on them.

The door to my wife's bedroom creaked open. I turned to see a disheveled Cherry emerge. Her pigtails were half unraveled and bunched up around her neck. Her round face scrunched in irritation, then she held a hand up to shield her eyes from the sunlight filtering through the window. She took a step forward and tried to brace herself against the door frame, missed, and fell flat on her face.

I held back a laugh as she whipped around to growl at the frame as if it was at fault for not anticipating her needs. Her scowl looked as if it had crawled its way out of the depths of the underworld to curse the door frame until it rued the day it had slithered its wretched little soul in front of her path.

In that moment I felt I could see into every facet of my wife's mind. If she had the ability, and if door frames had complex enough lives to warrant a family who would love and miss them in the event of their demise, she would send pieces of its body back to them in a methodical pattern. Then make wine from their tears. Instead of ever entertaining the notion that she may have just not looked where she was going. I was both in awe of and in deep fear of her.

If this wasn't love, it was damn close.

She gave the innocent wood a little kick and dragged herself toward me. Then her eyes zeroed in on the mug of coffee and she pounced.

"Good morning," I said.

Her gaze flicked to me. "I will under no circumstances speak to anyone until I have finished this coffee."

I had no desire to be added to her list of victims, so I remained quiet as she sipped. She let out a long, satisfied breath and sat down next to me. When the last drop of coffee slipped past her lips, she set down the mug and snuggled her small body against mine. Her sweet scent eased my frazzled senses. I put an arm around her waist and pulled her closer against me. When she didn't pull away, the magic bond between us thrummed with satisfaction. "You're rather affectionate this morning," I remarked.

"Your stupid dragon slut magic demands physical touch. It's been getting worse by the day," she grumbled, lacing her fingers with mine. "Did you not sleep?" she asked. "You look like you're held together by two strings and a ball of stress."

"Accurate," I admitted.

"Where are we?" she asked. "This doesn't look like your castle."

I stroked my thumb along her knuckles, relishing the small

touch. "We're in Kirkwall. I found us a house to rest in after you collapsed. The kobolds had just finished furnishing it before you woke up."

"You bought a house?" Cherry's brow furrowed as she looked up at me. "How in the world did you buy a house that quick? There's no way I've been out for that long."

"Bring enough gold to a bank and they'll do anything with haste."

She smiled and shook her head. "Why didn't you just get us a room at an inn? I imagine that would be much cheaper."

"Don't inns reuse the same sheets every time they have a new guest?" I asked.

"Yes?"

"That's disgusting. Just the thought of it had my skin crawling. Sleeping in the same bed as countless strangers with only a quick wash in between. Human cities smelled bad enough as it was. There was no way I could debase my wife by letting her sleep in something as filthy as an inn."

Cherry snorted before a stream of giggles rang through the air. "You are so weird."

"Hmm."

"What's with the boxes?"

"You had cuts on your heels. So I bought you new shoes."

"A lot of new shoes, apparently."

"Are you complaining?"

"Nope," she said, burrowing further against me.

Lying here like this felt like a dream I never wanted to wake up from. Even if it was only the result of the honeymoon magic's insistence. It would be a memory I cherished for centuries. Again, the need to steal her away churned in my gut with an awful sickness. A sickness that grew more intense with the knowledge that I had to be the one to ruin this moment. "Princess," I began.

She elbowed my gut.

"Honey badger," I amended. "I need to talk to you about our little trip."

"What's on your mind?" she asked.

"I'd like to…well, *like* isn't the correct word. But I need to take you to stay with a friend of mine. She's a human woman and she could take you home if you wish."

"Where will you be?" she asked, yawning.

I closed my eyes and allowed myself to breathe in the scent of her hair, filled with an ardent need to commit it to memory. "I'll remain in my castle until you've had enough time to decide what you want to do. Unless you ask her to, Usha will not tell me where you live."

She rolled to face me and settled her head on my arm. "Why?"

This was much harder to do with her facing me. All I wanted to do was pull her closer and kiss her full lips until I was the only thought that crossed her mind. "I spoke with Fallon the Shadow Dragon this morning."

"The one that you helped kill Myva?"

"The very same. He and Felix, a werewolf acquaintance of ours, both have human wives. They mentioned you would feel more comfortable if I left you in the care of another human woman and let you be."

Her nose scrunched as she searched my face. "Why would they tell you that?"

"They think you're scared of me." I gave in to temptation and traced my thumb along the rich dark skin of her jaw. "Are you scared of me, Cherry?"

"I suppose I should be," she mused. "Yet somehow I get the feeling that I'm not the terrified party here."

Hope was a terrible thing, and I stomped it down before I gave too much weight to her words. "Still, they think—"

She put a finger to my lips. "I'm not their wife, I'm yours. You promised to take me anywhere, and I want to see a unicorn." Her gaze drifted as she trailed off. "Maybe a cyclops too. Oh, wait, are ghosts real?"

I'm yours. The words echoed in my mind like a sweet caress.

My voice took on a strained edge as I resisted the urge to crush her to me. "You attempted to brave the horrors of Volsog to get away from me. What's changed?"

She raised her brow. "You and your little buddies released hordes of dangerous monsters into the world. Without the goddess' protective barrier, my home would be an easy target for attacks. I haven't decided if I trust you enough yet to protect us, but I am starting to like you. So I'm staying."

Such a practical little thing.

"Is there any more of that..." She paused, then twirled her hand as if she could churn the answer from thin air. "Dammit, I just said the word. The zippy bean juice."

"Do you mean coffee?"

She snapped her fingers. "That's the one."

I chuckled and nodded toward the kitchen. "It's on the counter."

Cherry slipped out of my arms to acquire more fast bean juice. Her gait was bouncy and significantly less cantankerous with the first cup doing its job.

"That's it then?" I called after her. "We keep sightseeing until you decide to believe me when I say I don't hunger for human flesh?"

She returned and handed me a cup of my own before sitting back down beside me. "Gotta better idea?" When I shook my head, she continued. "On that note, have you ever eaten a human?"

Oh gods.

Cherry's body grew tense. "That's an awfully long pause."

"I don't think so," I whispered, filtering through countless battles in my memories.

She bit her lip, her eyes narrowing. "You don't *think* so."

Lie. Make something up, you dullard.

As if reading my thoughts, a look of hurt marred the warmth in her eyes. "Don't lie to me."

My treacherous mouth opened of its own accord and sang like a canary. "I've been in three wars. Two of them were behind Volsog's gate, far away from humans. The first was against Myva's army. Some of which were human, though it was impossible to tell underneath all the armor. Most of my time was spent in dragon form spewing fire on enemy lines and well..."

"Well?" she prompted.

"Everything tastes the same when it's charred to a crisp."

For a moment, she simply stared, then gave a slow blink. "And you think *inns* are gross?"

Chapter 14

Cherry

Everything's better with a pocket full of money. I know the saying is money can't buy happiness, but I feel whoever came up with that never had a shopping spree on someone else's gold. Cause I felt pretty damn happy.

"Try the spongy thing next!" Alexis called from her seat beside me. The other restaurant patrons kept sneaking glances at the talking sword, who was floating happily above the chair that had been pulled out for her. After she loudly demanded that a chair be pulled out for her. I wasn't entirely sure what the point was seeing as she had no ability to sit, but it wasn't my place to deny her happiness.

In truth, I think she just wanted to show off her fresh

polish. Soon after Dante fell asleep, Alexis and I hit the town. The first stop being the blacksmith, who balked at the idea of touching a cursed object. A few silver pieces on his counter removed his prejudice, and he happily polished Alexis until she shone. Then threw in a fancy red sheath at her request.

The talking sword turned heads at most of the shops we visited. Not that I could blame them. But thankfully the people of Kirkwall were simple and the gold in our pockets gleamed brighter than any curse.

I moaned contentedly around the bite of flan. "Sweet dancing fireflies, it's like a cloud in my mouth." A drop of caramel drizzle landed on my new skirt, and I quickly wiped it away. The expensive fabric was softer than the fluff on a baby lamb and made my old clothes feel like a personal attack against comfort. Even the trousers underneath were fur-lined for added comfort.

The people of Kirkwall did fashion right. Back home, women's clothing mostly comprised simple skirts and blouses, as our climate was far too hot for much else. But this far north, the dominant weather this time of year seemed to be colder than a witch's tit in a brass bra, and the layered clothing offered more styling options.

My dress coat was a pretty pale blue, similar to the one that had been ruined in the harpy attack. Decorative lines adorned the edges of the sleeves, while a similar pattern raced along the hem. A pale sectioned underskirt sat on top of brown trousers for added warmth. In a wonderful bout of serendipity, I was able to find a red blouse that matched the boots Dante had bought me. It even came with a decorative sash around the middle to keep everything in place. All in all, the outfit made me feel fancy and fashion-forward while still being practical enough to travel in. I fucking loved it.

It wasn't even just the outfit. Spending the day shopping and chatting made me feel like a real person again. When I stepped outside and heard the voices of people milling about the streets, I almost burst into tears. It'd been so long since I'd heard the voice of someone else who wasn't a dragon or a sword. It may have just been an angry mother screaming about the price of tomatoes, yet it was still the most beautiful sound I'd ever heard. I was free, and I had Dante to thank for that.

"We should probably order something for Sleeping Beauty on the way back," I said, shoveling another scoop into my mouth.

Alexis tilted ever so slightly to the side. "Oh right, I forgot about him."

I laughed into a napkin at her nonchalance. "Isn't he your friend?"

"Look, I can't be expected to keep track of every flesh being I associate with. Let's just find him something lemon-flavored and hit up more shops."

"Sounds like a plan."

We spent most of the day at boutiques, and I was keen to

hit up the farmers' market on the way back. With my food resources no longer limited to the island, I could finally cook some of the homemade food I'd been dreaming about for years. The smell of my ma's cinnamon rolls had been haunting my dreams for too damn long.

I hailed the server over to us. In an instant, John flung himself over to our table with the speed of a man who could smell a fat tip coming his way.

He and the rest of the servers at The Royal Mockingbird wore grayish blue outfits with pristine, puffy white sleeves. The restaurant sat on the edge of a cliff overlooking the ocean. If the large sign they had out front was to be believed, this was the best view in Kirkwall, second only to the castle garden itself. As soon as we had entered, John had taken one look at my fine new clothing, and the tiara sitting proud on top of my head, and guided us onto the terrace with a wide customer-service smile.

The man in question now halted in front of our table with a practiced snap of his heels and gave a polite bow. "I trust everything has been to your liking, ladies?" he asked.

"Everything has been delicious, thank you," I said, with the most polite smile I could manage. "Could we get a lemon tart and the roasted chicken to go?"

"Of course, ma'am. I'll fetch that for you right away." He turned to Alexis and inclined his head. "And for you ma'am?"

"None for me, thanks," she replied.

He gave another bow, then disappeared back into the

crowded restaurant. When I was sure he was out of earshot I whispered low to my companion, "I can't believe he hasn't asked why you can talk, yet."

Alexis laughed. "Listen, John is about earning that bread and I respect it. He doesn't have time for our games."

A short time later, John returned with our food wrapped neatly in a little basket. I thanked him enthusiastically and handed him a few gold pieces. "Keep the change."

He stared down at the coins in his hand with wide eyes. "Ma'am, did you hand this to me by mistake? Your bill was only ten copper."

"Nope. That's for you," I said, gathering up our food. When he remained frozen next to the table, I maneuvered around him and waved goodbye as we left. Sunset bathed the busy street in a warm glow, while a salty sea breeze blew against wind chimes.

"I SAID I QUIT!" a voice bellowed. Alexis and I turned to see John kick open the doors to the restaurant and flee down the street, laughing in joy.

"Aww, look how happy you made him," the sword cooed.

"I used to spend my winters working at a tavern in my hometown," I said solemnly. "People are always jerks to servers." Night after night of cleaning up after sloppy drunks had instilled a deep need in me to be kind to servers. I knew all too well how shitty the job was. Even though my boss, Sunbeam, took care of anyone that got too rowdy, I still had to deal with cruel insults and wandering hands. Being able to free someone else from that life felt fantastic.

I patted my full belly happily as we made our way through the busy streets and back toward our house. "What should we do after we drop Dante's food off?" I asked.

"Hmm. Looks like we're going to pass the coliseum on the way back, we could stop by and see if there's a match tonight."

"Oh, that does sound fun! I've never been to a gladiator match." From our spot on the cliff I could see the marble columns of the coliseum in the center of the city. No doubt the biggest tourist attraction in Kirkwall, the coliseum was surrounded by shops, taverns and restaurants. Even if there wasn't a fight tonight, there was no doubt we'd find something else to get into.

"Sorry, no demons allowed." The burly knight guarding the coliseum's entrance crossed his arms and scowled down at us, looking anything but actually sorry. His partner glowered in our direction before turning his attention back to the line of other patrons.

Alexis simmered into a burned orange before snapping back at him. "First of all, rude. Second, I'm not even a demon. I am a cursed object. If you're going to be prejudiced, the least you could do is get it right."

The knight rolled his eyes. "I don't care if you're cursed or a holy relic. No demons or demonic forces are allowed beyond this point."

"If there are no demons allowed, then explain that," I said, pointing to the sign advertising tonight's attraction—a snake-man and an ogre facing off. It read "Boomslang vs Barbarian" in bold red letters. I'll admit I haven't met a lot of demons, but I can say with confidence I've never met a human with half a snake's body.

I peered past the guard to see if I could spot any gladiators milling about. If today's fight was between a snakeman and an ogre, there could be even more types of demons working as gladiators. We'd been walking around for most of the day, and still hadn't seen any other demons.

Would it be weird to ask them to sign my book?

The knight rolled his eyes. "Gladiators are the exception. A bit of blood entertainment is the only thing demons are good for, anyway. So unless your cursed sword," he began, putting air quotes around the last bit, "plans on stepping into the ring, then you two need to get gone."

Alexis floated closer. Her blade pulsed with a magic aura. "Oh, I'll step into the ring alright. Why don't you join me? I'll show you a good time."

He shifted his weight to one side before placing a hand at the sword on his belt. His voice took on a frosted edge as if he was looking at something disgusting. "If it were up to me, you and the rest of your filthy ilk wouldn't be allowed past the city gates."

Alexis gasped. "FILTHY? LOOK HERE, YOU POT-BELLIED

BITCH!" She tipped herself forward until her blade pointed directly at the knight's throat.

Quickly, I grabbed her by the hilt and pulled her back. "Whoa, let's all calm down a notch, huh?"

"See!" he sneered. "This is exactly what I'm talking about. You can't trust a demon further than you can throw them. First, we get orcs and minotaurs stinking up our streets, and this morning a freaking dragon of all things lands in the middle of uptown as if he owns the place!"

"Alright!" I shouted, holding up a hand to cease his rambling. "We get it, we're going." Alexis thrashed in my hold, nearly taking me off my feet. I dug my heels in when she tried to lurch forward, then slowly dragged us backward away from the coliseum's entrance.

"Cherry, what the hell?" she snapped.

I pulled her in front of me to whisper closer to her hilt. "I know, he's a piece of shit. But he is also not the only guard in this area. I don't know how many of them it's going to take to throw us in a dungeon, but I can guess how many they're going to use."

Her hilt grew red hot under my grip and I released her. "Fine," she hissed. "But I will not forget this transgression." The angry coloring faded from her as we walked away.

"I'm sorry," I said, unsure of how to comfort her.

The sword giggled in a way that sent a shiver down my spine. "Oh, don't you worry, I'll get back at him. One way or another."

Well, at least she's optimistic.

Alexis remained silent the rest of the way back to the house. I stayed quiet and let her be. Clearly, she needed to work through her frustrations. When we finally made it back inside, I set the chicken and lemon cake down on the table. Almost as if they had a mind of their own, my feet carried me to the bedroom, eager to see Dante again. It was ridiculous, seeing as I had only left him a few hours prior, but I missed him. Whether it was from the magic bond or actual feelings, I wasn't sure. The ache between my legs was easy to identify. That was obviously magic.

I think.

The door to the bedroom was cracked open, and I peeked inside to see Dante still in the bed. His face was scrunched up as if he was having a nightmare. Just before I opened the door to wake him, I noticed a large shadow cast on the side of the wall. Fear gripped my heart, and I swung the door open.

Instead of a large shadow creature, Rebekah sat on his chest. Candlelight from the bedside lantern cast a wide shadow on the wall and I let out a breath of relief. The kitten stared down at Dante's face with intense concentration. She had slowly turned her head to face me after the door had creaked. The intensity in her icy blue eyes made the hair on the back of my neck stand up and I shivered. "Geez, no wonder Alexis thought you were some terror creature."

"Oh, perfect!" the sword chirped behind me. "Just the little monster I wanted to see." She ducked underneath me and floated next to Rebekah. "Up you go," she said as an orange glow appeared around the kitten and lifted her off of Dante.

Flailing, the kitten swiped uselessly at the sword, hissing and spitting in an adorable fit of rage only a kitten could manage. Alexis ignored her protests and moved to leave, the kitten floating helplessly behind her. "Excuse me," she said.

I stepped aside allowing her to pass. "Where are you taking her?"

Cackling evilly, she raised the kitten up higher, showing off her prize. "I'm going to put kitty cat here in the knights' barracks. That'll show those disrespectful little shits."

I tilted my head. "So she pees on their stuff?" I asked. As far as petty revenge schemes went, it wasn't a bad idea. Cat piss was damn near impossible to get out. The smell was so rancid it could make your nose curl.

There was a pregnant pause. "…Yes. Don't wait up for me." Rebekah gave one last yowl of protest before she and Alexis disappeared back into the busy streets.

A deep voice whispered my name close behind me.

"Ah!" I whipped around to see Dante looking down at me with tired eyes. He raised a brow at my outburst and I quickly covered my heart to smooth its frantic beating. "Hissing pumas, you move like a ghost."

"Alas, I'm still alive," he said, sardonically, then tilted his head toward the table. "Please tell me that food is for me."

At my nod he wasted no time in helping himself. Growing up with two brothers had gotten me accustomed to watching men eat their food with gusto. Yet it still didn't prepare me for how quickly Dante tore apart that chicken like it owed him a debt. "No one's gonna take the chicken from you, Dante. You can slow down. Maybe taste it a little."

"Hmm." He cracked a smile but didn't slow down. It wasn't long until he finished it off and moved on to the neatly wrapped dessert. His lips parted on a gasp. "Cherry, I didn't think you'd be so forward in your advances."

"What are you going on about?"

"If this lemon tart is your way of seducing me, it's working."

"You are shockingly low maintenance if that's all it takes."

He ignored me in favor of dramatically eating a spoonful. "And there's caramel glazed drizzle on the top? Oh, you saucy minx."

"Are you feeling any better?" I asked, draping my coat around a chair. When I pulled it out to sit, he held out a hand to stop me.

"Hold on, this is new," he remarked, gesturing at my outfit. "Give us a turn, I want to see it."

Smiling, I twirled around showing off my new outfit. Part of me was a little worried about what he'd say when he found out we had gone on a shopping spree with his gold, but the way his eyes kept roaming over my body gave me the distinct suspicion that he didn't give a damn.

"Why do you look so damn happy?" I laughed.

He tugged me into his lap and toyed with my gold bracelet. "Why shouldn't I be? I was half worried you would flee while I slept. Yet here you've returned, with food no less."

Unable to resist, I reached up and coasted my fingers down the strands of his silver hair. Even disheveled with sleep, he still looked irresistible. Honestly, it was unfair. How's a girl supposed to keep her wits about her in the face of a jawline that strong? "If I left, who would keep me in my fineries?"

He grinned. "Does this mean you'll finally tell me where you live?"

"Hmm, not yet."

"How about a last name?"

I gave a light slap to his shoulder. "Easy, big guy, you haven't even taken me on a date yet."

"How presumptuous of me." He slid my sleeve up to my elbow and kissed at the skin below the bracelet. The gentle caresses sent flutters all the way down to my toes. "Why don't we see what kind of taverns Kirkwall has to offer?"

"I could go for a drink." Understatement of the century. I was half counting on Alexis to be a bit of a buffer between us. Being alone with Dante in all his…everything, had me feeling a little lightheaded. Nothing a bit of liquid courage couldn't fix.

"Excellent," he said, helping me to my feet. "Hopefully, the food is halfway decent as well."

I took his arm as we headed out the door. "You just ate a whole chicken dinner."

He chuckled and a sharp fang poked out of his upper jaw. "If I had to survive on your meager human portions I'd be dead in a week."

"Is that how you lost your horn? Too little food and they just start falling off?"

"It was cut off in battle during the hydra attack." His response was believable, yet the red tint in his ears told me otherwise.

"No it wasn't."

"Cherry, if you're psychic just tell me."

I gave him an incredulous look. "And reveal all my secrets? Never."

"Fine," he said, sheepishly. "I may have gotten my head stuck in a ravine after flying under the influence."

Laughter bubbled in my throat. The thought of a mighty dragon, drunkenly crashing into a ravine was too much. "So you're just stuck like this?"

Dante shrugged. "They shed every fifty years anyway, so it will grow back sometime next spring."

With the sun waning in the distance, the streets of Kirkwall came alive as everyone flooded the area looking for a night of drinks and fun. Coliseum vendors wore huge signs promoting tonight's match. They stood on crates and shouted over the crowd detailing the fight of the century. People flooded toward them, laughing and placing bets.

I doubted Dante would be as easy to pull away as Alexis if he got pissed off about their business practices, so I dragged him further away from the vendors and into a tavern called The Real Golden Vine.

He eyed the sign above the door and cocked his head. "Do you think that implies the existence of a fake Golden Vine?"

"THERE IS A FAKE GOLDEN VINE!" a man shouted from behind the bar. His meaty hands furiously scrubbed at the counter with his rag. His face was adorned with a mustache I imagine most men could only dream of; it added to his dramatic demeanor as he huffed out his irritation.

Several patrons lining the barstools collectively groaned and waved him off. "Don't start on that nonsense now, you old bastard!"

The barkeep swatted at them with his rag. "The man asked a question. Questions deserve answers," he argued. Wiping his hands on his shirt, the barkeep motioned for us to have a seat at a table. I looked to my companion, who shrugged and made his way over. Dante pulled out a seat for me before taking his own.

"Somebody go get Viti before this one gets going," another man at the bar said. He ran a hand through wild red hair while he sipped his drink. Clearly having fallen victim to the story too many times prior.

"Viti is busy!" the barkeep barked back, then turned to a younger-looking man waiting tables. "Jenson, get these two the house special!" Jenson rolled his eyes, but did as he was told.

"Dammit, Neil, it's been a year already, let it go."

"Bah!" Neil, the barkeep, swatted at the redhead and came around to our table. "Now you two listen here," he began, crossing his arms over his chest. "My tavern has the best mead in the city! You could try a brew at every damn tavern in Kirkwall and you'd wind up spitting it out in favor of coming back here."

Jensen came by the table and set our drinks down. Before he could leave, Dante asked for an order of roasted meat and bread. I shook my head to show I needed no food, and he nodded and left.

"Go on, take a sip," Neil ordered.

Dante took a tentative sip. "Damn, that is good."

Neil preened under the praise and smiled wide. "Damn right it is! That recipe has been handed down for generations. Which means nothing to that gluttonous demon down at the other Golden Vine."

The door behind the bar burst open and a woman came in carrying a jug of mead. "Dad, stop pestering the customers!" she bellowed. Her hair was cut short in a boyish fashion, yet it was the same deep black as her father's mustache. If you squinted hard enough, you could see the resemblance. Thankfully for her, she hadn't inherited her father's strong chin.

Neil's tongue caught in the middle of his tirade and he

flinched as he looked at the young woman. "Viti, it's fine, they asked me."

"No they didn't," the redhead cut in.

"Shut up, Rufus!"

Viti groaned and set the jug down on the counter. As if sensing his time was at an end, Neil slammed his hands down on our table and babbled. "That other Golden Vine is a lie. I've been running this tavern for twenty years since I inherited it from my father, then suddenly this damn spitaur shows up and opens a new tavern down the road using *my recipe* and *my Golden Vine name* claiming it's been in his family for generations."

He yelped when Viti grabbed his ear and began dragging him away. "Alright Dad, that's enough out of you."

"Ow, ow, ow, release me you freakishly strong wench. I'm tired of my tavern name being tarnished by that eight-legged bastard!"

Her response was to slap him on the shoulder before shoving him into the back room with her.

"Well," I said. "That was a lot."

Dante took another long swig of his drink and eyed the glass. "This is the spitaur's recipe."

"How do you know?"

He swirled the mug around then leaned in closer and spoke low. "There was a tavern in the south end of the Mirrored Summit. It was run by a family of spitaurs and their specialty mead tastes exactly like this. I'm guessing they had a similar business here before Myva banished us, and came to reclaim their old territory."

"Damn, that would mean this feud probably goes back 600 years." I nursed my drink and thought about a tavern run by spider people. Now *that* would be a sight to see.

"As long as the food is good, I'll have no complaints," Dante said.

"I see. We'll have to ask if they have any fried humans."

Dante grinned and shook his head. "I knew I should've lied."

"Don't you dare," I warned, pointing a finger at him. "I'll see right through you."

"Oh, I don't doubt that for a second."

"No?"

"Let's be honest, we can both see that you'll be leading me by the ear."

"Yeah, how do you figure?"

He leaned on the table and rested his head in his hand. "Cherry, you've got me chasing phoenixes through snow banks. Another day and I'll be holding down a griffin just so you can pat the damn thing."

"That actually sounds kinda fun." Mentally, I added griffin to my list of pit stops.

"I'll be the bane of every creature on this continent to get a smile from you," he said, smiling warmly. The declaration came out easily, like his devotion to my entertainment was the most natural thing in the world. To him, it just might've been. Dante's actions left no room to misinterpret his intent in taking me as his own. It was etched into every caress and look he sent my way.

The gravity of that realization sank in. I squirmed a little in my seat. My face heated, and I hid embarrassment with a laugh. "You lay it on pretty thick, don't ya, Dante?"

His eyes closed on an inhale. Molten lava flooded my belly when he opened them again. Those gray eyes may have looked cold, but the heat behind them could burn me to cinders. "I enjoy hearing my name on your lips."

I sent a mental scream down to my legs to inform them it was in fact *not* time to spread. *Eggs on rice, I'm in a public establishment.*

A plate of meat and bread was placed on the table, freeing me from the spell of his gaze. When he made no move to dig in, I fiddled with the rim of my drink and nodded toward the food. "Aren't you going to eat?"

"Gods, you're stunning."

My heart fluttered. His eyes flashed and his grin pulled wider.

Oh gods, did he hear that?

I licked my lips; his gaze followed the movement. Unmistakable hunger darkened his eyes and my belly coiled in response. I thought back to his hand on my hip when we'd been standing in his hoard. How quickly I had bent to his will.

He edged closer and whispered quietly, "I'm getting through to you."

"Maybe a little," I admitted, taking a large gulp of my drink. It was meant to come out light. But the words sounded hoarse and desperate. The room felt too hot. The people were too loud, and I wanted nothing more than to be back in his bath with his face buried in between my legs.

Fuck, pushing him away was damn foolish.

"Careful, badger," he warned. He leaned back in his seat and I realized that I had leaned forward, trying to get closer to him. "I'm not a patient man. Show me a crumb of interest and I won't give a damn where we are."

I sucked in a breath and looked around at the busy tavern. Flaming peppers, he was serious. In an effort to diffuse the charged desire in the air, I laughed and shook my head. "Sometimes I worry about you."

"You should always worry about me. I'm your husband," he said, digging his fork into the plate, taking his first bite.

"Occasionally isn't enough?"

"No. I won't rest until I've consumed your every thought."

"You're a greedy thing."

"You have no idea," he drawled.

This was turning into less of a date and more of a "How long can Cherry last before she runs out to dunk her head in a pail of water?"

Unless I didn't run.

There was no rule that said I couldn't touch him without being completely sure if this was for me. It's not like anyone I knew was around to judge the decisions I made. I sure as hell didn't spend all that time locked in a tower only to get out and not live a little.

"How about we go check out the other Golden Vine? I want to test out your theory."

He didn't bother to look up from his second dinner. "You mean you want to see a spitaur."

I clasped my hands together. "So bad!"

Fresh air would be an added bonus. The air in this tavern had me choked up with a dragon's scent and the desire to disregard public decency with reckless abandon.

"Finish your drink," he said, then pulled two silvers out of his pocket and placed them on the table.

What it must be like to be too rich to have any concept of money.

I reached out and replaced it with the proper change.

Chapter 15

Cherry

The usurper Golden Vine was packed. A group of men cheered as they rolled dice on a nearby table. Every corner of the tavern was filled with drunk patrons having the time of their lives. Swing benches hung from the rafters on golden silk vines. A woman on the bench laughed hard at something her friend said, spilling mead down below.

It was no wonder the other Golden Vine owner was so pissed off. Though I imagine it was hard to compete when your competition served drinks while hanging upside down from a golden web that spanned the entire ceiling. My brother Cumin would have run screaming into the night, but I thought it was fucking wicked.

"One blueberry and one spiced apple," a voice called from above me. I looked up to see a spitaur lowering down our drinks on a golden thread. Thankfully, the thread came out of his hands, not his ass.

His lower body resembled that of an orb weaver. Gold and black bands decorated each of his eight long legs. The human-half looked normal enough, aside from the pointed ears and fangs most demons shared. His hair was cropped short and coordinated with the banded coloring of his legs. If I wasn't so blindsided by my growing obsession with Dante, I think I would've found him handsome.

My companion reached up and grabbed our drinks without a word. The spitaur clasped his hands together and gave a friendly smile. "If you like, we could set up a table for you in our private section?" he asked.

Dante shot him a dismissive glance and wrapped an arm around my shoulders. "No thank you, we won't be staying."

"We won't?" I asked, as he steered us out the door. Dante glanced back at the dejected-looking owner then pulled me further away from the tavern and into the busy street.

"Absolutely not. They're about to launch into a sales pitch to get me to claim Kirkwall as my territory and I am in no mood. Besides, I'd like to see the castle gardens while we're here."

"Does that happen often?" I asked.

"More than I'd like."

"Huh, you must be a decent landlord."

He shrugged and took a sip of his drink. "Some dragons like to be more involved with what goes on in their territory than others. I prefer to be left alone unless there's an actual threat."

A king that does his job and leaves. No wonder he had demons kissing his ass.

His head snapped up as he spotted something in the crowd. "Oh look, fire dancers."

"What? I want to see!" I tried peering over the crowd, but the most I could make out was a ball of fire being swung high to the rhythmic drumming filling the air. I wiggled a little further into the crowd and tried jumping up to spot the dancers. "Damn these short legs!"

"Give me that," Dante took my drink and crouched in front of me. Needing no further invitation, I hopped onto his back, wrapped my legs around his torso and took my drink from him. He stood, locking his arm around my leg and finally the fire dancers came into view.

Women dressed in clothing not nearly warm enough for this weather twirled balls of flames around their bodies. The crowd cheered as one swung her ball at her counterpart, who flipped out of the way in the nick of time.

The beat of the drums picked up its pace and Dante tapped along against my leg. While the rest of the crowd was enamored with the fire dancers, his gaze remained transfixed on the drummer. "Do you play drums, too?" I asked.

"Drums, piano, most string instruments, it'd be easier to

tell you what I don't play. An obsession with a musical theater group plagued most of my 400s." His gaze turned wistful as he watched the drummer. "I mostly played the cello. But picking up other instruments became useful in case someone else couldn't perform."

I gasped, nearly spilling my drink. "Dante, are you telling me you used to be in a band?"

"A long time ago."

I took a sip of my drink. "Sing me a song!"

"Sing? Never." He untangled us from the crowd and set me down. More people flocked to the fire dancers' performance, leaving us with plenty of room to make our way past them and further out of the marketplace and toward the castle. With everyone else so distracted, it almost felt like we were alone. Moonlight lit up the cobblestone streets in a soft glow, while lanterns glowed orange in the night.

An icy chill rustled the fallen leaves around us and I hugged myself against his arm. Pushing as much of my body against him as I could to steal his warmth. Gods, he always smelled so good. "Pretty please? You can't just dangle that juicy bit of information in front of my face then snatch it away."

"We have all done regrettable things in our past. I'll play you a song on any instrument of your choosing. Singing is off the table."

"Dante, my love. My one and only," I cooed.

"Now who's laying it on thick?" he asked dryly.

"I beg you, one song."

Winding streets gave way to more opulent houses until we reached the castle gardens. Knights were stationed at the main entrance to the castle itself, but the garden entrance seemed to be open to the public, if the people walking in and out were any sign to go by. An old couple nodded politely at us as we passed each other through the gate.

Archways covered in yellow and orange roses imitated a setting sun as we walked in. Noble women dressed in fine gowns laughed and whispered to each other in a gazebo surrounded by beautiful flowers. Evergreen hedges were trimmed back into proud pegasi. In the distance, I could see marble sculptures poking out of the maze.

"I tell you I've been in three wars and this is what you fixate on?" Dante said, incredulously. "One of them was against the sea people. Ask about that." A flush of red spread across his ears.

The same dragon who had gone down on me after our first meeting with no hesitation...was blushing. My soul would never know peace until I heard him sing.

"What about a drinking contest?" I asked as we entered the maze. "If I win, I get one song. If you win, you can have whatever you want. Aside from my hometown name, of course." He may be bigger than me, but if his reaction to liquor was the same as it was to my drugged tea, then it was safe to assume Dante was a lightweight.

He glanced down at me with a wolfish grin. "You can't be intoxicated for the things I want, Princess."

Dammit. Now I'm blushing. I looked away from him, only to find that we had happened upon a statue of a woman entangled in the embrace of two men. Her head was thrown back, eyes sealed shut on a gasp as her first lover worshiped her breasts. The man kneeling at her feet had her leg thrown over his shoulder as he gazed up at her in worship while his hand dipped underneath her robe. The title read "Fall From Grace" but, if you asked me, I'd say my girl was doing just fine.

"You and that damn nickname," I muttered.

"Here, try my spiced apple, it's good." He set his mug against my lips, then tilted it back when I drank. It lacked the sweetness of my blueberry mead. Yet the apple flavoring was enhanced by spices of cinnamon, clove and nutmeg. "That's it, little Badger," he murmured softly, petting my hair. "Drink. Drink and forget."

I pushed the drink away, trying to rein in my laugh before I spit it out. "I thought I had to be sober for the things you wanted to do?"

"Oh? Is that the direction this date is headed?"

"Could be," I teased. The moon was full, the mead was good, and dammit all, I just wanted to throw my brain out the window for a night and kiss the hell out of him until we ended a tangled mess of mouths and limbs. To feel him sink into me until I finally got a reprieve from the alarmingly feral infatuation I had for him. "For a song."

"So insistent." Dante grabbed me by the throat and dragged me against the base of the statue. My breath hitched when his thumb ran along my lower lip. "How about a different bet?" His gray eyes roamed over my body until his mouth curved on a grin at my shiver. "If you can stay quiet for me, I'll sing for you. If you can't, you'll allow me to call you whatever I like."

I looked around our corner of the maze. No one was within eyesight, but I could still hear the laughter of the noble women in the distance. "Here?" I let out a gasp as his lips found my throat.

Dante's dark chuckle reverberated against my collarbone. "Didn't I warn you I lacked patience?"

"But someone could see," I scolded, trying to beat back the rush of excitement in my voice.

"I know. That's why you'll have to be extra careful, won't you?" He paused his movements to gaze down at me with a devilish grin. "Do we have a deal, Princess?"

Somewhere deep in my soul, the moral compass guiding me through life shriveled up and died. Public decency? Never heard of her.

"Deal."

"That's my girl," he rasped. His mouth clamped over mine, and he kissed me as if he'd perish if I pushed him away.

My knees buckled, and he guided me down to sit on the

statue's base. The pressure of his tongue coaxed my lips apart, deepening the kiss with tender impatient caresses that sapped my strength until I clung to him like a lifeline.

He took advantage of my weakness, parting my legs with his thigh to settle himself in between. The tip of his tongue swept across my own. Playing against my teeth before it marauded its way deeper, tasting my throat.

Startled by the intensity, I shrank back, but he followed, his hand sliding up to grip my hair and force my head back, trapping me open for him. Heat rushed through me until a fevered moan threatened to slip past. I fought it back, refusing to lose the bet.

His mouth broke from mine to skim along the arch of my throat, sending tremors of pleasure that left goosebumps in their wake. A rustle of leaves snapped my eyes open; I bit my lip to control my breathing and scanned the neatly trimmed shrubbery for signs of an interloper. Dark shadows beyond crisp green leaves accompanied the voices of men locked into a discussion regarding a gambling house. Dante's hand slipped beneath my blouse to knead my breast, stroking over the peak until I nearly lost myself and cried out. The men continued on their path, too engrossed in their conversation to notice our tryst on the other side of the yew.

"Well done," he murmured. "Wrap your arms around my neck. Yes, just like that." Rough hands made quick work of removing my trousers. Cold air nipped at my exposed skin, highlighting the searing heat of his touch as he settled me back down against the marble. He moved lower, the silken strands of his hair tickling my thighs.

I threw a hand over my mouth, cutting off a gasp as his lips brushed over my pussy through the thin layer of my panties. His tongue darted out to drag against the slit. My body bowed forward, quivering as his mouth closed over my clit and sucked gently.

Dante shuddered, then ripped my panties from my body. I watched on, entranced as he brought them up to his face and breathed deep. "Fucking hell, Cherry. Do you know what your scent does to me?" He threw the garment aside and spread my legs further apart. "Of course not, how could you? Stay quiet if you don't want an audience, love. I'll fuck you in full view of the court if need be."

Sweet mother of mercy.

His breath teased over my pussy, and I shrank away, hit with a wave of bashfulness at my lack of experience. What was I supposed to do with my hands? What if it didn't taste good? I nearly worked up the courage to ask, but Dante gripped my hips and dragged me to him, mercilessly plundering the swollen flesh until all questions faded into the stars above.

"Don't hide this from me," he growled. "It's mine." Quivering thighs spread further, desperate to give into the demanding mouth hell-bent on wrenching a scream from my throat.

I bit down on my finger as my free hand grabbed his horn.

When his tongue dove inside me again, my hips jerked, trying to drag him deeper. "That's right, sweetheart…use me how you like," he whispered wickedly, lavishing attention over my clit.

Nearly at the edge, my head fell back, mirroring the silent scream of the woman carved in eternal rapture.

My, what a pair we made.

The stone was cool beneath me, though I couldn't tell if it was because of the chill or the raw heat of Dante's mouth working me over. I wanted more, needed more, and Dante kept going, drinking from my body as if it were a fount of water. My toes curled, threatening to trip me off balance as he licked and sucked with abandon. The pleasure was a drug that burned down my spine, spreading to the tips of my fingers and toes.

As if he could taste the need in my blood, a smile tugged at his lips as he thrust two fingers inside of me. He began to move them slowly, in and out, withdrawing only to plunge back inside. "Is this what you need, Princess?" he asked, before drawing his tongue over my clit. He thrust harder, drawing a small whimper from my lips. "Careful, someone's coming."

I glared down at him to see a sinful glint in his eye. "Do you hear that?" he whispered, as if I could hear a damn thing past the blinding pleasure. Tears pricked my eyes as he curled upward, finding a place deep inside me that had my eyes rolling back. "Go on, break for me, sweetheart. Let them all hear the pretty noises you make when your husband's inside you."

"Fuck you," I gritted out, biting back my scream in a fit of defiance, even as I convulsed, shuddering and grinding my hips against his hand. I gasped, hanging limp in his arms as he continued to stroke, prolonging the release until I thought my heart would stop beating.

When I opened my eyes, he was watching me, grinning.

"Such a stubborn thing." His voice was thick, full of hunger and promises of more to come.

I smiled, tucking a strand of hair behind my ear as I glanced around. We were still alone, but I could just make out the sounds of people chatting somewhere in the maze.

His eyes darkened, and he pulled me close. "I can't get enough of you. You have no idea how many nights I dreamt of this moment before we even met, of touching you the way I do now." He kissed me again, his hands tearing at his pants before he grabbed my ass and lifted me up, then laid me down in the grass. I forced myself to remain still as the head of his cock pushed against my lower lips.

"Wait," I rasped.

"Dear gods, why?" His breath was ragged as if he were struggling with control.

"Could you start slow? I...I haven't exactly done this before." If the feel of his length was any indication, I was about to take something a lot bigger than his fingers. I'd heard the first time was often a little unpleasant, and the promise of pain sent a nervous shiver down my spine.

"Of course, love." Crouching over me, Dante teased his cock against my core. "Whatever you need of me," he whispered, kissing my throat. "I'll be so gentle…open up a little further for me…yes…gods, you're so perfect." As the head of his cock pushed past my lower lips, I did my best to relax. He deepened his entry with careful strokes, gently coaxing my body into accepting him.

"You're so tight, Princess." His whispers became frayed as his hands gripped my hips. I could feel every inch of his shaft stretch my insides, my body quickly adjusting and welcoming him. His pace increased, and soon he buried himself completely within me. My muscles tightened around him, milking him for more.

Pleasure built quickly, amplified by the magic simmering in our veins. I grabbed him by the back of his head and kissed him, drowning out my groan. Dante pulled out and shoved his cock back in with more force, testing my reaction. I whimpered and bucked against him, pleading for more.

"You are beautiful," he whispered as he slammed into me over and over again. His eyes were wild, his face flushed, as he plunged into me without mercy. His hands clawed at the ground, digging into the dirt as he pounded me.

Each thrust sent a jolt of pleasure through my body, making my muscles tighten and my breasts bounce. I dug my nails into his shoulders, my head tipping back as his mouth found mine and devoured me. His tongue tangled with mine, and he fucked me hard, fast, and deep until the pleasure built into an blinding force.

He broke the kiss to whisper in my ear. "Forgive me, Cherry, but I have no intention of singing."

Before I could ask what he meant, I felt the magic from our bond erupt. Tiny bursts of electric sensations mingled with the thrust of his hips, sending a tidal wave of blinding euphoria through my body. There was no fighting the scream that tore from my throat. The sound echoed through the garden, followed by cries of surprise from the couple I'd heard in the distance.

Dante groaned, burying his face in my neck while he thrust deep. Those damnable little shocks lit up my nerves until I was mewling and clawing at his back like some desperate animal. Dante tensed above me. With a strangled groan, he gripped my hip and ground his cock against the end of my well until my legs shook with a violent orgasm, and he emptied himself inside of me. Our bodies were covered in sweat, our clothes strewn across the grass. He collapsed onto my chest, leaving me breathless. I ran a hand up his back, unable to resist touching him.

"You cheated," I huffed.

I felt his lips curve into a smile. "We never established rules."

"We need to get out of here," I said, but my limbs were boneless goo. The mere thought of standing seemed like an impossible task. Was it possible to orgasm your way into an early grave? What the fuck was that shock thing and when could we do it again?

"I KNEW IT!" a woman screamed. Panic solidified my bones once more as I shoved Dante off me and tried to shield my ass. I spotted my trousers a few feet away and scrambled toward them.

"YOU TWO-TIMING BACKWATER BARON, I KNEW I'D FIND YOU HERE!"

Backwater Baron? Confused, I looked around for the screeching woman, but no one else had entered the clearing. Dante lazily tucked himself back into his pants, and peered over the garden wall. I followed his gaze just in time to see a parasol whip though the air before coming down with a hard thwack.

"Ow!" a man cried. "Rachel, honey, it's not what it looks like."

"Really, Clayton? Tell me what it looks like then, cause from where I'm standing it looks like YOU'RE FUCKING MY SISTER!"

Oh my. Guess we weren't the only ones having a bit of fun.

Dante and I shared a look, before he waved me over to kneel by the hedge to better listen.

"She just fell!" the man cried.

"On his dick?" I whispered.

"ON YOUR DICK?" Rachel cried. "We both know that's bullshit. Everyone just heard her scream! Shocking since the most you've ever gotten out of me was a pity moan."

Dante covered his mouth as his shoulders shook. I tamped down my own laughter and nudged his side. "Come on, we need to go."

He raised a brow at me and nodded toward the screaming pair. "And miss how this ends?"

Another, softer voice spoke up. "We didn't want you to find out like this."

The parasol came down with another hard thwack. "Oh yeah? Well, I guess now that we're all sharing secrets, every time your little shrimp dick left me wanting, I fucked the stable boy. Enjoy your syphilis!" Rachel roared.

I gasped loud.

"What was that?" Clayton murmured.

Shit, shit, shit!

"Who's there?" Rachel yelled.

Gray fog pooled over the area, blinding my vision. In a flash Dante scooped me up and leapt over the hedges until we were out of the garden. When we were free and clear, he slowed and set me down in an alleyway to catch our breath. Laughter burst out of me until I was clutching my sides. "Enjoy your syphilis," I wheezed.

"I told you human cities are disgusting," Dante murmured, laughing along.

"Oh gods, I shouldn't laugh," I said, trying to rein myself in. "Syphilis is a terrible way to go."

Dante held no such shame, and braced himself against the

alleyway in his hysterics. "Go?" he asked. "She'll be fine after a few rounds of tonic."

"Demons have a cure for that?" I asked, bewildered.

"Do your people not? Gods, what have humans been doing in the past century?"

"…Dying of syphilis?"

He ran a hand through his hair and threw an arm over my shoulder as we made our way out of the alley. "Clearly we've been gone too long. Remind me in the morning and I'll send a kobold to bring the cure to whoever's in charge around here."

Chapter 16

Alexis

Aggravated yowls rose from the terror beast floating beside me. The sound echoed off the walls of the dingy hallway of the coliseum. "Hush! You'll blow our cover," I said.

The swirling mass of dark magic and id only thrashed harder in response. Why, was a total mystery. The damned thing hadn't escaped the first few times she'd tried to wiggle away. Some creatures just didn't know how to accept their fate, I guess.

"Alright, so here's the plan," I began. A door to my right opened. Quickly, I stashed the loud beast behind a wooden crate and laid myself against a wall.

Two men dressed in dirty work clothes appeared. The taller

one tossed a mop and bucket down and sighed heavily. "If I have to mop up one more puke puddle today, I'm gonna quit."

His companion shot him a bored look. "No you're not."

He slumped. "You're right, I'm not. But dammit, I wish parents would watch how many sweets their little monsters ate."

"Tell me about it."

Thankfully, the workers were too caught up in their bitch fest to notice me. Which, honestly, was a little insulting. It's not every day you see a sword of such brilliance. But that was their loss. When their voices faded, I rose up and lifted Rebekah from her hiding place.

The swirling mass of black fog surrounding her body hid her face from me, but I could tell she was glaring. Curious, I brought her closer, trying to see through her magic. With a rumbling hiss, two sharp fangs lurched out of the darkness to bite at my steel.

"Alright, damn! Keep your secrets," I said, backing away. "Anyway, back to business. The knights' barracks should be around here somewhere…" I pushed my way through a door that smelled of sweat and mediocrity to find a room full of bunk beds and various weapons and armor thrown about. "Ah-ha!" I yelled, triumphantly.

Floating closer to one of the bunk beds I gently set the horror beast down as well as my can of paint. "Alright, this is how this is gonna work. I don't know what you are, but I know you're dangerous and probably hungry, right?"

"Mrrrrm."

"I don't know what that means, but I'll take it as a yes. Long story short, a couple knights pissed me off, and you're going to help me take revenge. When you see any knight come through that door, I want you to unleash whatever hell you've been cooking up. Show no mercy, spare no expense. In exchange, I won't tell Tweedledee and Tweedledum that you're not really a cat. Provided you don't hurt them. Deal?"

I stared into the void patiently. After a moment a voice spoke up. **"Deal."**

"Excellent!" I cheered. Wasting no time, I took my paintbrush and wrote "THESE KNIGHTS SOME HOES" in big red letters across the wall.

A creak behind me alerted me to an interloper. I turned to see the two cleaning men from before standing in the doorway staring in awe. As they should. I am amazing. But also, fuck. How dare they interrupt my plans? "Get out," I said.

Instead of listening, the one in front just stared at me slack-jawed. "Who are you?" he rasped.

"Me? I'm not real, I'm just a figment of your imagination. You should probably leave and go rest. You're seeing things."

The other man poked his head out and shouted, "That can't be right, I see you too!"

"I am a shared delusion."

The man in front glared. "That doesn't even make sense."

Annoyed, my blade glowed orange and hot. "Do you really

want to argue this point, or do you want to live to see tomorrow?"

He blinked, then looked around wildly. "Oh gosh! I've somehow been struck blind."

"Yeah, me too!" said the other one. He slapped his friend on the shoulder and pointed behind him. "You know, Sam, we should probably take the rest of the day off. Seeing as we've gone blind."

"Yup, right behind you, Mac," he said, slamming the door shut.

"That's the spirit." I turned back to my art piece, adding tasteful ejaculating dicks around the word "KNIGHT." When the door creaked open again, I let out a frustrated growl and whipped around. "Dammit, what now?"

The words barely left my being before Rebekah sprang into action. The black mist surrounding her body parted to reveal a boar-like creature with a mouth full of tentacles and fangs stretching along its back. Her maw opened and tentacles lunged at the unsuspecting knight who had walked in. Screaming, the redheaded man was dragged into Rebekah's waiting mouth. Blood spurted from his head as she clamped down. His legs flailed, but escape was futile.

More knights rushed in to try to pull their friend from the horrific creature. "What the hell is that thing?" one screamed. Rebekah hissed, then threw the body of the guard she had bitten to the floor, turning her attention to the newcomers.

A tall dark-haired knight grabbed a spear from the wall and tried to jab it into her side. "Just get it away from Mark! Dammit, is he even still alive?"

Mark rose from the ground and stumbled up to his struggling companions. "Oh, thank the gods!" a freckled knight yelled. "Mark, are you OK, man?"

Mark groaned in response, then sank his teeth into the cheek of the freckled knight who screamed and backed away. Mark turned to face him, and I gasped when I saw the back of his head. His skull was torn open and half his brain looked like it had been slurped up and eaten. Whatever the fuck that thing was, it sure as hell wasn't Mark.

The freckled knight jerked where he stood, his eyes rolling into the back of his head. With a gurgling rasp, the man dragged himself into the demon's waiting jaws.

I watched the fight with growing concern as Mark turned on his friends to help Rebekah. Another knight that Mark had bitten rose with an unearthly groan and took a bite out of another guard. "Um…OK. Not quite what I was expecting."

Chapter 17

Cherry

Baked cinnamon goodness floated through the air like a siren's call. Morning sunlight filtered through the windows, casting a warm glow into the kitchen. If I closed my eyes and focused hard enough, I could just picture the apple-embroidered curtains of home.

I scooped a large portion of icing onto my knife and delicately spread it over the cinnamon rolls. They weren't as fluffy and perfect as when Ma made them, but I felt like I got close.

"Oh good, you're up," I called, seeing Dante drag himself out of the bedroom.

The dragon-shifter looked half asleep. His pants sagged on his waist, leaving a tantalizing view of the silver hair trailing from his navel before it disappeared down his pants. Immediately, thoughts of last night flooded my mind, making my face heat.

Flaming ghost peppers! I lost my virginity to a dragon-shifter in the middle of a public maze.

Fuck, it was so hot though.

He blinked slowly at me, before his gaze drifted to the counter. "You know how to bake?" he asked in a gruff voice.

"Simple things, at least. Do me a favor and punch the bread dough over there." I pointed to a bowl of dough on the side table in the corner. "I'm making twisted sweet bread later. It'll make an easy snack to have on the road...air...whatever."

"You...need me to punch dough?"

"Yeah, you gotta let the air out or it won't rise right. Haven't you ever made bread before?"

When he shook his head, I couldn't help but roll my eyes. With those little helper kobolds always at his beck and call, I'd be surprised if that rich boy ever even made his own sandwich. "Welp, first time for everything. After we eat, you can help me roll it out and braid it."

He approached the overinflated bowl of dough with apprehension, then rolled up his sleeves. "How hard?" he asked, glancing back.

I shrugged. "Just give it a good wallop."

"Alright," he said before slamming his fist in its center. The wooden table snapped like a twig, sending loose bits of flour, dough, and splinters all over the floor.

"Fuck," he gritted out. Dante fumbled with the shattered corpse of the bowl, trying to salvage whatever he could out of the obliterated mess.

Probably should have seen that one coming.

I laughed, looking at the dragon frantically trying to pick up the chaos. "Sweetheart, just go sit down."

"Hold on, I can—"

Crash.

"Dante. Back away from the dough."

Slowly, he raised his hands and backed away a few steps.

"Further," I called.

He sighed, then dragged himself over to the couch and slumped into the soft cushions.

I took a couple of cinnamon rolls out of the pan and joined him, leaning against his side. He threw an arm around my shoulder, dragging me against his chest. "Here, try one. You woke up just in time."

He took the treat without a word, his eyes closing as he took the first bite. I leaned further against him, getting comfortable. His hand slid to my side and I laced my fingers with his and traced small circles with my thumb. It felt so nice to lie here like this. Kirkwall's chilly air was chased away by the warmth of his body holding me. The delightful aroma of coffee, baked treats, and Dante made me feel so at peace it was almost unnerving.

Dammit, I'm crushing so hard.

Tap tap.

Fat droplets of rain pattered against the window. Odd. It was sunny just a moment ago. "Feeling alright?" I asked.

"Please excuse me." He shifted me upright, then made his way into the spare room and shut the door. The sound of howling wind filled the air, then promptly cut off.

I opened the door to see what had happened, only to find the room completely empty. "...Was it something I said?"

Dante

"Come on, pick up, dammit." I paced in front of the mirror, waiting for the magic to stop swirling.

She called me sweetheart.

Butterflies—fucking butterflies of all things—burst into song and started dancing in my stomach. The cinnamon roll in my hands was still warm. I took another bite, savoring its impossibly sweet taste. Nothing had ever tasted so right in all my long years.

Finally, the image cleared revealing the captain's quarters of the *Banshee* and its puzzled-looking captain. "Dante?" Usha called, brushing a dark red lock behind her ear. "How are you in my mirror?"

"It's scry magic," I said, quickly. "Is Felix anywhere near you?"

"Um, yeah. He's out on the deck with the others." She stood, and picked up the mirror before nudging open the door. A group of demons sat around a table, laughing and playing dice. "Felix, Dante's in my mirror for you."

The werewolf looked up from his game and grinned before leaping over the table. He took hold of the mirror and placed it on a barrel, then slid a chair over to sit. Felix crossed his arms over his chest and leaned back. "So, what did you do now?"

"How did you confess your love to Brie?"

Behind him, the menagerie of demons that made up the *Banshee*'s crew peeked over with interest. Felix's eyes widened. "That's a big leap from where we last left off. Weren't you going to bring her here so Usha could watch over her?"

"We're past that now," I said. "Tell me what you said to Brie to make her accept your feelings."

"Whoa," he held up his arms. "Slow down, it's only been a day. There's no way she suddenly lost her fear of you. What the hell happened?"

I held up the half-eaten treat. "She made these for us."

Felix's blue eyes remained wide as he waited. After a moment he gave a curt nod. "OK?"

"OK?" I parroted back. How is he not getting it? "Everything has changed. She agreed to stay with me. I destroyed her sweet bread by accident and she just giggled, handed me a cinnamon roll then cuddled with me on the couch. I don't know what to do with myself. I need sappy words. How am I supposed to convey these emotions? Poetry, sonnets, anything, what do I say?"

"Do you think maybe you're just reading a wee bit too much into the cinnamon rolls?"

"No," I growled. "These are clearly a sign of affection after our date last night. I just need to figure out how to tell her what I'm feeling so she knows she's mine and fully accepts me as her mate."

My hand still tingled from where she had brushed her thumb against it. I didn't know how I was supposed to go back and act normal around her when all I wanted to do was take her back to my castle, bind her to my throne with a golden chain and fuck her until she couldn't breathe without me.

This was madness.

I was prepared for the incessant need to claim her when I found her. There were plenty of accounts from other dragons discussing how feral they became around their fated mate. But nothing could have prepared me for the visceral hatred I felt for the sun who dared to set on my days with her. I wanted to fly up in the sky, rip the sun god's still-beating heart from his chest and lay it at Cherry's feet so the days began and ended at her discretion. Nothing less would be good enough.

A knowing grin tugged on the werewolf's face. "Gods, it's like looking in the twisted mirror of my past."

"So you understand?"

"All too well. Alright, let's get started. Tell me what

happened on your date. Are we talking a kiss goodnight, or did you just chat and get to know each other?"

"We got drinks, explored the city, then fucked in Kirkwall's castle gardens."

He whistled. "Seems like it's going well. Why are you so frantic?"

"Because I don't know what to say to her! What if I mess up and she pulls away again? I need the perfect love confession. You said you were good at this kind of thing."

"Whoa, wait," Warwick cut in. The minotaur clopped over to Felix and sat beside him. "If you're still getting to know each other, maybe a love confession would be too much at this point. We're not sure where she's at with this. Humans don't imprint like we do, so they probably fall in love at a slower rate."

"I can't take much slower than this," I groaned, running a hand through my hair.

"Oh, what does he know?" Balabash appeared at Felix's other side and sat down. "That idiot can't even walk in a straight line without tipping over. Don't listen to him. Go up to this woman, grab her by the throat, but not enough to choke her, and push her against the wall. Slide a leg in between her thighs, pushing them apart, and kiss the hell out of her. When she's properly dazed, tell her you love her and that she's yours."

Oh, I like that idea. I like it a lot.

"Should we really be telling the man who until recently

couldn't even shake hands, to grab someone by the throat?" Felix cut in. "Never mind that." He waved a dismissive hand and continued. "That's too aggressive this early on. The whole reason she was pushing him away before was because he was coming on like a wyvern in heat and she has issues with dragons. A slower approach would work better."

"Who are you to talk about coming on too strong?" Bash countered. "You came on stronger than moonshine made in a dirty bathtub and your wife fell immediately."

"First of all, I was drugged and you know that," he snapped. "Second, Brie is level-headed and had no issues telling me exactly what she wanted."

"Bash's idea doesn't sound half bad. It's not like she's a blushing virgin, guys," said Warwick.

I let out a breath, my fingers tapping nervously on my knee. "Well...not after last night."

The men froze.

"Are you serious?" Felix asked. At my nod, he buried his head in his hands and sighed. "Shit. This might change things."

"It does?" I asked; concern dripped on the wings of the butterflies in my stomach until they sank to the bottom. Perhaps I had taken it too far in the garden.

Demon women were so few in number that they are always in high demand. It never even occurred to me to ask if any of them placed importance on virginity. Was there some kind of ritual that I missed?

More men gathered around the werewolf and began shouting about proper courting rituals. "Take her on another date first and play it cool!"

"No, strike while the iron is hot!"

"Toss her an apple!"

"Nobody does that anymore, you old bastard."

"Maybe we should just find a human virgin and ask?" Ambrose piped up from the back.

Everyone turned back to look at the lamia in shock. In the year I'd spent upon the *Banshee* I don't think I'd ever heard Ambrose say more than three words. His snake half coiled tightly at the attention and he shifted his gaze away.

"He's right!" called an orc, whose name I'd forgotten. "Let's just find a human virgin. There's gotta be at least one in Boohail."

Warwick clapped Balabash on the shoulder. "What about your barmaid, Sunbeam?"

The large orc grabbed his hand and twisted, causing the minotaur to cry out. "If any of you lot darken my Daybringer's doorstep, it will be the last mistake you ever make."

"I was just asking," he whimpered.

"Look, we'll just ask around," called the nameless orc. Issah? No, that didn't seem right. "Everybody spread out and try to find a virgin woman."

I heard the door to the captain's quarters slam open. "STOP SCREAMING ABOUT FINDING A VIRGIN," Usha hollered. "THE

VILLAGERS ARE ALREADY WARY OF YOU LOT AND THIS IS EXACTLY HOW RUMORS START."

"But it's for Dante," Warwick answered.

"How is that better?" Usha snapped. "Fuck, y'all stress me out." She stomped over to the mirror and shoved Felix off his barrel and sat down. Usha closed her eyes and breathed deep. "Alright. Fill me in."

Chapter 18

Cherry

How dare he just leave! Just vanished without so much as a "Hey, thanks for last night," or even just telling me if or when he was coming back. I took my anger out on yet another cinnamon roll. My stomach would be a raging mess later, but fuck it. The man I just slept with had upped and left me and—snapping gators—that entitled me to eat my goddamn feelings!

I didn't even have Alexis around to scream to. I had figured she and the kitten would have been back by morning at least, but still nothing. Well, whatever. Maybe I'd just pack up and leave too. It's not like he'd even taken his stuff with him, so I still had all the gold.

Yeah, that's what I'd do. I'd forget all about him, buy a big fancy carriage with his money, and ride back home on my own in style. Fuck dragons and their mixed signals!

The sound of howling wind erupted from the spare room, then fell silent. Dante appeared a moment later, then paused when he spotted me by the counter. "You look upset," he said carefully.

"Of course I'm upset," my words practically came out in a hiss. "You just left me here."

His eyes widened as a grin tugged at his mouth. "Did you just stomp your foot?"

"...No."

"Do it again."

"I said I didn't stomp!"

Dante closed the distance between us and wrapped me in his arms. "You missed me," he said, looking entirely too pleased with himself.

I folded my arms, but didn't pull away. "I'm just annoyed you disappeared out of nowhere."

He placed a kiss on my forehead before whispering in my ear, "Look at you. I leave for a few minutes and you're beside yourself. I enjoy this needy side of you."

"I'm not needy, you were just gone a while."

He reached behind me to pluck a sugary treat from the counter. "The cinnamon rolls are still warm."

"Fuck you."

He barked out a laugh, his normally somber features

lighting up into something reminiscent of sunlight breaking through storm clouds.

The view tugged at my rage-fueled heart until the anger simmered away, and I wrapped my arms around him. "OK fine, I missed you. I'm not used to having people around me anymore. So don't just vanish like that."

"Understood," he smiled, and my tummy did a sappy little flutter like the smitten bitch I am. "I promise I'll never leave you alone for too long, Princess."

Oh. That did something to my heart-places. My arms tightened around his back. His hand trailed along my spine, soothing away the loneliness I'd held on to for too long.

Don't you fucking cry on this man, Cherry.

My savior came in the form of a knock at the door.

"I'll get it," Dante sighed.

I nodded and quickly pulled away, rubbing at my eyes. The front door creaked open, followed by a hissing noise. When I turned around, green smoke billowed from the doorway and into the room. Harsh wet coughs erupted from Dante before he fell to the floor.

"Oh shit!" I snatched a cloth from the kitchen and put it to my face, trying to block out the smoke, then dove for him. Something hard hit my side, and I crashed to the floor. I gasped, taking in lungfuls of the smoke before the coughing fit started. My limbs grew heavy, and it was a struggle to so much as lift my head.

Dark silhouettes filled the doorway before the hushed voices of men filled the room. "You sure this demon is worth any money?"

"A big fella like this has gotta be better than nothing. Besides, do you have a better idea? I can't lose any more coin to that damn Boomslang. If he dies, it's not like we'll be any worse off."

The taller figure reached down to grab Dante, who was still unmoving on the floor. "Dammit, this fucker is heavy. Grab his legs."

My nails dug into the wood floor as I tried to drag myself over to them. "Back off," I croaked.

The man behind the one grabbing Dante froze. "Shit, man, there's someone else in here? Let's just go."

"Stop being a fucking coward and just take that one too. Two fighters are better than one."

The man at the back cursed, then stepped around his cohort to approach me. "Oh fuck no, this one's a human. I'm not catching that charge."

"Well, obviously don't take her, then." He shrugged Dante off like a dirty sack of potatoes and approached me. "I have to do everything myself," he said. His foot came down, and the world went black.

Chapter 19

Cherry

When I came to, Dante was gone, and I had a wicked bruise on my head. "Shit, shit, shit! OK, deep breaths, Cherry, don't panic," I said, clearly panicking. Fear had turned my blood to ice under my skin. Dante had been kidnapped. Actually fucking kidnapped, and I had no idea what to do.

My limbs still felt sluggish, but I struggled to my feet and called out for Alexis. No answer. Dammit, if she was still gone too, it was possible something could have happened to her when she had gone to the barracks. That just left me. Which...didn't bode well for anyone else.

A plan. I needed a plan. The two men mentioned fighting and...Boomslang? Where had I heard that name? Realization dawned and my stomach dropped. "The coliseum."

As expected, the coliseum was packed. The announcer regaled the roaring crowd with tales of their reigning champion, Boomslang. Banners painted with the snakeman's likeness hung all around the coliseum walls. Some patrons in the stands held up signs cheering for their favorite fighters while others had painted their faces in a lime green that matched the snake's scales.

In an effort to unseat the undefeated champion, tonight's match would be open to all challengers from far and wide. The announcer paused to offer anyone in the crowd a chance to step forward and face the champion. Surprise, surprise, no humans stepped forward.

Buying a ticket to get in had been easy enough, but the section where they kept the gladiators was completely closed to the public. Which made sense if you were forcing demons to fight against their will. Can't imagine that was great for their public image.

Guards holding rather pointy-looking lances stood firm at the door. One glanced my way when I stared too long, and I quickly averted my gaze and rounded the corner.

Absently, I thumbed the travel stones in my pocket. I hadn't really thought past finding Dante and having him warp us out of here. But the travel stones and cinnamon weren't much use to him if I couldn't get near him. Snapping gators, I wasn't even sure if cinnamon would work on this curse. They may have been using a different one from the false goddess.

"Now I wish I'd spent more time looking through his big book of magic rather than the one for the beasts. A sleeping spell would be great right now," I muttered. I worried at my bottom lip and ducked into a seat in the stands.

I needed something to distract a whole mess of people at once. The more guards I could drive away the better. What gets a crowd of people running?

"Gah, there's so many bees over here!" A woman in a fine green dress waved her fan at the pesky bees surrounding her. Her waving only aggravated the insects further, and they began attacking her in earnest.

I grinned. "That'll do."

I abandoned my seat and ducked into a dark corner away from the crowd. Fishing the travel stones out of my pocket, I placed the return stone on the ground and held the other one with both hands. "Alright, I'm pretty sure I have to leave one of you here, which means you should be able to take me to the third stone back in his castle."

The stone in my hand gave no response.

"Or you should," I muttered, narrowing my eyes at the rock. "As soon as I figure out how to use you."

I hit it.

Nothing.

"Damn."

I closed my eyes and tried to focus on the magic flooding through my veins. It was risky, considering what had happened last time I tried to use Dante's magic. But beggars can't be choosers. "Please don't blow up in my hands this time."

Swirling wind pulled around me, and I damn near cried in relief. When the wind cleared, I found myself standing on the golden coin-covered floor of Dante's hoard. "Yes, I did it!" I cried out, throwing my hands up.

"Why yes. Yes, you did."

"Dante?" I asked, turning around at the sound of the deep voice. It belonged to a dragon alright, just not the one I was used to seeing.

This one was far paler than Dante, with hints of violet tipping the larger scales running down its back. The dragon lay upon a pile of coins and looked down at me with an almost bored expression. It lifted itself off its perch and slinked forward like a cat stalking a mouse.

Nothing is ever easy, is it?

"Tell me, little human, what would cause a frail thing like you to make the foolish mistake of breaking into the hoard of the Lord of Storms?"

Knees shaking, I swallowed the fear back and straightened my spine. "Hello," I greeted cheerily. "You must be Kohara. I'm your new sister-in-law, Cherry."

My greeting was met with laughter that clattered the coins at my feet. **"Of all the excuses I've heard over the years, that may just take the cake."** Kohara took another step forward, her mouth glowed with orange flame.

I quickly backed away behind a treasure chest. "It's not an excuse! I really am your sister-in-law. As a matter of fact, Dante needs your help and—"

"Enough," she barked. **"I grow weary of your excuses, though I commend you for being brave enough to get this far. Come out from behind your little hiding place and I'll grant you a swift death."**

"Wow, that is so generous, but I think I'm just going to stick with living for now."

Smoke hissed around her snout. **"Fine then, I'll come to you."**

"Oh that's so not necessar—" The last of my words were cut off in a high-pitched scream as I dove out of the way of her claws.

"Hold still, you little vermin," Kohara growled. She took another swipe at me, nearly taking off my head before I ducked and rolled down a pile of coins and took off running.

"If you could just listen to me for a second!" I cried, ducking behind a column to avoid the stream of flames my sister-in-law shot forth. When the flames dissipated, I bolted toward the exit, only to be stopped by a wall of pale scales as she slammed her tail down in my path.

Skidding to a halt, I veered away and ducked behind the large throne sitting on a dais. "Listen dammit, Dante is in danger!"

"As if I would believe the words of a lying thief," she

hissed. **"Any idiot could see you're just trying to save your own hide."**

When she lunged forward, I dove under her arm before snatching a trident off a pile of gems. Then whipped around and poked her armpit with it.

"Ow!" she yelped. She snapped her head to glare at me before her eyes grew wide, her dark pupils turning into thin slits. **"Put that down now! You have no idea what you have in your hands."**

"The hell I will!" I thrust the trident forward again, nearly clipping her chest before she slunk back.

Angry rumbling erupted from her throat before a stream of flames shot forth. Panicked, I held the trident up in front of my face. All at once, the magic humming in my blood came alive and surged into the cool metal of the trident. The flames parted around me as if blocked by an invisible shield. Kohara reared back in shock, and I took the opportunity to run through her legs and poke her at the base of her tail where the scales turned thin. When she leapt out of the way, I bolted toward the door.

"OW! You little shit, that hurts!" she hissed, darting after me.

"Yeah, so does being set on fire!" I called over my shoulder. Flames singed my side, causing my heart to drop into my gut. A small bit of fire caught on the side of my coat and I frantically patted it down as I turned down the hall and kept running.

The dragoness burst through the doors behind me, denting the wall she crashed into. Her claws made terrible screeching sounds as they scraped against the marble flooring.

When she was nearly at my back, I flattened myself on the floor, causing her to skitter over me as she tried to stop. I shot up and jabbed my weapon at the base of her tail as hard as I could. This time, blue lightning raced up my arms and into the fork of the trident.

Kohara screeched, then jumped to her side before crashing into the dining table. She flailed among the chairs before righting herself with an angry hiss. By the time she had gotten up, I was already halfway up the steps, nearly to my destination.

"You'll pay for that, you little snack!"

"I fucking knew they ate people."

I threw open the doors to the bee room and ran toward the giant purple honeycombs as fast as I could. The sound of screeching claws on marble grew closer.

"Oh, this part is gonna suck so bad," I whimpered. My hand grazed the traveler stone in my pocket, reassuring me that it was still there before I moved on to phase two. Phase two being pissing off giant venomous demon bees.

Totally fine, no pressure.

Swallowing the lump in my throat, I raised the trident up, and smacked the shit out of the purple beehive. Angry buzzing erupted from the comb and I darted over to the next one and slapped that too. Then a third one for good measure.

Kohara slammed through the doors just in time to see a reckoning of bees swarm out of the hive. Her jaw fell slack, as her body coiled away. **"Are you insane?"**

Although phase two was going according to plan, my flight response kicked in and I couldn't help but run away screaming from the horde of angry bees. I snatched the traveler stone from my pocket and poured as much magic into it as I could.

"No, don't run toward me!" Kohara screamed. I tried running around her, but she turned to escape and I ended up slamming against her side. Wind picked up around us, accompanied by ferocious buzzing.

We came out on the other end of the portal in an explosion of rubble. Kohara's dragon form was far too big for the little corner I had left the return stone in, and the surrounding walls crumbled against her hard scales. A demon bee was caught under her chin, and she reared up with a scream. A horde of demon bees flew out from around us and into the stands of the coliseum. Screams of panic broke out all along the stands as people started fleeing. The announcer in the center of the stage looked on at the chaos in horror before he too turned and ran.

Before the dragon could realize I was within squishing distance, I crawled out from underneath her and snuck toward the door leading to the gladiators' quarters.

To my ever-changing luck, a demon bee had beat me to my destination and picked a fight with the guards. The shorter guard put up a valiant effort; however, his partner immediately dropped his lance and ran away screaming. The shorter guard looked back at his fleeing companion, which was his downfall. His shining armor did nothing to stop the giant stinger from running him through. I gasped as the demon bee retracted its stinger and flew away, leaving the guard with a gaping hole in his chest before he fell to the floor.

Welp, that's going to add to my list of nightmares.

Kohara righted herself and shook off the rubble before whipping around to glare at me. **"You!"**

"Oh shit," I turned and shoved my way through the doors. The sight that greeted me on the other side was much, much worse. The gladiators' quarters beneath the coliseum looked more like a dark and dingy dungeon. Rows of cages lined the walls, each filled with dazed-looking demons. My body felt numb as I took in the sheer amount of them.

There was no way I had brought enough cinnamon for everyone. I ran up to the first cage and peered inside to see a large orc and a spitaur slumped inside. The orc's dark red skin was mottled with bruises, while his hair sat in a disheveled heap that may have been a bun in a former life. The spitaur didn't look much better. I gasped, seeing the gold and black bands on his legs. "Holy shit, it's the tavern owner!"

To my shock, the cage was unlocked. "Right, I guess mind-controlled captives don't do much to escape."

I stepped inside and slowly approached the orc. "Hey, can you hear me?"

No response, not that I expected one. I leaned the trident against the wall then reached into my pocket and took out the bag of cinnamon before waving it under his nose. His lips twitched, and I raised the cinnamon closer to his nose. When his body jerked, I stepped back and did the same to the spitaur. No sooner had I backed away, the orc leapt to his feet with a snarl, causing me to stumble further back.

Wild eyes fixed on me. I held my hands up and tried to look as friendly as possible. "Welcome back. Is the curse out of your system?" I asked.

The orc rubbed a hand on his face and groaned. "Where am I? What happened?"

"You're beneath the coliseum in Kirkwall. Though I'm not sure what happened to you. Can you tell me your name?"

"Yala," he muttered.

"Great. Well, Yala, I'm looking for a dragon-shifter with silver hair."

"The one that wanted all those shoes?"

"Shoes? Um, sure. Have you seen him down here?"

Yala blinked slowly before shaking his head. "I remember nothing past waking up this morning."

Beside me, the tavern owner groaned, and struggled to his feet. "Wha...what's going on?"

"So you weren't lying," a feminine voice called. I turned to see a statuesque woman with long silver hair and matching horns standing outside of the cage. Kohara glanced around the room of cages with clear disgust.

"I'm not," I snapped, turning to her. "Will you stop trying to kill me?"

The barest hint of a smile tugged at her lips. "For now."

Great first impression.

"Snack," she called, turning back to me.

"Cherry," I corrected.

"Disregard the others for now and focus on finding my brother."

Rage simmered in the pit of my stomach. "You expect me to just leave them?"

"Not for long," she sighed, placing a hand on her hip. "I'll find whoever's controlling the magic and kill them. But that's going to be a lot harder to do if I have to babysit my brother's wife. So find him, rub that cinnamon on his face, and stay out of my way."

"You are just lovely," I drawled.

"I am, aren't I?" she said with a serene smile. Kohara reached into the cinnamon bag and put some of it in her mouth. "You two, if you want to live through the day, make sure she does." Her tone came out light and breezy, but Yala tensed behind me. His eyes never left her back as she left.

"Bit of a character, that one," I muttered.

I picked up the trident and headed out of the cage, pausing

when I noticed both of them struggling behind me. "If you're too tired, just stay here."

Yala snorted. "And piss off that dragoness? There are easier ways to die, lass."

Can't argue with that logic.

The spitaur wobbled, before catching himself on the bars of the cage. "We'll be fine. Just lead the way."

"Right," I said, peering down the hallway. "Let's check further down while everyone is distracted outside. What's your name?" I asked, offering my arm when the spitaur stumbled again.

He took a deep breath and rubbed the remaining cinnamon off his nose. "Cyser."

Footsteps pounded toward us. "We got company," Yala called, stepping in front of me. I peered over his side to see a guard sprinting toward us. The orc cracked his knuckles before he took a fighting stance. "If you wanna dance, then bring it on!"

The guard didn't slow from his breakneck pace. He cast a glance behind him before tripping as he tried swerving around Yala. He went down hard, his armor scraped against the stone floor as his spear caught on the bars of the cage beside him. He scrambled up, forgoing his fallen spear to burst through the doors. No sooner had he stepped outside, a demon bee swooped down and carried him off, screaming.

Yala crossed his arms with a satisfied grin. "Huh, guess I scared him off."

Cyser rolled his eyes. "I imagine whatever he was running from scared him off, you oaf." He shoved passed Yala to grab the fallen spear. "Let's just hope for our sake, it's just another demon."

Yala's lips pursed, then he glanced down at me and shrugged. "Well, I bet I scared him a little bit."

"I'd be terrified," I offered. Shuffling footsteps accompanied by pained groans rose from the end of the hallway. Through the dim torchlight, I could make out the silhouette of more men rounding the corner.

"Don't humor him," said Cyser.

"Hey, fuck you!"

"Fellas please! Can we focus on the task at hand?" I yelled, gesturing to the encroaching silhouettes.

Alexis flew around the corner. "Hi, Cherry," she chirped. "Run, Cherry," she called, as she spirited past us. She used her magic to push open the doors, only to see the screams and havoc of the Kiboon Bees. "Nope," she said, closing the door.

"Alexis? What's going on?"

The sword swayed back and forth in the air. "Um...long story, and trust me, I'd love to tell ya. You know I love spinning a good yarn. But first, you're going to need to figure out that zap thing. Right now."

"What, why?"

She pointed behind us.

A horde of guards shambled into the hallway. Blood leaked

255

from a gash on the side of one's head. The guard next to him had a face that looked half eaten, with his left arm gnawed off at the elbow. Those behind them didn't look any better off. Mr. Half Face noticed us first. His mouth fell open into a horrid groan before he flung himself forward, the rest of the horde following suit.

"Alexis, what the fuck?" I screamed.

"Less screaming, more shocking!"

Cyser turned around and shot a stream of golden thread at our attackers. Those in front went down in a sticky mess, but the guards behind them wasted no time in clambering over their fallen comrades.

Yala charged forward, only to skitter to a halt when Alexis flew in front of him. "Wait, don't let them bite you!" The sword stabbed herself through the eye of the closest guard. Then pulled free to plunge into the next.

Cyser yanked Yala back and shoved the spear into his hands. "Here, make yourself useful."

Yala recovered quickly and impaled a guard through the chest. He didn't go down. The half-eaten man paid no mind to the spear in his chest, and grabbed Yala by the hair, trying to bite at his face. "What the hell are these things?" he screamed. He planted a foot on the guard's chest and shoved him off his spear.

Another golden thread shot out, trapping several guards against the bars of a cage. A man with a large gash on his stomach leaped over the thread and lunged for me. Without thinking, I jabbed him with the trident. Blue sparks radiated against the tip until a blast of lightning shot his head clean off. Its harsh recoil sent me flying back with a scream. I crashed into Cyser, taking us both to the ground.

Dazed, I stared up at the ceiling unmoving. Yala yanked me to my feet and pulled me in front of him. "Do it again!"

"Ah, fuck!" I thrust the trident out in front of me waiting for the sparks. When none came forward, panic raced through my veins. "Oh, come on you son of a bitch!"

Alexis shot out and stabbed the guard in front before he could reach us. "Try again! Put your back into it!"

Sweat nearly made the trident slip through my grasp and I fumbled to keep hold. "I don't think it works like that!"

"Try it anyway," Yala said.

Heart pounding in my chest, I tried focusing my breathing and called upon Dante's magic. The trident thrust forward and...nothing.

Snarling in frustration, I jabbed the trident into the neck of the nearest guard. "Oh you picky ass-end of an anaconda, just FUCKING LIGHT!" A blast of lightning shot forth, decimating the man and those behind him, leaving only two remaining. My back hit Yala's chest. The orc grunted and dug his heels in, ensuring I didn't fly back again.

The three of us stood there, wide-eyed. Alexis doesn't have eyes, but I'm sure if we had asked her, she would have said she was also surprised. "Well damn," Cyser whispered.

A wave of exhaustion hit me like a ton of bricks. I slumped forward, using the end of the trident to keep myself upright. "Snapping gators, that took a lot out of me. I'm not sure how many of those I have left, y'all."

Alexis and Yala charged forward, making quick work of the remaining two. The half-dead guards stuck in Cyser's web groaned and snapped their teeth. But none possessed the strength to pull themselves out of the sticky mess.

"You want to tell me what the hell's going on now, Alexis?" I asked, panting.

Unearthly moans sounded off in the distance.

"Umm...long story short, Rebekah did it. But we should really walk and talk," she replied. Alexis darted down the hall and veered to the left, away from the groaning. The rest of us followed suit, Yala half dragging my tired ass.

"What do you mean, 'Rebekah did it'?" I stared at Alexis in abject horror.

"Hey, don't look at me like I'm the crazy one," she snapped. "You're the one walking around with a vorswine like it's a pet."

The spitaur's face grew ashen at her words. "There's vorswine here?"

"The hell is a vorswine?" I asked, exasperated. "Rebekah's just a cat!"

The sword froze in front of us; we all skidded to a halt. The kitten in question slowly appeared, head first, from around the corner. Except she was bigger than the last time I saw her. A lot bigger. Her pristine white fur was spotless, which was odd considering the floor was covered in blood. An armored foot peeked into view, and I had the sneaking suspicion that I did not want to see what the rest of the body looked like. The foot twitched before chopped grunts sounded off from the body. Alexis' voice grew quiet as she spoke. "Cherry, I promise you, that thing is not a cat."

Rebekah caught sight of us and sat. Her bobcat-sized body vibrated with a delighted purr. Tail swishing, she took in each of us with her beady blue eyes until she fixed her gaze on me. Her head tilted to the side and a deep voice sounded off from somewhere around her. **"Too sour."**

A man in a long black cloak came out from a room flipping through a stack of papers. He looked up at Yala and Cyser before frowning. "Hey, what are you lot doing out of your cages?"

Rebekah turned her gaze to him, **"Sweet."**

The kitten's body cracked in half. Spindly black hands shot out of the opening and grabbed the man by the throat. He cried out and clawed at the floor before her jaw unhinged like a snake and bit into his head.

...*Nope.*

Screaming, we took off running in the other direction. Yala tripped over one of the tavern owner's legs, nearly taking me out with him. I pulled him to his feet, and we took off after Alexis, deeper into the coliseum.

"The east side of the building is completely shot; we're

going to have to see if we can get out from the west exit," Alexis called as she led the way.

"What do you mean it's shot? Are you telling me there's more of those things?"

"Well yeah," she replied. "That's where the barracks were, so we started off there."

"You wanted her to do this?" I screeched.

"Look, I knew she was something bad, I just didn't know she was a damn vorswine. I thought she would just eat them, not turn them into mindless zombies with an appetite for human tartare. Though in my defense, those guards were very, *very* rude. And, you know, turns out they were kidnapping demons, anyway. If you think about it, I'm kind of a hero. A vigilante if you will."

"You just released a vorswine into the city!" Cyser shouted.

"No, she did!" Alexis said, pointing to me. Like a rat. "I just took her to the knights' barracks."

The two men looked at me in disbelief.

"I...I thought it was a cat."

Cyser clenched his fists at his side. His face contorting in an enraged scowl. "You thought it was a—"

Boom.

The wall in front of us exploded, followed by the deafening sound of a dragon's roar. My stomach sank as a Kiboon bee launched at us from outside.

"Run!" Yala cried. He sprinted down the hallway and

opened up the door at the end. A horde of zombies greeted him on the other side.

He shut the door.

"Not that way. Other way!" he screamed, charging back toward us. With a speed surprising for his massive frame, the orc leapt up, using the wall to spring himself higher, and stabbed his spear through the bee. Thankfully, the bee stayed dead. Unlike the damn zombies.

With a sickening creak, the door burst open and a sea of zombies piled through.

Chapter 20

Dante

"I will not ask you again," I said. The mage beneath me cried out as I twisted his broken leg. "Where. Is. My. Wife?"

His response came out through broken whimpers. "I told you, I don't know. You're the only one those men brought in."

"Hmm. I don't believe you." He screamed in pain as the bone splintered. Black on black clothing hid a fair amount of the blood seeping through his wound. Though it painted the floor a pretty shade of red. Similar to my wife's boots.

Movement caught my eye, and I sent a bolt of lightning at the man drawing his wand. He fell to the floor dead. I sighed, stood up straight and addressed the mages lined up against the wall. "You fools must be hard of hearing. No one is leaving this room until my wife is brought to my side safe and sound. If I find one mark on her body, pray to any god you like. They will not save you."

We'd been at this nonsense since I awoke strapped to their pathetic offering table. If there was anything more unpleasant to awaken to than the mumbled ramblings of half-witted mages, I didn't know of it. Still, if it weren't for the fact that I had just eaten Cherry's cinnamon rolls, their holding magic might just have been enough to bind me.

For that, they couldn't be allowed to live.

"Please," one mage begged. "We know nothing about another dragon. You are the only one they brought in."

"A human!" I roared. Lightning crackled up my legs until it danced at my fists. The itch to shift tore at my human form until scales grew along my forearms and back. "My wife is a human. With big brown eyes, adorable dimples and a laugh that makes everything right with the world. And if anything happens to her, I will make you live through horrors so vile your grandchildren will weep!" Frustration caused my hands to clench, crushing the mage's ankle. He let loose a pained wail and fainted.

Through the chaos, a calm authoritative voice spoke up. "Now, now. Can't we discuss this like reasonable men?"

I turned to see a man dressed in royal attire step out from the balcony ringing the second floor. His golden crown sat proud and polished atop his head. A white cloak held together by golden talismans trailed behind him as he moved. The king held his head high, doing his best to maintain an air of indifference. I imagine the confidence was strengthened by the soldiers that flanked his sides. Foolish. They'd be dead before they so much as touched their swords.

"King Andor!" The mages along the wall fell to their knees.

Lightning struck the wall just above their heads. "I didn't tell you to move," I said.

They stood.

To his credit, the king didn't flinch. Yet the stench of fear rolled off him in waves.

Good. He should be afraid.

The king cleared his throat and stood a little straighter. "I am King Andor. Ruler of all of Kibar and its surrounding seas."

"And I am in no mood for your long-winded exposition. Let me cut to the chase. You're going to find out what these idiots have done to my wife and bring her to my side. Then, you're going to kill every mage involved in this mind control curse. Starting with whoever is in charge of its power source. Do so quickly, and I'll consider leaving this city intact."

A look of disbelief crossed his face until it settled into fury. He closed his eyes and schooled his features before speaking again. "Clearly we've angered you with our gladiator games." He waved his hands in a dismissing gesture. "I'll admit, we should've put an end to the games as soon as the goddess was destroyed. Yet, it's rather hard to convince businessmen to give up their income. As a dragon, I'm sure you understand the allure of good coin."

"As a dragon, I understand you're wasting my time. Bring me my wife, now."

His lips twitched as he chuckled. "I'm sure there will be time for that. First, I'd like to discuss a proposition with you."

"Here it comes," I said, rolling my eyes.

"Swear your loyalty to me and become the Dragon of Kibar. With your might added to our royal army, none of our enemies would stand a chance." He smiled wickedly and spread his arms wide. "Mokyr, Foli, even the mighty Kinnamo will fall with you at our side."

"Not interested."

"Don't be so hasty. We can give you anything. Gold, jewels, as much land as you could dream of! Swear your loyalty to me and I'll even give you one of my daughters to marry. That will solidify our alliance."

I pinched the bridge of my nose to avoid setting him on fire. "Did you completely ignore the fact that I already have a wife? It's like you're trying to die."

Gods, I hate solicitors.

"Surely a princess is more valuable?"

"IN HERE, QUICK!" A door on the east side of the balcony flung open. Cherry burst through, waving in Alexis and two men before slamming the door shut. A chorus of banging and groans sounded off from the other side. The four of them all pushed against the door, panting heavily.

"What is the meaning of this?" the king snarled.

Cherry turned toward him, bewildered before her eyes caught sight of me. She smiled wide and flung herself against the railing. "Dante!"

For a moment I could do nothing but stare at her in disbelief. King Mokas the Blight's trident was clutched firmly in her hand. Telltale signs of magic drain dulled her normally bright features. The ends of her sleeves were singed, while blue sparks flickered at the ends of the trident's prongs.

The door pushed open enough for a bloody hand to come through, slashing at the orc. "Cherry, a little help?" he cried.

"Oh crap," she cried, shoving her shoulder into the door.

I leaped to her side and pulled her to me. Then took the trident and pointed it at the door. "Move."

Her companions backed away quickly. In an instant the door flung open, revealing dead men charging toward us. I didn't bother to ask questions. Thunder boomed, and a ray of light obliterated every last one of them.

Alexis sighed dramatically. "Sweet shining polish! It's over. Welp, I'll leave the rest of the bad guys in your claws. Let me on that belt, big guy. I'm taking a nap," she said, then slid her handle into the O-ring on my belt.

The orc threw himself on the ground and breathed deep, while the spitaur slumped beside him, gasping just as heavily.

"Are you alright?" Cherry asked, cupping my face. "I brought cinnamon if you need it."

"I'm fine. More importantly, how did you escape?"

She tilted her head. "Escape? They never took me. I was just knocked out."

"We told you!" a mage shouted.

Lightning shot through his chest, and he crumpled to the ground. It was rude to interrupt.

"Well see!" The king smiled wide, his posture relaxing into a state of undeserved nonchalance. "Your wife is fine so there's no more need for concern. Now about our deal—"

"Fine?" Cherry snarled. "We just spent the past hour running through your coliseum full of zombies and enslaved demons!"

"Of course," the king nodded. "We regret that our gladiator games have caused you and your husband distress. Please understand that any large-scale immigration comes with its trials and challenges. My advisers and I would be more than happy to discuss the reformation of the coliseum in exchange for you and your dragon's cooperation."

She turned back to me and jutted a thumb at the king. "The hell is this condescending prick talking about?"

"How dare you speak to me that way, I'm your king!"

"I'm from Kinnamo, you popinjay," she snapped.

I stifled a gasp. "So your home *is* in Kinnamo?"

She let off something between a grunt and squeak before

shooting a glare back at me. Her voice rose several pitches. "Now is not the time for that!"

"Which part?" Kinnamo was a vast country. Its territories spanned most of the southern part of the continent. Fallon's territory was located on the very end of the southern tip. If her home was anywhere close, then Fallon and I would have no issues forming a united territory. That being said, if her home was in the ruined city of Wandermere, then I'd have some explaining to do.

Her foot stomped. "Can you please focus on the task at hand? What does this guy want from you?"

The only task I wanted to focus on involved bending her over the railing until she talked. Yet I suppose patience had its virtues. "He's trying to sell me his daughter in exchange for military enlistment," I said.

Cherry simply stared at the king for a good moment, then wagged her finger at him. "Lightning. I'm gonna use lighting on your ass." She snatched the trident from my hands and aimed it at the king. "Yala, brace me."

"Now we're talking!" The orc laughed and positioned his large body behind her, his hands on her shoulders. Fear pricked under my skin as sparks danced around her forearms. If it backfired like it had done in the wilderness, Cherry could blow her arms clean off. Before I could reach out to stop her, the trident absorbed her magic into its prongs, effectively saving her from death.

Wide-eyed, the king and his guards dove just before a bolt of lightning struck the wall behind them. Bits of rubble and sparks rained down on the terrified men, who wisely chose to stay prone. Seemingly mollified by their cowardice, Cherry leaned the trident against the wall and returned to my side. "Are you sure you're alright?"

My chest lurched, seeing her big brown eyes full of concern. "Did you come to save me, princess?" It was a ridiculous question the more I thought about it. Cherry was human. With a body as fragile as her lifespan. Even if they did somehow manage to bring me under their thrall, no human mages could hold me for long. Yet here she was, charging in after me into the unknown.

Her brow furrowed. "Of course I did. Don't look so surprised."

I grinned, like a love-struck fool. "'Of course,' she says." A sense of warmth spread over me, as if I had been dunked in the healing waters of a hot spring. I brushed a curl from her face. She flinched when my hand grazed the side of her head. A pained expression marred her features. I drew my hand away, ice freezing my veins when it came back red with blood.

Rage.

"Dante?"

Her mouth kept moving but all I could hear was thunder. **Rage.**

Chapter 21

Cherry

Dante's eyes bled from gray to violet. His body trembled as gray smoke rose from him like steam from a kettle. He stroked back a few tendrils of my hair, just below the bruise on my head. **"Who did this, Cherry?"**

I flinched, having never heard his dragon voice when he was still in human form. Its deep timbre blanketed the room with tension. My human hearing may have been nothing compared to that of a demon, but I swear on my life I heard everybody's ass clench.

Cherry. Not princess, badger, or even sweetheart. Well fuck. "Umm."

He smiled, the fangs of his upper jaw elongated, while

silver scales plated up the ridge of his nose. **"Doesn't matter. I'll drown this land in fire and you can point out their ashes later."**

He touched my face softly, his thumb passing over the dry surface of my lips. His expression was reverent, the look on his face held promises of adoration and unspeakable violence. Heat flooded my lower belly. I pushed it away, refusing to think about what that said about me.

I'm not attracted to this. I'm not.

I chewed on my bottom lip, unsure how to respond to such a promise. "Or, ya know, you could just *not* do that."

Wind howled around us, ripping tapestries from the walls. The king shouted for his guards to run us through, then promptly disintegrated in a flash of white.

"Dante, stop!" I cried.

"Don't worry," he soothed. **"It will be over soon."** With a flick of his wrist, flames engulfed the lower floor of the room, barely giving the men below a chance to eke out their last scream.

Slap.

My hand stung from where the palm met hard scales. I was fairly certain the action hurt me more than it did him. But it got his attention. "I don't want you to drown anything. Please, just help us fix this mess so we can all be done with it. The king is dead, and your sister is off somewhere finding the head mage. There's no need to kill anyone else."

"I'd also like to not drown in fire," Cyser called behind us. "Just saying, if he's taking it to a vote."

The wind stilled. Hard scales receded into soft russet skin. Before I could breathe a sigh of relief, the roof tore off. "Dammit, what now?"

Kohara poked her massive head through the hole in the ceiling. Rebekah was clutched firmly in her clawed hand, yowling and spitting at the dragoness in indignation. **"I got 'em!"** Kohara cheered, the words muffled by something in her mouth. She swallowed it down, then lifted her chin in pride, as if expecting praise.

For my own sanity, I decided to pretend it was a loaf of bread and humored her with a weak clap. "Great job!"

Dante regarded her with a long-suffering expression. "What are you doing here?"

She snorted, shooting flames into the sky. **"Is that any way of thanking me for saving your wife?"**

Debatable.

Yala rose from the floor and stretched. "Well, that's done. Are we raiding the king's liquor cabinet or what?"

We all looked at him in silence.

"What? He's dead. No use to him now."

I like Yala.

With the king and his mages dead, and Rebekah sealed in some sort of magic cage of Kohara's making, things settled pretty quickly. Even the bees were quickly brought to heel.

Turns out there was a bee flute Dante kept next to their hive that allowed him to control them. Live and learn, I guess.

All the demons trapped in the coliseum came to their senses and seemed to be more than willing to join in Yala's plan to storm the castle and raid the king's liquor cabinet.

For you know, penance or whatever.

Half the city's guards had been turned into zombies at Rebekah's doing, so there wasn't much resistance along the way. When I followed the party through the gates, most of the remaining guards were forming a blockade around the king's daughters and a few people who I assumed were important members of the court.

The king's eldest was locked in discussion with Dante, but the discussion was full of political jargon I didn't understand and sounded an awful lot like not my problem. It didn't take long before I bailed on the conversation and followed Yala to the castle bar.

"Alright, next question." Yala took a heavy swig of his beer and slammed the mug on the table. "You're trapped in an abandoned castle for an entire night with either a basilisk or fifty pissed-off pixies. Which do you pick?"

"Oh that's easy. I choose the basilisk," Basil replied. The lamia, formally known as Boomslang, poured himself another shot of whiskey. His snake half was coiled neatly underneath him and I did my best not to stare. Or reach out and touch the bright green scales. His body was covered with bandages, and there was a spot on his tail that looked like someone or something had tried to take a bite out of him.

It made my heart sink to think about how long he had been stuck fighting in the coliseum. Yet instead of rage or tears, the first thing out of his mouth when he came to was "Where's the bathroom?" Even the few remaining guards were met with bored nonchalance. Instead, the promise of following Yala on his quest for expensive whiskey far outweighed any thoughts of vengeance.

The orc gaped at the man as if he'd grown a second head. "You can't be serious. You'd rather take on a basilisk—the giant snake creature known for spitting deadly venom—than a gaggle of pint-sized nuisances?"

Basil shrugged, "I also spit venom."

Exasperated, the orc flattened his hands on the table like he needed something to tether him down. "That doesn't mean you're immune to basilisk venom!"

"Yeah, but pixies could sneak up on you. What if I'm trying to find a snack in the kitchen and one pops out of a cabinet and stabs me in the eye?"

"Why are you trying to find snacks? The name of the game is hiding. You're only trapped in there for a night."

"I get hangry. Food is always the number-one priority."

"Hmm. He's got a point there," I said, sipping my beer. "Besides, I think I'd be more concerned about the possibility of torture. Like, I don't know how vindictive pixies can be, so I'm not trying to find out." Basil pointed at me in agreement.

"No!" Yala slammed a fist on the table. "You are both so wrong! You shouldn't be getting snacks, you should be worried about ending up in the belly of a basilisk."

"Alright but you can see a basilisk coming. I have no idea where those pixies are."

I held up a hand. "Wait, are basilisks the ones where their stare kills you?"

Basil shook his head. "No, that's a cockatrice. Completely different beast. Anyway, let's say I'm in the treasure room trying on jewels, and boom! Caught in a pixie net. Now my tail is being turned into a hundred tiny lamia-skin boots."

"Why are you looting when there's danger afoot?!" Yala shouted.

"Waste not, want not," Basil replied.

The chair beside me screeched and Dante slumped into the seat. *The Big Book of Beasts* dropped on the table with a loud thump as he leaned back.

Yala flashed him a wide grin and pounded his fist on the table. "Ah see, now there's someone with a bit of sense." His face grew serious as he leaned into the table, resting his chin on his hands. "Same question, which would you rather be trapped in an abandoned castle with at night: a basilisk or fifty pissed-off pixies?"

"You can't ask him!" Basil hissed. The scales lining his

lower body rose like a puff adder. "He's an apex predator. You may as well ask me if I'd rather deal with mosquitoes or flies."

"I'd choose the basilisk," Dante said simply.

Basil's scales lost their poof. "Oh, never mind. Ask away."

"You too?" Yala threw up his hands in disbelief.

"The basilisk is the obvious choice," Dante began. "Sure the bite hurts, but it is not going to kill me. But having to spend an entire night with fifty enraged pixies judging my every move? A flesh wound hurts far less than emotional manipulation."

I shot him an incredulous look. "You're picking the basilisk so your feelings don't get hurt?"

"Pixies can be very cutting," he said, as if it was the most obvious thing in the world. Images of a murder of crows harassing an eagle came to mind and I had to stifle a laugh.

The orc groaned in defeat. "Alright, fine. Basilisk it is then."

"What did you bring this for?" I asked, nodding at the book.

The dragon-shifter reached across from me to grab the bottle of whiskey and poured himself a glass. "I figured you'd want to record Rebekah now that we know that she's not a cat."

My head perked up at the idea. "Oh, I didn't even think of that!"

Wasting no time, I snatched up the book and approached the cage housing Rebekah. The ball of fluff lay in the center of the cage with her feet tucked neatly beneath her, resembling a loaf of bread. Runes were scratched into the metal bars, each of them pulsing with a pale green light. From what the dragoness had mentioned, the runes made up a sealing spell that had the ability to drain the not-cat of her magic. After an hour in the cage, the guards in her thrall had dropped dead, and her form had shrunk back to the small kitten I remembered.

Her ears flattened at my approach. Clearly she was still holding a grudge at my involvement in spoiling her fun. I ignored her death glare and raised the book in front of her. Its pages flitted as a blue glow erupted. When the glow faded, I turned to see a page titled "Vorswine."

"What the...fuck?" The horrific creature illustrated on the page looked nothing like a cat. It was like someone took a wild boar, carved a gash into its back and filled it with teeth and protruding hands. Its maw opened up into segmented parts, almost resembling a blooming flower. If flowers were made of nightmares and three tongues.

I returned to my seat and read the description. Vorswine: a shape-shifting creature that feasts on the minds and brains of its prey. Those who have been feasted upon can be used as puppets to drag more prey back to them. Vorswine will grow in both size and threat level with each mind eaten until they are capable of subduing larger prey. If no smaller food is available, they will begin poisoning the minds of larger creatures until they can be consumed.

Signs of possible vorswine poisoning include: headaches, a desire to eat brains, indigestion, nightmares and, in rare cases, an inability to digest strawberries.

"What's with that book?" Basil asked.

I glanced nervously at my new companions. Now that I had the book in my hands, it was extremely tempting to ask if they'd allow me to record them as well. Yet such a question might seem offensive. Still, the commandeered castle bar was filled to the brim with all different kinds of demons I had never even dreamt of seeing in person. Lion-shifters were talking animatedly with a dour-looking vampire. A man that looked more bird than human guzzled beer while a centaur manned the bar. It was like I had stepped out of the real world and into all of the fantasy novels I had coveted as a kid.

Pushing down my nervousness, I flipped open the book to show off our previous entry. The shocked face of the phoenix made me giggle, thinking about what we had had to do to get that picture. "It's basically a monster manual that will record whatever demon you point it at."

"Really? Let me see." Yala wiped beer foam away from his mouth and grabbed the book. He lifted it to his face and smiled wide. The pages glowed and flipped to the section on orcs and Yala's profile appeared on a new page. His mouth fell open in astonishment as he watched the page fill out. "Unbelievable, it has my height, age and everything." As he scanned the page, his eyes grew wide. "Damn, it even records that," he said, glancing down at his crotch.

Basil shot him a disbelieving glance. "You're kidding," he said, before taking the book. The lamia held it up high and smiled like he'd seen Yala do before. When the page finished glowing, he read what was written while lips curved into a shit-eating grin, before he handed it back to Yala. "I win."

Yala sputtered and grabbed the book back before looking over Basil's page. He snorted and pushed the book away from him. "It doesn't count as better just because you have two of them."

Two?

"Jealous?" he asked, sipping his drink.

"Let me try." I looked up to see the tavern owner descend upon the book. With the flex, he struck a pose and waited for his page to clear. Before I could stop myself, I cast a glance down at his spider half, wondering where exactly his dick would be.

Beside me, Dante chuckled and shot me a knowing glance.

Damn, caught red-handed.

It didn't take long before more men gathered around and started shoving each other to grab at the book. Each striking poses more ridiculous than the last and bragging about the results.

"Beat that," a centaur shouted. He crossed his arms over his chest and his tail flicked in a way that resembled my childhood horse after he'd completed a difficult jump. His showboating caused a few men to jeer at him and discredit his merits on the fact that he was half horse. Which…did seem unfair.

It wasn't until a minotaur stepped up and declared himself superior that the centaur finally stopped his gloating.

I didn't think I'd get my wish in the form of a dick-measuring contest, but hey, a win is a win.

"Gods, what a beautiful time to wake up," Alexis said. The sword unhooked herself from Dante's belt and floated next to the table with a relieved sigh. "Truly, it must be my birthday."

"I'm telling you, mine is bigger!" someone shouted in the crowd.

"FROM THE BASE, I SAID!"

A small scuffle broke out and Alexis wasted no time in floating over. "Fellas, let's all calm down," she said cheerily. "I'll be the judge. It's only fair, seeing as I have no genitals. Now form a line. We're not savages."

"Always the opportunist," Dante sighed.

"So, what are you two planning on doing now this is all over? Are you going to stay in Kirkwall?" I asked.

Basil shrugged. "Currently, I have no plans beyond this drink."

Yala let off a loud burp. "I've had quite enough of Kirkwall. The plan is to keep looking for my brothers and the rest of the Monet clan. We got separated the last time Volsog Gate opened."

"Did you say Monet clan?" We all looked at Dante, who suddenly looked more irked than he had a moment ago.

Yala's posture straightened, his voice taking on a more

nervous note. "...Yes. Has one of my kin done something to offend you?"

The dragon's eyes narrowed dangerously. "Every damn day." He stood. Yala flinched. Dante walked over to a decorative mirror hanging on the wall and raised his hand. He muttered something I couldn't catch, and the mirror's image started swirling. He beckoned us closer then stood aside.

When we made our way over, the swirling purple and gray of the mirror faded to reveal a blond man staring curiously back at us. "Dante?" he asked.

"FELIX!" I jumped at the orc's shout. Yala all but crashed into the mirror in his excitement, nearly knocking it off the wall.

Mirroring the orc's excitement, Felix's body shook rapidly and then, bam, a werewolf sat in his place. "Yala! I can't believe it's you!" Behind the massive wall of fur, I saw the tip of a rapidly beating tail smack the shit out of whatever innocent furniture was next to him. "Wait right there, I should have a travel stone that links to Dante's."

Dante tensed beside me. "What? When the hell did you get that?"

The sound of drawers opening and closing filled the air as the werewolf rummaged through his things. "When you let Fallon borrow your Hearthstone stones to move his hoard, he figured out how to copy the spell. It's much easier to get around this way."

He glowered at the man in the mirror with clear suspicion. "But how did you link it to mine?"

"Don't worry about it, bestie," Felix called over his shoulder. "Ah ha!" he shouted, before a whirlwind enveloped his body.

"You're friends with my brother?" Yala asked.

"Let's not get crazy," Dante said flatly.

"He's right!" came a chipper voice next to us. "We're more like boon companions."

The werewolf launched himself at Dante, who sidestepped him with practiced ease. Felix grinned as if that was the expected reaction, pivoted, and leapt on his back, wrapping his arms around Dante's neck. "Get off me," the dragon growled.

"I missed you too, buddy."

Yala bounced excitedly on his feet. When Felix clambered off his irritated boon companion, his brother was the next in line for his aggressive hug. The orc greeted him with open arms, falling back when the weight of the werewolf slammed into his chest.

Felix's head tilted back until his red eyes fixed me. He jumped up, and I instinctively widened my stance to brace for a tackle that never came. Instead, he calmly walked over and offered me a clawed hand. "You must be Dante's mate. I'm Felix, Dante's best friend for life."

"No he's not," the dragon quipped.

Unperturbed, Felix gave him a lopsided grin. "We're best friends, we're buying a shrimp boat, and starting a business."

"Go to hell."

I took his hand and offered a friendly smile. "Nice to meet you, I'm Cherry."

The smile faded from his face and his head tilted to the side, reminding me of a confused dog. He brought my hand closer to his snout and sniffed. "You smell like Cinnamon."

Awkwardly, I drew my hand away and placed it at my side. "Well, I was carrying around a bag of it for most of the day. So that's not too surprising."

"No, I—"

A large red hand slapped on his shoulder, snapping Felix from his thoughts. "Oh, stop bothering her and come drink with me," Yala beamed at his brother. "I haven't seen you for a year!" He half dragged the werewolf back over to the table and the two soon lost themselves in catching up.

I slid an arm around Dante's and leaned against him. "You want to get out of here?"

Silver eyes looked down at me with clear relief. "More than anything. There are an awful lot of people here."

"You love me!" Felix bellowed.

Dante rolled his eyes, the barest hint of a grin tugged at his lips. After we collected *The Big Book of Beasts*, we bid the rest of the gang farewell and headed out into the cool night. Despite the chaos of the day, the stars shined as they always did. Unbothered by the squabbles of those beneath them.

He stopped us near the castle's entrance before we made

it onto the street. "Cherry, I know today has been a lot, but there's someplace I'd like to take you. It's a tad far, so you may want to sleep on the way there."

I looked up at him curiously to see concern lining his eyes. Almost as if he was worried I'd say no. I squeezed his hand in mine. "Alright, let's go."

"Good." He stepped away from me, smoke enveloping his body. It spread out along the courtyard like a thick fog until it faded, revealing a dragon.

Smiling, I went up to his side and ran my fingers along the soft hair of his mane. "Don't need me to turn around anymore?" I asked.

His large body rumbled as he lowered his head to the ground. A long claw pushed my feet up, helping me climb onto his neck. **"You risked your life to come and save me. I think we've grown past that."** With a powerful kick of his hind legs, we were airborne. Soaring through the night like a playful wind.

Laughing, I snuggled further into the warmth of his mane. "It didn't seem like you really needed my help. By the time we got there, you pretty much had them on their knees."

"You didn't know that when you came in."

"No, I suppose I didn't."

"That meant more to me than I know how to say."

To be honest, I hadn't even thought about leaving without him. Seeing him drop to the floor had filled me with more fear than I've ever felt in my life.

This, whatever this is, it's still new. Still very new. But the thought of anything taking him away from me is terrifying. Even before I was kidnapped, I don't think I've ever felt this sense of… ease? The feeling was hard to place. If I had to give it a name, I'd say it just felt right. "Leaving you was never an option."

Dante hummed. The soft mane beneath me radiated a soothing heat, and I found my eyes drooping. **"Get some rest,"** he murmured. **"I'll wake you when we get there."**

Chapter 22

Cherry

"Wake up."

"Nmrm." I rubbed at my eyes with a groan and tried burrowing closer into the warmth at my side. Cold slapped against my senses when the heat slipped away from me.

I looked up to see Dante grinning down at me. "Stop your growling and get up, or you'll miss it."

"You took all the warm," I said petulantly.

He chuckled and held a hand out to help me up. "I am the embodiment of evil. Now get up, you've got walking to do."

The temptation to flip him off and go back to sleep was palpable, but I took his hand anyway. Dante hoisted me to my feet and guided me toward a staircase carved into the side of a rock. I looked around, but the area was covered in a thick fog. The dim glow of dawn did little to help me see past a few feet.

"Where are we?" I asked.

"This is the Whispering Isle, and you'll need to make it to the top before the sun rises, so get moving."

Grumbling, I took the first few steps, then glanced back when I noticed he wasn't following. "You're not coming?"

He shook his head. "I can't help you reach the top. You'll need to do it on your own."

"Are you going to tell me why?"

"You'll see when you get there."

"Cryptic sayings should be illegal before sunrise."

He laughed and gave my back a light push. "And they say I'm impossible if woken too early. Get moving, honey badger."

My hand skimmed across the rock wall as I trudged my way up the steps. Pillow-soft moss crept along the wall as the staircase veered along its curve. Legs aching, I grumbled a slew of insults at the impossible man forcing me to exercise so early in the day. Truly, the original plan of absconding into the wilderness grew more tantalizing with each step.

Panting like a dog on their last legs, I caught my breath. A bushel of blueberries protruded from the path a few steps up, so I struggled up a few more steps to try a few. "Hmm. That's good shit."

Dante

"Absolutely not," I said.

Kohara's mane bristled. **"Don't be stingy! I brought what you asked for. The least you could do is let me test her."** The unicorn clutched in her talons was courtesy of the King of Kibar's personal zoo. The creature let off a pitiful noise as it tried to buck out of her hold. Its dark eyes looked at me, as if pleading for help.

"No. You'll break her. Just like you're about to do to that poor unicorn. Let it go. It's no use to me dead."

Sparks crackled down Kohara's spine. **"I will not break her!"** she hissed. With a snort, she released her death grip on the animal, who fled into the surrounding fauna.

I sighed, already tired of dealing with her antics.

The dragoness shifted on her feet. Then looked up at the mountain where Cherry was still climbing. **"It's not a real challenge if you just let her up there,"** she whined. Kohara lowered her massive head like a dog denied a bone. Her tail swished behind her as she took on a sweeter tone. **"Just let me chase her a little. Please?"**

A harmless suggestion from anyone else. But I knew my sister better than that. As expected, when she glanced up at my wife again, her pupils dilated with predatory excitement.

"Cherry needs to do this on her own."

"She's not even walking, she's just eating berries."

"What?" I turned around to see Cherry slumped against a rock, stuffing her face. "Less snacking, more walking!" I shouted.

Cherry screamed her discontent, but kept moving.

"See?" Kohara said with a laugh. **"I bet I could make her run."**

"The answer is no. Go play with one of your men and leave my wife alone."

"But I'm bored of them! I wanna play with Sna— Cherry," she whined. Her body shook as she tried to rein in her excitement, and I did my best not to kick her ass off the island. Kohara was a few years older than Fallon. Yet from what I'd seen, the shadow dragon was leagues better at controlling his instincts. I'd hoped that she'd gain a bit of maturity in my absence, but that clearly wasn't the case. Perhaps we coddled her too much. She was the baby of the family after all.

"Cherry is a human. They are incredibly fragile creatures."

She snorted. **"You didn't see her face-off against me in your hoard."**

"What?"

"Nothing," she said quickly. **"But listen, I've never even been to one of the floating isles before. I know you and our brothers all took the challenge, but I never got to. I grew up hearing stories of the trials you faced together. That's something I'll never get with them gone. Mother and Father**

are dead, which means Cherry is the only sister I'm ever going to get. Let me be a part of this."

My chest ached at her words. The only world Kohara had ever known was behind the oppressive walls of Volsog. At the very least, I had memories of the time before to look back on fondly. Taking the floating isle challenge was one of the best times of my life.

I gazed up at the mountaintop, where I'd left my mark over 600 years prior. Lockjaw the Fierce ruled over the isle as its lord. My brother Lo, being the little shit that he was, alerted him to my approach and teamed up to stop me. Lockjaw nearly took my head off in our battle, yet the pride I felt when I won his challenge was indescribable. So much so that I used to dream of becoming strong enough to take over an isle as its lord.

Now Lockjaw and Lo were dead. As were the lords of every other isle. Kohara would never get the chance to know what that was like.

"I can't risk you hurting my wife."

"Dante—"

I held up a hand to silence her. "However, this isn't the only isle, and knowing Cherry, she'll never be satisfied until she reaches each one. If you can show me that you've learned restraint, I'll let you come up with a trial of your own another time."

Her eyes glowed with excitement.

"However, I suggest you worry about your own challenge."
"What?"

I grinned, letting my lightning crackle around my feet. "Did you think I'd take it easy on you just because you're my sister?"

With a wide smile, Kohara turned to leave, then paused just before taking off. **"Can I at least finally meet those pirates you've been traveling with?"**

My shoulders tensed. "No."

She snorted. **"You never let me play with your things."**

"Because you break them!" I snarled.

She had the decency to lower her head. But not enough to let it go. **"What about that blond werewolf at the castle?"** Her eyes took on that feral glint as she gazed off. **"He looked fast."**

She yelped when my foot hit her side. Kohara's body flew back and plummeted into the clouds below.

Cherry

"Less snacking, more walking!"

His voice caused me to jump, dropping my handful of berries. Frustrated, I snatched a few of them up and threw them in the direction of the voice below. "How long are these damn steps?!"

The sound of his snickering echoed through the area but

he didn't answer. When I rounded the corner, I could see the barest hint of pale scales beneath the fog below. Kohara was muttering something to the blob next to her. Smaller figures shifted beneath the fog but I couldn't make out what they were. The dragoness slumped on her side, her long tail flicking like an irritated cat.

Her body jerked to the side with a loud "Oof!" followed by the sound of claws scraping on stone. She let out a low cry, before her body plummeted into the mist.

Did he just punt his sister off a cliff?

After climbing for what seemed like forever, the steps finally arrived at the peak. I half crawled up the last step before collapsing into a heap. A pair of black boots appeared out of the mist. "This had better be good, Remnac." I spat out his last name like a curse.

"Why don't you tell me?" he asked. Dante waved a hand through the air and the fog began to melt away. The summit was shaped like a bowl with a high arch on one side. Fruit trees lined the edges of the bowl, their branches weighed down by heavy-looking apricots and cherries. On the east side, a long balcony was carved into the mountain.

Dante lifted me from the ground and carried me over to the arch. I reached out to snag a few cherries as we passed by. "Careful," he warned. "They're incredibly sour."

Curious, I popped one in my mouth anyway, then spat it out. "Snapping gators, I've eaten lemons less sour."

"You just don't listen." He plucked an apricot from a nearby tree and I wolfed it down, trying to chase away the sour.

He set me down at the base of the rock wall and I looked up to see it completely covered in red handprints. They ranged in size from that of a small child to hands big enough to belong to a bear. "What is this?" I asked.

Dante's eyes softened as he gazed at the wall of hands. "This is the Whispering Isles marker point. One of seven. Do you remember when I told you that dragons age slowly?"

I nodded.

"Well, our dragon forms are exceedingly hard to control at first. Some take as long as two hundred years simply to fly straight. Even longer to make it long distances." He paused and retrieved *The Big Book of Beasts* from a spot on the ground. "In order to prove our worth as a fully realized dragon, many of us take the Floating Isle Challenge. Seven high peaks spread across all of Mytheglin. If you manage to make it to all seven isles and put your mark on the wall, you are granted the title of Lord of your element."

He bit his thumb, and smeared a drop of blood on the index page of the book. "Back when the world was full, it was often the only way you'd be considered strong enough to hold a territory all your own. To make the task more difficult, it was common for a lord or lady to have their territory overlap one of the isles. In order to get to it, you'd have to face them in combat or make it through whatever challenge they threw your way. Guarding an isle was considered a great honor, reserved for only the strongest. The isles aren't grounded to anything. So a particularly powerful dragon could even move it into their territory with the help of a mage."

He paused, glancing over the sea of hands. When he spoke, the words came out in a soft whisper. "When my brothers were alive, we made a game of sabotaging each other whenever one grew old enough to take the challenge."

"Did you still make it?" I asked.

His smile was wistful. "Yes. They didn't make it easy, but I made it." He lifted the book up to his face, then handed it back to me.

When the book stopped glowing, its pages flipped to an entirely new section: Dragons.

Its first entry held the image of his two-legged form with a winding silver serpent behind him. I stared at the page in wonder until I felt a hand at the small of my back. Dante pushed me forward, nodding at the wall of hands.

I lifted the book up. The second entry appeared in the form of a red dragon with flames licking at her feet. "She was Idalia, Lady of Flames. I only met her once, but someone had made the mistake of angering her and she wound up melting the side of a mountain."

When the book moved over more handprints, dragons of every shade and power filled the book until my arms ached from holding it up. I rested it against a nearby rock and flipped through the entries. "Dante, this is amazing."

"I'm glad you like it."

"Like it? Are you kidding me, I love it!"

"Good, come here then." I turned to see him crushing something in a small bowl. When I approached, he bent down to kiss me, then dipped my hand into the red paste.

"Wait." I pulled my hand away when he guided it to the rock. "Is this allowed?"

He raised a brow at me. "You made it up the steps, didn't you?"

"But I'm not a dragon. I didn't fly here on my own."

He set the bowl down then retrieved the book. Its pages lit up when he held it to the hand the size of a bear paw. When the page finished, he held it out to me showing off the orc it belonged to. "The challenge is only to climb to the summit of the isle on your own and put your mark on the wall. No one said you had to be a dragon. Besides, it's not uncommon to find your fated mate outside your race."

My heart thumped heavily in my chest as I looked up at the wall of ancient handprints. "Where's yours?"

He smiled and guided me further down the wall until we stopped at one hand in particular. It was clustered in a group of prints of similar size, but there was just enough room below it to fit my hand. I pressed my palm to the cool stone, holding it firmly in place before lifting away.

"It's time," he said, snatching my wrist. Dante pulled me over to the balcony.

"Time for what?" I asked.

He waved at the dark sky in front of us and darted away. "Just watch the sky."

"…OK," I said, turning back around. I leaned against the railing, scanning the sky for anything of note. Just before I turned back to ask him what to look for, it happened.

Sunrise came in a golden tunnel through an endless sea of clouds. Its first rays blanketing over the sky in time with the first string of a cello. Soft music joined the sun's ascent as if welcoming home a dear loved one. The night's chill died away in colors so warm it broke my heart. Tears fell down my face, but I didn't dare wipe them away. Not wanting to miss a second.

Dante's song quickened in tempo and the sky responded in a chorus of pink, purple and gold. Right before my eyes, a cloud swirled and took the shape of a massive stingray that glided over the sky as if drinking in the sun's rays. I gasped as another swirled into a school of flying fish. They chased after the stingray in a playful dance, illuminated in a rainbow of colors.

"How…" the question died on my lips as I turned back to the dragon. His eyes were closed. Face serene in concentration as sure as he played his cello. Wisps of silver slowly rolled off him and into the sky.

Of course. This is the song of The Lord of Storms.

The stingray dove to burst through a fluffy cloud until it dispersed in fades of white. I blinked, trying to make sense of the lush green hill in the middle of the sky. When more clouds parted around it, my jaw fell open. "Is…that…is that island *floating*?"

Sunlight illuminated the world around me until I saw more tiny islands floating peacefully in the sky. I peered over the railing to try to see the ground below. But the mountain disappeared into the sea of clouds. Breathless, I gazed at the islands in wonder. "The floating isles." The thought of six more of these spread across the continent was almost unthinkable. I wanted to see every last one.

Just above us, the stingray and flying fish swirled together to form a herd of unicorns. They galloped across the sky, some veering close enough to reach out and touch. I did, letting the cool wetness break against my palm. The cloud unicorn reared up, then raced down the side of the mountain. I ran after it, laughing away the tired ache in my legs. When its hooves hit the ground below the steps, the fog parted revealing—

"Oh, no fucking way."

A unicorn. An actual unicorn stood in the meadow at the base of the mountain. It wasn't until I felt his arms slide around me that I realized the music had died away. Dante brushed a braid behind my ear and kissed my temple. The action was so soft and gentle, my heart practically leaped out of my chest to beg to be held in his hand. His arm hooked beneath my knees, and he settled me against his chest before he leapt down the cliff.

I bit back my scream of surprise and clung to him when he set us down in the meadow. The unicorn flicked its head in our direction as if assessing a threat. I let Dante guide me down in the grass to sit between his legs. "I'm afraid this is as close as we can get before it runs off," he said.

Tears choked my throat, so I simply nodded and clutched the arms around my waist. He pulled me in tighter to whisper in my ear. "I love you, Cherry. Our story may not have had the best beginning, and the middle has gone off the rails, I'll admit. But we're nowhere near the ending. I'll have centuries to find out all the little things that make you tick. Then, just when I think I've finally got you figured out, you'll do something outrageous to throw me off your tracks. And I'll fall a little more in love with you each time."

He lifted my hand to kiss my palm. "I only ask that you stay with me long enough for me to get the chance to make you love me too."

This is it.

This was the feeling I'd been so desperate to find since that day in the river. The ache of isolation melted away with the warmth of his kiss. Arms strong enough to shatter the stone walls of my nightmares pulled me tight against him until all I could feel was safe.

I felt safe.

Something in me broke at the realization.

His nearness consumed my every thought until I shook with the need to touch him. To satiate the growing inferno of hunger and bliss that came anytime I caught sight of him. I broke free of his arms, turned around, and kissed him. His body shuddered, before he responded in kind. Unlike our frantic coupling in the maze, this kiss was gentle. Soft in a way that granted us the peace and time to get to know one another. The way his lips molded against mine, the taste of his tongue answering the call of my own.

Breathless and dazed, I pulled away. Gasping when his lips found my throat. My hand slid to the nape of his neck and tugged on his hair. "Dante…"

"Don't tell me to stop," he begged. "Please, not now."

I held his face in mine, kissing away the furrow in his brow. "My name is Cherry Hotpepper. I live in a small village called Boohail in the tail end of Kinnamo. Please take me home."

For a long moment, he simply stared. His mouth quirked, "Hotpepper, huh?" A small laugh escaped his throat, and he rested his head on my shoulder. "Do you have an older sister named Cinnamon?"

I stilled. "How do you know Cin?"

"I don't know how I didn't notice before. You two look so much alike."

"Answer my question," I demanded.

He leaned away to meet my eyes. An amused grin lit up his features. "Your sister is Madam Shadow."

His words sank in, and I buried my face in my hand. My sister, the same girl who screams at the sight of snakes, married a dragon and helped kill a goddess. "Which means Boohail already has protection?" He nodded. "Son of a bitch."

Dante barked out a laugh.

"This whole time!"

"This whole time," he said. "I had just left Boohail the morning I met you. We could have been back before the evening if you had simply told me."

"Unbelievable." I closed my eyes, a long-suffering sigh escaping. Yet, in the same breath, relief flooded through me. Boohail was fine. I didn't need to worry about anyone's safety or how to get home. I had a dragon more than willing to take me there, or anywhere. "Guess that means I'm free to do as I like."

"And what would that be, Princess?"

"Hmm. Got any ideas?"

His eyes flashed with something dark and hungry. "Careful, Princess. Leave the decision-making up to me and you'll end up bent over my throne with a pretty collar around your throat."

Oh my filé powder, yes.

"How pretty are we talking?"

The speed at which he tossed one Hearthstone to the ground and pulled out the other was almost comical.

A gust of wind and rush of movement was all it took before

I was standing in the middle of Dante's hoard. Gold and precious gems pitted their shine against one another. Each of them failed to garner my attention for more than a passing glance. Not when my dragon's eyes bled from their calm gray to feral amethyst. Flecks of silver dotted his eyes, like stars in the night sky. A hand lifted my chin, drawing me further into the hypnotizing smolder. So deep, it took a second to register the click around my neck.

I touched my throat and was greeted by cool metal. My fingers snagged on a divot, and I raised them up to see a thin gold chain running from the collar. Dante released his hold on me to chain the other end to his throne.

Wow. Doesn't waste time, does he?

I gave the chain a small tug and eyed him with suspicion. "Did...did you just have this in your pocket?"

He turned back to me with a grin that could send any woman to her knees. "Is it so wrong for a man to hope?"

I raised a brow. "I guess not. Unless this is the part where you tell me the unicorn was a ruse to trap me here forever?"

Dante always had a regal air about him. From the masculine cut of his jaw to the deepness in his voice. He moved in a way that commanded obedience better than any king. A light tug on my chain and my feet drew me to him of their own accord. The intoxicating scent of rain and man that was so uniquely him, unleashed a hot tide of lust within me, a need so sharp and aching it stole my breath away.

"You may be the one chained, Princess, but make no mistake, I am always at your mercy." Voice smooth and dark as night, he gripped the back of my neck and dragged me closer until he could run his lips along my temple. "Nevertheless, I am a dragon through and through. I want to take the treasures I hold dearest and hide them away, deep where no one else could dare lay eyes on them. You most of all. Just for a night, let me covet you in a way only one of my kind could understand."

Sweet dancing coyotes in the moonlight, just fuck me up, you beautiful bastard—

"Say yes, my treasure."

"Yes." The word came out in a broken whisper, but I was too needy for him to care.

Still keeping me firmly in place by the back of my neck, his free hand trailed down to the hem of my blouse. "How attached are you to these clothes?"

"They were quite expensive," I murmured. "Good thing my husband is rich."

His lips curved against my ear. "That's my girl." With a tug, I just was free of cumbersome things, like anything blocking Dante's impossibly warm hands. My breath hitched when the cool air hit my skin, only to be chased away by searing kisses. My trousers were next, putting up little resistance to Dante's crusade.

He knelt in front of me, groaning when he ran his hands along the thin fabric of my panties. That, he took his time with. Slowly sliding the fabric down from my ass, trailing the skin with his lips, before he slid it down my legs to toss away. Rough hands skimmed the curve of my ass as he placed a kiss against it. His fingers moved up my spine and trailed back down a tantalizing pattern that had me panting. He squeezed, not hard enough to hurt, but enough to make me gasp before he nipped at my hip.

The barest kiss on my stomach caused me to shiver. Large hands roamed up my sides, memorizing each dip and curve. He glanced up, eyes pleading as if begging me to let him continue. I stroked a hand through his hair and smiled in approval. Another small touch of his lips and he guided me to sit on his throne.

"Come here," he whispered, pulling me in for a soft kiss. His hands cupped my breasts as his tongue slipped against my lips. Moaning into him, I slid my hands down the waist of his pants, unbuckling them to feel the weight of his cock against my fingers. His hard length twitched beneath my touch. I traced my thumb along the vein protruding from the bottom. "Fuck." His hand came around my throat, squeezing gently as he whispered in my ear, "You don't know how many times I've imagined you reaching your hands down my fucking trousers."

With the gentle squeeze he stopped my wrist. "But this is my throne you're chained to. I'll be the one doing the worshiping." He kissed and sucked his way down my body. Silver hair tickled against my side. The sharp curve of his horn gave a delicious edge of danger to his appearance. I leaned back further against the throne, the gold chain clinked against metal as he brought my knees up, kissing each one before spreading them. Dante paused with hooded eyes. "You look so perfect spread out for me. Yes, something this precious should be coveted." He kissed along my inner thigh, before he let out a haggard breath and closed his mouth around my pussy.

"Oh gods."

Dante smacked my pussy, causing me to jump. "Oh no, Princess, you don't call anyone else's name in here but mine."

"Yeah?" I asked. "What happens if I do?"

A slow salacious grin curved his mouth, made all the more arousing with my wetness on his lips. "Oh, how I love it when you're difficult." Amethyst eyes stayed locked on mine. He slipped two fingers inside me, curving them up to tease against my sweet spot. I groaned, rocking against him. Something close to a sadistic glint lit his eyes, and that's when I knew I had fucked up.

All at once, the storm magic rushing through my veins erupted in small electric bursts. I screamed when he concentrated them on the tips of his fingers and drove them mercilessly against my sweet spot. My legs spread wide desperately trying to drive him deeper inside me. The beginnings of my orgasm raced through me like a raging river on a weakened dam. Just before I felt that tantalizing break, the sparks stopped.

"Dante!" I whined.

His eyes softened, "That's right, sweetheart. Tell me who is making this pretty cunt drip with want." His fingers dipped in me once more, offering a slight shock.

I whimpered, trying to buck against him. "You are," I moaned.

He buried his face between my legs, swirling his tongue around my clit as he thrust into me with the maddening electric current. "Louder, sweetheart."

"Dante, please," I panted.

"And who am I to you?"

"Fucking hell," I snarled, grabbing his wrist and grinding myself harder against his hand. I reached up and took hold of his horn, forcing him to look at me. "My husband. My infuriating, beautiful husband who needs to make me come right fucking now!"

He shuddered. "As you wish." My legs shook as the shock-waves returned in full force. He shook off my hand to bury his face between my thighs. Drawing his broad tongue up my folds before he drew my clit into his mouth and sucked.

"Oh, fuck!" I sobbed. "Yes, Dante, please just like that!"

"Yes," he growled, watching me break apart in front of him. "My treasure is so hungry for me, isn't she? Poor thing." Dante ate me like a man starved, delving his tongue to offset the rhythm of his pulsing fingers. My hands gripped the throne so hard my knuckles paled. Stars blinded my vision as his skilled ministrations brought me to the brink. "Break for me, Cherry. Let me taste your release on my tongue."

And because my body reveled in answering his commands, I did. The orgasm tearing through me in a violent euphoria. I cried out as his pace quickened, dragging the orgasm out to an almost brutal length before it rose again. "Please," I whimpered.

"I have you. Give me another, I crave the sweet taste of you." My back arched, head falling back in a scream of a second orgasm that may have to be arrested for murder, because I died and came back.

When he finally released me, I collapsed against the stone. Resting my forehead against the cool surface.

Gaze ravenous, he skimmed one big hand down my side, my body trembling beneath his light touch. Gently, he guided me to face away from him, kneeling on his throne. Much to my relief, the plush cushion shielded my knees from the hard gold. "Oh Princess, by the time I'm finished with you, you'll be a sweet little puddle at my feet. If you ask nicely, I may consider letting you catch your breath before I do it again."

He drew a hand over the curve of my ass, squeezing it as he got rid of his pants. His thick length dragged against my folds, making me moan with anticipation. Just before the head dipped inside, he brushed my hair back, leaving gentle kisses on my shoulder. "Is this still alright?"

"Yes, don't make me wait. Please."

Needing no further invitation, his thick cock buried inside of me, stretching my walls until I shuddered. He gripped my hip, driving himself further before his hand slid to my throat, bending my head back to kiss at my temple. "Fuck," he groaned. "You feel so good, Princess."

"Oh, god—*ahh*!" A sharp slap to my tit caused the word to die in my throat. In a quick motion, Dante removed one of the ties on my pigtails, used it to bind my hair in a bun, then seized it like a rein to yank my head back.

"What did you say?" he asked in a whisper. His gentle tone at odds with the rough treatment of my body.

Shameless, my back arched, driving my ass higher as I mewled out a response. "I said, 'Please fuck me, Dante.'"

"Atta girl," he groaned, grinding himself deep into me until I was crammed full. Blinding sensation swirled through taut flesh until I was left stuffed and bare and oh so right. My chain tinked against his throne when he thrust deep.

The slight pain of his fist in my hair, the controlling way his fingers dug into my hip, and that telltale *tink* of the chain on his throne had me crying out his name.

"That's it." *Tink.* "Sing for me, my beautiful wife." *Tink.* "Never have I heard something so sweet." *Tink.*

His cock was relentless, slamming into me with a speed that made it impossible to keep track of time. But I didn't care. All I wanted was more. More of his cock, more of his hands, and most of all, more of his voice.

"I love the way you speak," I moaned.

"Do you?" He bit my neck. Sparks of electric fire raced down my nerves until my body sizzled with pleasure.

"Yes," I moaned.

He ground his hips into me, sending those sinful bursts of lightning pulsating through his cock. My nails dug into the throne, a keening sound ripped from my throat. "Does it excite you that I can make you feel like this?"

"Oh yes, yes, yes!" I begged. My vision watered as the pleasure grew intense. I blinked tears away, letting them roll down my face.

Dante shuddered behind me. "Look at those pretty tears." His arm came around my waist and he used it to flip me around. Using his hand to guide the back of my head down to the throne before he buried himself back inside with a harsh thrust. "My Princess is trying to make a monster out of me," he bit out in a hard thrust. "Give me more. Tell me what you need, my treasure."

"I need you, Dante," I groaned out. This new position drove him deeper until I was a shuddering mess beneath him. My legs shook, another orgasm threatening to snatch the soul from my body. "I need you so fucking much."

"Then take me, love. Take all of me." He released my hair to wrap his arms around my hips, holding me tight as he drove hard and fast into me. The chain on his throne rattled against the stone floor. Every single strike of his hips sent waves of pleasure thrumming through me. His arm tightened around my waist until it threatened to snap.

"Dante! Oh, fuck!" I cried out as he drilled into me, deep and fast. One last thrust, and my body exploded, my mind going blank with pleasure. My entire body spasmed, and I felt the rush of my release around his cock.

Then he broke, thrusting into me with force and ravishing my mouth with a scorching kiss. He forced my knees up to my shoulders, giving himself deeper access, then threw his head back and ground his cock into my giving pussy. All at once, every muscle in his large body contracted, sinews and tendons straining, until he grunted, his release burying deep inside me. Dante panted and languidly continued to thrust inside me, before he finally slumped against the throne.

He sank to his knees and lovingly kissed my thigh. "I love you, Cherry."

I meant to say I love you too, but the back-to-back orgasms had strained my throat so much it came out more like "I lerph me ner."

He snorted, shoulders shaking as he laughed. "What?"

Giggling, I held up a finger, showing I needed a minute. I took a deep breath, forcing my brain to come down from the high to remember what words sound like. "I love you too."

Chapter 23

Cherry

After a well-deserved nap and closet raid for new clothes, we warped back to the Whispering Isle. With Felix still at Kirkwall, the easiest way to get back to Boohail was to simply find the werewolf and use his stone to take us all back.

We sank through the clouds until they parted into a glittering sea. The high trees of Kibar's forests looked like pin needles in the distance. It almost felt surreal to finally be heading home.

I fiddled with the strands of Dante's mane and sat back to enjoy the ocean view rushing beneath us. Its water shimmered like diamonds in the morning light. The waves were calm, giving the water an almost glass-like appearance.

. . . Wait.

Dread pooled in my stomach. I sat up and scanned the water's surface. "Dante, pull up."

"Hmm?"

Ahead of us, I saw a bubble float to the surface, disturbing the water. Panic set my nerves on fire. I gripped fistfuls of his mane and pulled, desperately trying to steer him as I screamed, "DANTE, PULL UP RIGHT NOW!"

With a jerk, the dragon veered upright, just as a wall of teeth shot out of the water. The jaws snapped shut, clipping a few scales from Dante's neck. Sparks nipped at my legs and lightning raced down his body. He whipped around and slammed his tail at the larger creature, who roared at the bite of his lightning.

Before I could so much as blink, our attacker slammed into my dragon's side. His mane slipped through my fingers and my body was flung into the air like a rag doll. Dante reached for me, but was thrown back when a blue dragon rammed into his side.

My back hit the water hard, stealing the air from my lungs. Stunned, I did nothing but sink. Watching on in horror as Gideon sank his fangs into Dante's leg.

Something grabbed my legs. I kicked. Searing pain shot through my foot and I cried out, the last of my breath turned to bubbles around my face. I looked down to see the needle-like fur of my worst nightmare dragging me deeper into the water.

No, no, not again!

Frantic, I thrashed at the water dog. Slamming my foot into its crooked face until the hand on the end of its tail released me. I swam to the surface as fast as I could, gulping in precious air as soon as my head broke free.

The dragons crashed into the water, the resulting wave sucking me up into the swell. My heart leaped into my throat as the world spun. Brief glimpses of sky filled my vision before an enormous explosion of white water and force dragged me down. Deeper and deeper until I feared I'd never see the sky again.

Muffled roars hit my ears before the surrounding water turned red. *Oh gods, please don't let it be Dante.* I flailed, trying to right myself to see which dragon the blood came from. But a cold thin hand grabbed at my ankle, yanking me to the side. Enraged, I grabbed at the water dog's hand, trying to pry it off me. The hideous black dog whipped around with a snarl, its needle-like hairs stood on end.

Hatred boiled in my blood, and I snarled back. Air escaped my lungs, but I didn't give a shit. I'm not going back to that tower. Never. My hands wrapped around the dog's throat. Squeezing tight as I forced lightning through my palms. Its body seized, face contorting in a violent scream before its tail-hand finally released me.

Lungs burning, I kicked to the surface again, panting hard. "Dante!" A wave sucked me up again, and I was dragged back under water. Something solid scraped against my side, and I clung to it. It closed around my waist, lifting me completely out of the ocean. Coughing up water and salt, I sagged against a giant talon before whipping the water out of my eyes. My heart sank when my vision was clear. "You?"

Gideon's sea-foam green eyes stared back at me. He ducked down, narrowly avoiding a ball of lightning. Dante charged toward us, but swayed in the air and fell back into the water. Blood seeped from a gash in his side.

A terrible sound of anguish ripped from my chest as I watched Dante sink beneath the waves. Gideon moved to hover in the air above him, looking down. And then he dove.

"No!" Bolts shot from my hands and struck the side of his face. Gideon dropped me, crying out as he clutched his face. My feet started kicking as soon as I hit the water. I reached out, grabbing hold of a long whisker and pulled myself toward the sinking dragon. Unsure how to rouse him, I tugged harder at his whisker and kicked at his jaw. Yet he kept sinking.

Shitballs. Shit, shit, shit!

Desperate, I gathered sparks into my fist and socked him as hard as I could on the snout. Violet eyes shot open, and I nearly sobbed in relief.

"Cherry." His hand closed around me, and Dante flung us back into the air. Storm clouds churned angrily in the sky. With a roar, they billowed around us, blinding Gideon. The air churned with immense force, swirling in a spiral until a tornado formed.

With a pained groan, Dante turned and shot off toward the horizon, using the storm as cover. Within seconds, we hit the shoreline and dove into the trees.

Dante set me down, then collapsed into a heap. His voice came through labored breathing. **"Take the Hearthstones and return to the castle."**

"Right," I said. Quickly digging the small stone out of my pocket. "Hurry and shift back so we can go!"

He shook his head. **"I'm not going."**

"What?" I snarled. "Don't be stupid, of course you are."

"Cherry, if I don't cut him down now, he's only going to try again. Next time he might succeed in ripping out my throat before you spot him." He rolled, dragging himself to his feet. **"Listen to me for once and go."**

"You know damn well I'm not doing that!"

The ground shook with a thud. I turned to see Gideon land a few paces away from us. Dante snarled, blocking me from his view. The air crackled, blue sparks dancing across silver scales as a ball of light filled his mouth.

"I yield," Gideon said, lowering his head.

"What?" Dante and I asked in unison.

I poked my head around my dragon to see smoke swirl around his blue counterpart. The smoke faded into mist, revealing a tall haggard man with sea-foam green locks reaching down to his waist. Forlorn blue eyes slowly looked between us. Without a word, Gideon retrieved a dagger from his pocket, bundled up his long locks and sliced through them. He tossed the severed hair at Dante's feet.

"I yield," he said again, then turned and walked away.

With a heavy breath, Dante collapsed onto his side. Hissing noises issued from the gash in his side and the broken skin slowly began stitching itself back together.

"Wait a damn minute," I snarled, chasing after Gideon. "What do you mean you yield? What did you even attack us for?"

Sighing, the dragon-shifter paused and turned back to me. "I came to retrieve you and return you to the village you were taken from. Yet I see you've taken the Lord of Storm's magic. So there is no need."

"You can't be serious." My fists balled at my sides. "You say you came to take me home, but why now? Why did you take me in the first place? What the fuck did you want from me?" The words spat out like a curse. Years of hatred and rage caused my vision to blur with tears.

"I'm sorry," he said, solemnly.

"If you're sorry then tell me why!" I snapped. "You took five fucking years of my life. I deserve that much at least!"

"You were loud." Gideon turned away from me, his eyes flinching in pain. It was then I noticed the dark circles under his eyes, almost hidden by the deep umber of his skin. "My wife was an exceptionally loud woman. Her fury could shake the ground beneath you, and she possessed laughter so booming it could make the gods themselves take notice." He added with a faint smile pulling at his lips, "It was mesmerizing."

"People were drawn to her like moths to a flame wherever we went. She was always off somewhere in a crowd, telling noisy jokes until everyone was hysterical with laughter. I could always locate her by sound alone." He slowed down. A feeling of awful melancholy washed over him. So potent in the air that it made my heart constrict.

"And after her death…every day was silent. I cannot imagine a worse form of torture. When my servants delivered you to her keep, you made such a racket that I could hear you from the opposite end of my domain. I was aware that you were not my Lotti. Nevertheless, I thanked every god for the noise."

His final words were expelled with a trembling breath. His piercing blue eyes were filled with unshed tears. He blinked them away and then brought his attention back to me. "I realize you might not believe me. However, I never intended to hold you for so long. Each day I meant to wake up and bring you home. Yet, I lacked the strength to confront the stillness."

Gideon knelt and bowed so deeply that his forehead met the ground. "I'm deeply sorry my weakness has caused you pain."

He still wasn't crying, but I sure as hell was. I sniffed, wiping away fat tears before I spoke around the lump in my throat. "Dammit. It's really hard to stay mad at you after a story like that."

"I do not expect your forgiveness."

"Good, I don't want to give it." My lip trembled as I struggled to hold on to my anger. Despite my best efforts it slipped away from me, leaving only a bleeding heart for his loss. "I can't believe I'm saying this, but next time just come visit."

Finally, Gideon lifted his head from the ground with a quizzical look. "I'm not saying I forgive you yet, because I don't. But thanks to you, I understand how painful silence can be. If you need to be around a bunch of loud women, come to the Hotpepper farm in Boohail. Loud people are never in short supply in my family."

The dragon's eyes flashed with something that might have been warmth. He gave me one last bow and stood. He turned to leave, and then stopped. "I might just take you up on that."

I watched in silence as his figure disappeared into the trees. And when he was gone, I let out a breath. I slumped against Dante's side, pressing my face into the warmth of his scales.

A warm, gentle breeze blew over me and I shivered. Turning my head, I found my dragon watching me with a soft gaze. I smiled at him, and he tilted his head.

"Are you OK?" he rasped.

"I should be asking you that," I murmured.

He lifted his chin and snorted, sending flames to singe the neighboring branch's leaves. **"This is nothing. I had him on the ropes the whole time."**

"Oh, well of course. How could I have been so foolish as to doubt you?"

"It's fine," he sighed. **"Assuming you have learned your lesson."**

"Naturally. So that part where you almost drowned was all part of an elaborate scheme?"

A sparkling blast of wind encircled me. Dante took me into his arms and kissed me passionately. He trailed his fingers over my jaw, causing wonderful tremors to travel all the way down to my toes. "Do you think I'd pass up the chance to see my princess come to save me?"

I laughed as he nuzzled my neck. "Well, that was a bit dramatic."

"I'm a dragon, remember? Drama is our middle name."

"Oh, how right you are. Just never stop being so..." I searched for a suitable word. "Big and dramatic and everything else."

"Even if I must drown myself to show you how serious I am?"

"Yes, giving me heart attacks is the preferred method."

Dante chuckled. "Very well, my princess. It shall be done."

"I love you, you fucking weirdo."

Epilogue

Cherry

Crisp winter air filled my lungs with the familiar scent of wood-burning stoves, and the muted fragrances of our spice fields. The long winding cobblestone roads were so familiar and comforting I wanted to bend down and kiss them. I wouldn't, because *gross*, but I thought about it.

Cinnamon stared at me, wide-eyed. In the five years I'd been gone, she hadn't changed much. The same round face, the same wild curly hair, even the way she walked had stayed the same. Yet she had an air of confidence about her that I hadn't seen before.

I took a step forward, but Cin stood frozen in place, her mouth slightly ajar as she looked me over from a safe distance away. She turned back to the raven-haired dragon-shifter standing behind her. Who nodded and placed an encouraging hand on her back. At his assurance my sister turned back to me, eyes watering before she flung herself into my arms.

Brie stepped forward, and I reached out to collect her into our mess as well. She may not have been my sister by blood, but I loved her all the same. Like Cinnamon, few things had changed about my favorite cheesemaker. The most notable being the doting werewolf standing at her side. Though, when I thought about it, the fact that she married a werewolf should not have surprised me.

We spent a good moment like that, just sobbing outside Felix and Brie's house.

Behind me, Dante attempted to leave, no doubt trying to give me space to catch up with my sisters. But that only alerted Cin to his presence, and soon he too had his arms full of sobbing women as we migrated him into the crying collective. His eyes narrowed at Felix, who joined in on the huddle, but he bit back the tic in his jaw. "Thank you for bringing her home," Cin wailed against his chest.

Dante placed a tentative hand on her back and patted gently. It was obvious to anyone that crying women was a new concept for him, but I gave the big lug points for trying.

We walked down the winding road arm in arm to our parents' house. The cinnamon fields were barren at this time of year but they filled my heart with joy all the same to see them. Smoke rose from the chimney of the house, as the smell of gumbo wafted through the air. Too excited to hold back, I burst through the doors.

My ma froze in her kitchen; the apple-embroidered apron I had helped sew years ago was stained with the remnants of the dinner she was making. She dropped to her knees, jaw hanging open. A fresh crop of tears spilled from my eyes as I flung myself into her arms and hugged her tight.

"Hey, Ma, I'm home."

extras

orbit

meet the author

Kimberly Lemming

KIMBERLY LEMMING is on an eternal quest to avoid her calling as a main character. She can be found giving the slip to that new werewolf that just blew into town and refusing to make eye contact with a prince of a far-off land. Dodging aliens looking for Earth booty can really take up a girl's time. But when she's not running from fate, she can be found writing diverse fantasy romance. Or just shoveling chocolate in her maw until she passes out on the couch.

Find out more about Kimberly Lemming and other Orbit authors by registering for the free monthly newsletter at orbitbooks.net.

if you enjoyed
THAT TIME I GOT DRUNK AND SAVED A HUMAN

look out for

FOR THE WOLF
Book One of the Wilderwood

by

Hannah Whitten

The First Daughter is for the throne.
The Second Daughter is for the Wolf.

As the only Second Daughter born in centuries, Red has one purpose: to be sacrificed to the Wolf in the Wilderwood in the hope he'll return the world's captured gods.

Red is almost relieved to go. Plagued by a dangerous power she can't control, she knows that at least in the Wilderwood, she can't hurt those she loves. Again.

But the legends lie. The Wolf is a man, not a monster. Her magic is a calling, not a curse. And if she doesn't learn how to use it, the monsters the gods have become will swallow the Wilderwood— and her world—whole.

Chapter One

Two nights before she was sent to the Wolf, Red wore a dress the color of blood.

It cast Neve's face in crimson behind her as she straightened her twin's train. The smile her sister summoned was tentative and thin. "You look lovely, Red."

Red's lips were raw from biting, and when she tried to return the smile, her skin pulled. Copper tasted sharp on her tongue.

Neve didn't notice her bleeding. She wore white, like everyone else would tonight, the band of silver marking her as the First Daughter holding back her black hair. Emotions flickered across her pale features as she fussed with the folds of Red's gown—apprehension, anger, bone-deep sadness. Red could read each one. Always could, with Neve. She'd been an easy cipher since the womb they'd shared.

Finally, Neve settled on a blankly pleasant expression designed to reveal nothing at all. She picked up the half-full wine bottle on the floor, tilted it toward Red. "Might as well finish it off."

Red drank directly from the neck. Crimson lip paint smeared the back of her hand when she wiped her mouth.

"Good?" Neve took back the bottle, voice bright even as she rolled it nervously in her palms. "It's Meducian. A gift for the

Temple from Raffe's father, a little extra on top of the prayer-tax for good sailing weather. Raffe filched it, said he thought the regular tax should be more than enough for pleasant seas." A halfhearted laugh, brittle and dry. "He said if anything would get you through tonight, this will."

Red's skirt crinkled as she sank into one of the chairs by the window, propping her head on her fist. "There's not enough wine in the world for this."

Neve's false mask of brightness splintered, fell. They sat in silence.

"You could still run," Neve whispered, lips barely moving, eyes on the empty bottle. "We'll cover for you, Raffe and I. Tonight, while everyone—"

"I can't." Red said it quick, and she said it sharp, hand falling to slap against the armrest. Endless repetition had worn all the polish off her voice.

"Of course you can." Neve's fingers tightened on the bottle. "You don't even have the Mark yet, and your birthday is the day after tomorrow."

Red's hand strayed to her scarlet sleeve, hiding white, unblemished skin. Every day since she turned nineteen, she'd checked her arms for the Mark. Kaldenore's had come immediately after her birthday, Sayetha's halfway through her nineteenth year, Merra's merely days before she turned twenty. Red's had yet to appear, but she was a Second Daughter—bound to the Wilderwood, bound to the Wolf, bound to an ancient bargain. Mark or no Mark, in two days, she was gone.

"Is it the monster stories? Really, Red, those are fairy tales to frighten children, no matter what the Order says." Neve's voice had edges now, going from cajoling to something sharper. "They're nonsense. No one has seen them in nearly two hundred years—there were none before Sayetha, none before Merra."

"But there were before Kaldenore." There was no heat in Red's voice, no ice, either. Neutral and expressionless. She was so tired of this fight.

"Yes, two damn centuries ago, a storm of monsters left the Wilderwood and terrorized the northern territories for ten years, until Kaldenore entered and they disappeared. Monsters we have no real historical record of, monsters that seemed to take whatever shape pleased the person telling the tale." If Red's voice had been placid autumn, Neve's was wrecking winter, all cold and jagged. "But even if they were real, there's been *nothing* since, Red. No hint of anything coming from the forest, not for any of the other Second Daughters, and not for you." A pause, words gathered from a deep place neither of them touched. "If there were monsters in the woods, we would've seen them when we—"

"Neve." Red sat still, eyes on the swipe of wound-lurid lip paint across her knuckles, but her voice knifed through the room.

The plea for silence went ignored. "Once you go to him, it's over. He won't let you back out. You can never leave the forest again, not like...not like last time."

"I don't want to talk about that." Neutrality lost its footing, slipping into something hoarse and desperate. "Please, Neve."

For a moment, she thought Neve might ignore her again, might keep pushing this conversation past the careful parameters Red allowed for it. Instead she sighed, eyes shining as bright as the silver in her hair. "You could at least pretend," she murmured, turning to the window. "You could at least pretend to care."

"I care." Red's fingers tensed on her knees. "It just doesn't make a difference."

She'd done her screaming, her railing, her rebellion. She'd

done all of it, everything Neve wanted from her now, back before she turned sixteen. Four years ago, when everything changed, when she realized the Wilderwood was the only place for her.

That feeling was mounting in her middle again. Something blooming, climbing up through her bones. Something *growing*.

A fern sat on the windowsill, incongruously verdant against the backdrop of frost. The leaves shuddered, tendrils stretching gently toward Red's shoulder, movements too deft and deliberate to be caused by a passing breeze. Beneath her sleeve, green brushed the network of veins in her wrist, made them stand out against her pale skin like branches. Her mouth tasted of earth.

No. Red clenched her fists until her knuckles blanched. Gradually, that *growing* feeling faded, a vine cut loose and coiling back into its hiding place. The dirt taste left her tongue, but she still grabbed the wine bottle again, tipping up the last of the dregs. "It's not just the monsters," she said when the wine was gone. "There's the matter of me being enough to convince the Wolf to release the Kings."

Alcohol made her bold, bold enough that she didn't try to hide the sneer in her voice. If there was ever going to be a sacrifice worthy enough to placate the Wolf and make him free the Five Kings from wherever he'd hidden them for centuries, it wasn't going to be her.

Not that she believed any of that, anyway.

"The Kings aren't coming back," Neve said, giving voice to their mutual nonbelief. "The Order has sent three Second Daughters to the Wolf, and he's never let them go before. He won't now." She crossed her arms tightly over her white gown, staring at the window glass as if her eyes could bore a hole into it. "I don't think the Kings *can* come back."

Neither did Red. Red thought it was likely that their gods

were dead. Her dedication to her path into the forest had nothing to do with belief in Kings or monsters or anything else that might come out of it.

"It doesn't matter." They'd rehearsed this to perfection by now. Red flexed her fingers back and forth, now blue-veined, counting the beats of this endless, circling conversation. "I'm going to the Wilderwood, Neve. It's done. Just... let it be done."

Mouth a resolute line, Neve stepped forward, closing the distance between them with a whisper of silk across marble. Red didn't look up, angling her head so a fall of honey-colored hair hid her face.

"Red," Neve breathed, and Red flinched at her tone, the same she'd use with a frightened animal. "I *wanted* to go with you, that day we went to the Wilderwood. It wasn't your fault that—"

The door creaked open. For the first time in a long time, Red was happy to see her mother.

While white and silver suited Neve, it made Queen Isla look frozen, cold as the frost on the windowpane. Dark brows drew over darker eyes, the only feature she had in common with both her daughters. No servants followed as she stepped into the room, closing the heavy wooden door behind her. "Neverah." She inclined her head to Neve before turning those dark, unreadable eyes on Red. "Redarys."

Neither of them returned a greeting. For a moment that seemed hours, the three of them were mired in silence.

Isla turned to Neve. "Guests are arriving. Greet them, please."

Neve's fists closed on her skirts. She stared at Isla under lowered brows, her dark eyes fierce and simmering. But a fight was pointless, and everyone in this room knew it. As she moved toward the door, Neve glanced at Red over her shoulder, a command in her gaze—*Courage.*

Courageous was the last thing Red felt in the presence of her mother.

She didn't bother to stand as Isla took stock of her. The careful curls coaxed into Red's hair were already falling out, her dress wrinkled. Isla's eyes hesitated a moment on the smear of lip color marking the back of her hand, but even that wasn't enough to elicit a response. This was more proof of sacrifice than a ball, an event for dignitaries from all over the continent to attend and see the woman meant for the Wolf. Maybe it was fitting she looked half feral.

"That shade suits you." The Queen nodded to Red's skirts. "Red for Redarys."

A quip, but it made Red's teeth clench halfway to cracking. Neve used to say that when they were young. Before they both realized the implications. By then, her nickname had already stuck, and Red wouldn't have changed it anyway. There was a fierceness in it, a claiming of who and what she was.

"Haven't heard that one since I was a child," she said instead, and saw Isla's lips flatten. Mention of Red's childhood—that she'd been a child, once, that she was *her* child, that she was sending her child to the forest—always seemed to unsettle her mother.

Red gestured to her skirt. "Scarlet for a sacrifice."

A moment, then Isla cleared her throat. "The Florish delegation arrived this afternoon, and the Karseckan Re's emissary. The Meducian Prime Councilor sends her regrets, but a number of other Councilors are making an appearance. Order priestesses from all over the continent have been arriving throughout the day, praying in the Shrine in shifts." All this in a prim, quiet voice, a recitation of a rather boring list. "The Three Dukes of Alpera and their retinues should arrive before the procession—"

"Oh, good." Red addressed her hands, still and white as a corpse's. "They wouldn't want to miss that."

Isla's fingers twitched. Her tone, though strained, remained queenly. "The High Priestess is hopeful," she said, eyes everywhere but on her daughter. "Since there's been a longer stretch between you and...and the others, she thinks the Wolf might finally return the Kings."

"I'm sure she does. How embarrassing for her when I go into that forest and absolutely nothing happens."

"Keep your blasphemies to yourself," Isla chided, but it was mild. Red never quite managed to wring emotion from her mother. She'd tried, when she was younger—giving gifts, picking flowers. As she got older, she'd pulled down curtains and wrecked dinners with drunkenness, trying for anger if she couldn't have something warmer. Even that earned her nothing more than a sigh or an eye roll.

You had to be a whole person to be worth mourning. She'd never been that to her mother. Never been anything more than a relic.

"Do *you* think they'll come back?" A bald question, one she wouldn't dare ask if she didn't have one foot in the Wilderwood already. Still, Red couldn't quite make it sound sincere, couldn't quite smooth the barb from her voice. "Do you think if the Wolf finds me *acceptable*, he'll return the Kings to you?"

Silence in the room, colder than the air outside. Red had nothing like faith, but she wanted that answer like it could be absolution. For her mother. For *her*.

Isla held her gaze for a moment that stretched, spun into strange proportions. There were years in it, and years' worth of things unsaid. But when she spoke, her dark eyes turned away. "I hardly see how it matters."

And that was that.

Red stood, shaking back the heavy curtain of her loose hair, wiping the lip paint from her hand onto her skirt. "Then by all means, Your Majesty, let's show everyone their sacrifice is bound and ready."